PRAISE FOR SHIPWR

'*Shipwrecked* is the perfect book to settle down with this summer. I can't wait to read the next instalment!' *Bookbabblers*

'From a gripping plot, to laugh-out-loud moments and a heart-thumping romance, this is definitely a saga I will continue to read.' *A Day Dreamer's World, blogger*

'*Shipwrecked* is what I would look for in a Young Adult novel with equal amounts of sass, adventure, drama, and romance . . . Curham has really mastered older YA writing with this book.' *Just This Teenager, blogger*

'Siobhan really has a gift with making characters multi-dimensional, relatable and sympathetic.'
So Many Books, So Little Time, blogger

'[Curham] rolls humour, suspense and ethical issues all into one . . . I am genuinely looking forward to devouring the sequel to *Shipwrecked*.' *Guardian Children's Books Blog*

'An atmospheric read . . . I think this has the potential to be a brilliant series.' *Bookbag*

'Totally captivating in its uniqueness.'
Daisy, readgig.com

'A fab read and something really different and unexpected from an author I thought I knew.'
Overflowing library, blogger

'I enjoyed reading every single word. Wow! It is a true page turner . . . Siobhan is a truly wonderful writer.' *Emma is Reading, blogger*

More books by Siobhan Curham

Shipwrecked

Dear Dylan
Finding Cherokee Brown

DARK OF THE MOON

Siobhan Curham

Dark of the Moon
Published in Great Britain 2014
by Electric Monkey, an imprint of Egmont UK Limited
The Yellow Building
1 Nicholas Road
London W11 4AN

Concept © Egmont UK Ltd 2013
Text © Siobhan Curham 2014

ISBN 978 1 4052 6458 7

1 3 5 7 9 10 8 6 4 2

www.egmont.co.uk

A CIP catalogue record for this title is available from the British Library

Typeset by Avon DataSet Ltd, Bidford on Avon, Warwickshire
Printed and bound in Great Britain by the CPI Group

53081/1

EGMONT

Our story began over a century ago, when seventeen-year-old Egmont Harald Petersen found a coin in the street. He was on his way to buy a flyswatter, a small hand-operated printing machine that he then set up in his tiny apartment.

The coin brought him such good luck that today Egmont has offices in over 30 countries around the world. And that lucky coin is still kept at the company's head offices in Denmark.

For soul-mates everywhere . . .

Prologue

Hortense lights the final candle and steps away from the altar. Tendrils of incense smoke twist through the darkness like ghostly snakes, filling the air with the scent of sage. She takes a small wooden doll from her pocket and places it in the centre of the altar. A sudden breeze rushes through the trees like a nervous gasp, as if the island itself knows what's about to happen.

As Hortense stares at the doll, an unfamiliar brew of tension and anxiety begins bubbling inside her. She looks up at the crescent moon glowing hazily in the sky. In a few days, it will have disappeared completely. In a few days, the dark of the moon will have arrived, and she can finally finish what she began all those years ago.

Hortense turns and walks over to a wicker basket in the middle of the clearing. She slowly lifts the lid and a serpent's head appears, its burnished skin gleaming in the candlelight. She takes the serpent from the basket and holds it high above her. It hisses as it arches up to the sky.

'Papa Labas, bring me your strength!' Hortense cries. Lowering her arms, she brings the serpent down around her neck. She shivers as its cold skin glides against hers. Then she starts to dance, slowly bending and swaying, until it feels as if she and the snake are one. As she closes her eyes she feels strength rushing into her, hot and urgent like a forest fire.

She places the serpent back into the basket and strides over to the altar. She takes a small, curved knife from her belt and holds it up to the moonlight. Then she picks up the doll – and carefully gouges out its eyes.

Chapter One

I'm drifting in that weird no-man's land between awake and asleep. Cruz's arm is circling my waist, anchoring my body to the sand beneath us, but my mind keeps being sucked under, back into the dream.

There's no fire this time. No choking smoke or screaming baby. This time all I hear is Hortense singing, and all I see is a hazy yellow glow. Then a beautiful girl's face slowly appears, like a Polaroid picture. She has gleaming chestnut skin and dark brown eyes. She's smiling at me, but a tear is trickling down her cheek. She opens her mouth to speak, but before she can say a word a snake slithers out from between her lips, its fangs bared.

I wake with a start, my heart pounding. Cruz pulls me closer.

'Grace,' he whispers in my ear. His voice is husky with sleep.

I allow my body to sink into his, soaking up the warmth, and I start composing a checklist in my head to help bring me back to reality. The singing and the girl and the snake were all just a dream. I'm awake now. Cruz is right next to me. Belle, the Flea and Dan are sleeping on the other side of the palm trees. Everything's okay. Well, as okay as it can be when you've been shipwrecked on a desert island that's possessed by the spirit of a voodoo queen.

An icy sweat erupts on my skin as I think of Hortense. *Get a grip, Grace*, I tell myself, *don't go losing the plot now*. I think of the boat we found yesterday, and the fact that we'll be leaving in it at first light. But if Hortense can read my mind won't she know what we've got planned? Won't she try and stop us? I lie there, motionless, waiting for her whispered voice in my head. But all I hear are the hisses and creaks from the rainforest and the sound of the waves as they crash on the beach. I haven't heard Hortense's voice or sensed her presence since we rescued Belle yesterday and Hortense tried to lure me to her. Maybe Cruz was right. Maybe I did break the spell by refusing to go to her. Maybe the nightmare really is over.

Cruz grips me tighter, as if he can sense that I'm thinking about him. As his breath whispers through my hair, my skin begins to tingle. Very carefully, I turn over so that I'm facing him. Part of me wishes he would wake up, but another part of me is glad he's asleep. When he's awake I have to ration the amount I look at him, so that I don't appear too love-struck, but now I can gaze away to my heart's content. I look at the mass of dark curls spilling on to his face, the sharp curve of his cheekbones and the stubble darkening his jaw like a shadow. Then I look at his mouth and the places either side where dimples appear whenever he smiles.

It's hard to believe that the words 'I love you' came from that mouth just a few hours ago. Did he mean it? Can he really love me already? We've only known each other a few days, but so much has happened it's like we've condensed an entire lifetime into them. Once, when I'd been having doubts about my ex boyfriend, Todd, I asked my mom how you knew when you were in love. She gave me a real sad smile and said, 'Oh, don't worry, sweetpea, you'll know. There's a reason why they call it *falling* in love. It's like stepping off the Empire State Building with your eyes and arms wide open. You know you could end up with your heart all smashed to pieces, but you just don't care.' At the thought of Mom my eyes prickle with tears. How will she be coping now we've been missing so long? *I love you, Mom,* I say loudly in my head. *I love you and I'm gonna be back home real soon.* I pray that through some umbilical-style mother-daughter telepathy, she'll somehow hear me all the way in Los Angeles.

I blink my tears away and look back at Cruz. He looks so peaceful; it's like all the stress of the past few days has drained away into the sand while he's been asleep. He stirs and moves his face so close to mine our lips brush. My internal, incoming-Cruz radar kicks into action, making my heart pound.

'Hello,' he whispers, pulling me to him.

'Hello,' I whisper back.

His fingers start moving inside my T-shirt, trailing warmth up my spine. Then he moves one hand round so that it's cupping my breast. I can't help letting out a gasp and he instantly stops. I guess he's worried he's gone too far. But he hasn't, he hasn't at all. My lips find his again. If synchronised kissing was an Olympic sport our mouths would be going for gold right now. Cruz rolls on top of me and starts whispering something in Spanish in my ear.

'What does that mean?' I whisper back.

'You are so beautiful,' he whispers, breathlessly.

'Grace, Cruz. Are you guys awake?'

We both freeze at the sound of the Flea's voice. Cruz rolls back on to the sand beside me.

'What's up?' I call, pulling my T-shirt down. In the pale moonlight I can just make out the Flea's thin silhouette peering round the cluster of trees.

'It's Belle.'

My stomach lurches and I start scrambling to my feet. 'What's wrong with her?'

The Flea comes closer. His T-shirt's crumpled and his dark

6

hair is flat on one side from where he's been sleeping on it. 'She keeps moaning like she's having a really bad nightmare. But I can't wake her.'

I hold my hand out to Cruz to help him up and we hurriedly make our way around the trees to where Dan and Belle are sleeping. I can hear the soft purr of Dan's snores coming from within his cocoon of towels. Next to him Belle is twitching and breathing in shallow gasps. We crouch down around her.

'Belle,' I say in her ear. 'Belle, wake up.'

Belle lets out a low moan, as if she's in pain.

'What's wrong with her?' the Flea says, his voice trembling.

Cruz leans forward and grabs hold of Belle's shoulder. 'Wake up, Belle,' he says, gently shaking her.

Belle frowns but her eyes stay shut.

'Belle, honey, you have to wake up!' the Flea cries.

Dan sits bolt upright, like a horror-flick mummy rising from its tomb. 'Wass going on?' he yells, looking around wildly as if preparing for a fight.

'It's okay, we're just trying to wake Belle,' I explain.

Dan stares at me like I'm nuts. 'What the hell? It's the middle of the night.'

'I know, but she's having some kind of terrible nightmare,' the Flea says,

'I know the feeling.' Dan sighs and slumps back down on to the sand.

The Flea looks at me. 'Maybe we should sing her favourite song?'

'Say what?' Dan mutters.

'It's what they do to coma patients to try and bring them round,' the Flea says. 'I saw it on an episode of *World's Worst Diseases* one time. There was this girl who was in a coma after catching alligator AIDS and –'

Dan pokes his head out from under his towel. 'Catching *what?!*'

'Alligator AIDS.' The Flea frowns at him. 'It was *World's Worst Diseases* for chrissakes. Anyways, the girl was, like, a massive Beyoncé fan, so her mom made her a playlist on her iPod and she came round by the very next ad break.'

'I ain't singing no "Single Ladies",' Dan mutters. 'She's probably just wiped out after everything that happened to her. I say we let her sleep.'

I look down at Belle. Her face is glistening with sweat, but when I touch her cheek it's freezing. 'I don't know,' I say, 'she's not looking so great. Let's try sitting her up.'

Cruz helps me prop Belle into a seated position.

'What's that smell?' Belle murmurs.

The hairs on the back of my neck instantly prickle. 'What smell?' I stare down at Belle. Can she smell the same strange scent that I do whenever Hortense is near? I take a deep breath in through my nose, but all I can smell is the humid,

8

earthy scent of the rainforest.

'Beau-Belle!' the Flea says loudly. 'Come on, honey, you have to wake up.' He leans forward and starts shaking her.

Belle's eyes flicker open.

'Oh, thank God!' The Flea smothers her in a hug.

Cruz and I sit back and exchange relieved grins.

'Well, now you guys have woken her, how about we all go back to sleep?' Dan grunts from beneath his blanket of towels.

Belle frowns. 'Why's it so dark?'

'Because it's night time,' Dan sighs. 'You know? When most normal folk try and get some sleep.'

'There's not much of a moon tonight, hon,' the Flea says, putting his arm round her.

'But I can't . . .' Belle pushes the Flea away and stares around frantically. 'I can't see anything!'

The Flea frowns at her. 'What do you mean?'

Belle starts trembling, her eyes wide with fear. 'I can't see a thing. Oh my God! I've gone blind!'

Chapter Two

Quick as a flash, Dan is up and out of bed and crouching in front of Belle. 'What do you mean, you can't see anything?'

'Exactly what I said!' Belle stares at him blankly, looking terrified.

The Flea grabs hold of her hand. 'It's me, Jimmy. I'm right here, honey. It's okay.' He turns and looks at me, panic-stricken.

I lean forward and take hold of Belle's other hand. 'You can't see anything?' I look up at the sky. A crescent moon is suspended above us, glowing pearly white. 'Try looking up. Can you see the moonlight?'

Belle tilts her head back and blinks hard. 'No.' Her voice begins to tremble. 'What's happened to me?'

I glance at Cruz. He's frowning. 'I think maybe it is to do with the trauma you have been through,' he says to Belle softly.

'Sometimes our bodies can, you know, shut down when we have had a shock. As a kind of protection.'

Belle shakes her head. 'That doesn't make sense.' She grips on to the Flea's hand. 'It doesn't make sense, does it, Jimmy? How would going blind protect me?'

But the Flea is nodding. 'He could be right, hon. I'm sure I saw something like this one time on *Real Life Emergency Room*. There was this girl who'd been in a terrible car crash and she became mute because she was so traumatised at –'

'I just want to see!' Belle yells, wrenching her hand from his. 'I just – want – to – see.' She hunches over and starts to sob.

The Flea stares at her, distraught. 'I'm sorry. I was only trying to make you feel better.'

Belle just keeps on crying.

I look up to the top of the beach where the dark silhouette of the rainforest looms like a huge open mouth waiting to devour us. Anger floods my body. I leap to my feet.

The Flea frowns at me. 'What's up, Gracie?'

But I can't answer him – not without telling them everything about Hortense and freaking Belle out even more.

'I have to go do something,' I say, avoiding eye contact with Cruz. 'I'll be right back.'

I start running up the beach, ignoring the others as they call after me. My heart is pounding with fear, but anger forces me to keep going. Belle was abducted and now she's gone blind. Jenna, Cariss, Ron and Todd are drifting in a beat-up boat somewhere in the middle of the ocean — and all because of some stupid spell that I somehow managed to trigger. *Why can't you just leave the others alone?* I yell at Hortense in my head. *If I'm the one you want then go ahead and take me. I don't care any more. Just leave the others be.*

'Grace?' Cruz races up the beach behind me and grabs my shoulder. 'What are you doing?'

'I'm going to find her,' I gasp, trying to catch my breath. 'I've got to end this.'

Cruz pulls me round to face him. 'What are you talking about?'

'Hortense.' I lower my voice to a whisper so the others can't hear. 'She must have made Belle go blind. We thought it was over — but it's not. And it won't be until I go to her. I'm the one she wants. I'm the one who triggered her dumb spell.'

Cruz shakes his head. 'No. It is not you. It is not your fault.'

'But Hortense wants *me*. I don't know why . . . but that's why we're all here. That's why we got shipwrecked. She said so. I'm sick of seeing other people get hurt.' I start marching up towards the forest.

Cruz runs in front of me to block my path.

'Get out of the way.' I'm so mad that for a second I actually feel like shoving him.

He shakes his head. 'No.'

'You have to let me go.'

'Let you go to *her*? Are you crazy?' His eyes are filled with concern. 'I saved your life, remember? And that means that I am responsible for you forever. So, *no can do*.'

I think back to the moment on the boat when I was about to drown and Cruz pulled me to safety. And I think of everything he has done for me since. And my anger starts to fade. Tiredness rushes into its place.

I sigh. 'Dammit, Cruz! Why d'you have to play that one?'

He starts to smile. 'Come here.'

I frown at him. 'What do you mean? I *am* here.'

He opens his arms. 'I mean right here.'

I step into his arms and, as I do, the insanity of what I was planning hits me. How would tearing into the forest demanding Hortense take me guarantee she'd leave the others alone? How would it give Belle her sight back? How would it bring Jenna and the others to safety? The fact is, I don't have a clue what Hortense is up to, or what she actually wants.

'I just want to do something to fix all this,' I whisper into Cruz's shoulder.

'You will.' Cruz steps back and smiles at me. 'We all will. Look.' He points up. Behind the banks of charcoal-coloured cloud, the sky is turning an inky blue. 'The sun is on its way. As soon as it rises, we'll be out of here.'

I force myself to nod. I really wish I could believe it would be

13

so simple. But if Hortense has gone to so much trouble to get me on to the island, is she really going to let me leave without putting up a fight? I sigh and glance back over my shoulder at the rainforest. It's the quietest it's been since we got here, but for some reason this doesn't feel like a good thing. It feels like a calm-before-the-storm thing.

'So, no more running off like a *macaco-de-cheiro*?' Cruz says with a grin.

'Like a what?'

'A *macaco-de-cheiro*. It is a monkey that lives in Costa Rica. They run very fast – just like you.'

'Ah, I see. Okay, no more running off like a macaco de cheerio de whatever.' I grab hold of his hand and we start walking back down the beach. 'But no more reminding me how you saved my life either. It's not fair. How am I ever supposed to win a fight with you if you're gonna pull that one on me all the time?'

Cruz laughs. 'But it is the truth.'

'Cruz!'

'Okay, already.'

I squeeze his hand tight and we make our way back to the others.

'What happened, Gracie?' the Flea says as soon as we get back. 'Why'd you run off like that?'

He and Dan look up at me, Belle looks blindly from side to side.

'I'm sorry,' I mumble. 'I guess I just flipped out.'

Dan gets to his feet and comes and gives me a hug. 'Been a crazy few days, huh?'

I nod. Just the fact that Dan Charles is hugging me proves how crazy it's been – we barely said a word to each other back in our old lives at the dance academy. I guess I'd always been a bit wary, given all the rumours about his brother and gangs. But that seems really stupid now. I suppose one good thing about being stuck on this lousy island has been realising that when you judge someone without actually knowing them, you could really be missing out. I look at the Flea stroking Belle's hair. Another case in point.

Cruz goes over to one of the boxes of food we found on the boat and pulls out a couple of cans. 'How about we have something to eat since we are awake? We'll need all our strength for when we set sail.'

'Good plan.' The Flea grins. 'What do you say, m'lady?' he says to Belle in his fake British accent. 'Would you care for a hotdog surprise?'

Belle frowns. 'What's the surprise?'

'That it's not a frickin' coconut!' the Flea says, reverting to his native New York twang.

We all laugh and Belle nods and smiles weakly.

The Flea puts his arm round her and hugs her to him. 'We'll be getting out of here real soon, sweetie-pie. And then you can go straight to hospital and they'll figure out what's happened to you and have you right in no time.'

Belle nods again, but I can see tears shining on her face in the moonlight.

As Cruz passes round a can of hotdogs I can't help thinking about the man whose boat we found and whose food we're eating – and it pretty much kills my appetite stone dead. So many horrible things have happened since we got here, but seeing the man throw himself into the canyon right in front of us is almost too dreadful to comprehend. He'd written in his journal that he'd come to the island to see if the legend of Hortense was true – to see if she really did exist. I think of Hortense stumbling after us in the rainforest, her breath rasping like a bitter wind. What had she done to the man to make him so terrified of her – to make him jump to his death rather than face her? I shudder and look up to the sky, willing it to get light.

'I wonder how the others are doing,' the Flea says, staring down the beach at the sea.

I shiver as I follow his gaze. In the darkness the ocean seems to stretch on forever.

'At least there haven't been any more storms,' the Flea says. 'They'll have had a calm night. If they haven't been rescued already.'

My body relaxes a little. If the others have been found then the coast-guard might be on their way to get us right now.

'I still can't believe those guys left without us,' Dan mutters.

Cruz grunts in agreement, no doubt still furious that they took his boat.

'Well, hey, we'll all be gone soon too,' I say, my voice all fake cheery, like I'm doing the voice-over for a commercial.

Nobody replies.

A bird suddenly takes flight from the forest and swoops down over the beach toward the sea. If only I was a bird too. If only I could fly all the way back to LA — back to my mom and dad, and my cat, Tigger. I feel a lump growing in my throat. Cruz puts his arm round me and kisses the top of my head. I take a deep breath and make myself smile up at him. I can't fall apart now, not when we're so close to getting out of here.

'Should we start getting ready?' the Flea says. 'So we can leave as soon as the sun comes up?'

Cruz nods and he and Dan get to their feet and head over to the boat. After giving Belle a quick hug, the Flea jumps up and goes to pack his things.

'I'll sit with you, Belle,' I say, noticing that she's starting to look freaked out again. I shuffle up and put my arm round her. Her shoulder blades feel bony beneath her T-shirt. I think back to the digs Jenna and Cariss made about her being overweight before we left and it makes me feel sick

'Why did you run off just now?' Belle whispers to me.

I try to think of an answer that won't make me sound like

a fruit loop, and won't totally freak Belle out. 'I don't know. Frustration, I guess. I just wanted to find the person who's behind all the weird stuff that's happened here.'

Belle looks at me, but her eyes are blank. 'The person who took me?'

'Uh-huh.'

'Do you know who it is?'

My face instantly flushes. 'No, of course not.'

'Are you sure?'

'Sure I'm sure.'

Belle looks so stressed. Maybe I ought to tell her what I know — or at least, what I *think* I know about Hortense. But then I see Belle's mom's broken necklace glinting in her hand. And I remember what the Flea told us about her mom being diagnosed with cancer right before we left. I can't tell her anything. It'll just make her even more upset.

'We don't know any more than you,' I tell her. 'When we found you in the volcano whoever had taken you there had gone.'

Belle frowns. She doesn't look all that convinced.

'I'm just going down to the water to wash the sand out of my trainers,' the Flea says, coming over to us. 'You okay, Beau-Belle?'

Belle nods.

'Cool. I won't be long and then I'll help you get your stuff together, 'kay?'

18

'Okay.' As soon as he's gone, Belle turns back to me. 'Hold my hand, Grace,' she whispers.

Still keeping my arm round her, I take hold of her hand and squeeze it tightly. Despite the humidity it's as cold as ice. 'You're gonna be okay,' I tell her, softly.

She closes her eyes and leans into me. 'Thank you,' she sighs.

I glance over at Cruz. He and Dan are engrossed in checking out the sail on the boat.

I'm about to tell Belle what they're doing when I see the Flea racing back toward us, a look of horror on his face.

'What is it? What's wrong?' I call out to him.

'What's happening?' Belle says, gripping my hand tightly.

'It's okay, it's the Flea,' I tell her as he gets back to us, gasping for breath. 'What's the matter?'

The Flea just stands there, his mouth hanging open, but no words coming out.

'Hey, what's up?' Dan says, coming over with Cruz right behind him.

'Th-the boat,' the Flea stammers.

'It's okay, Dan and I just checked it again,' Cruz says.

'No, not that boat. *The* boat. *Our* boat. *Your* boat – the one the others took,' the Flea says, looking straight at Cruz.

Cruz instantly looks alarmed. 'What about it?'

The Flea gulps. 'It – it's been washed up on the beach. It's totally trashed.'

Chapter Three

As we run down the beach all I can think of is Jenna. And all I can hear is her voice, soft and scared, when we were trapped in the hold during the storm when this nightmare all began.

'*Grace, what's happening? Are we going to die?*'

I can see a dark shape at the water's edge. It looks like a beached whale. But as I get closer I see it's the hull of the boat. There's a huge jagged hole in the side, like something took a great bite out of it.

'Oh no!' My knees give way and I sink down on to the wet sand. My mind flashes back to the moment when I was left alone on the deck and I thought the waves were going to sweep me away. The idea of that actually happening to the others is so unbearable I can barely breathe.

The Flea starts pacing up and down. 'I don't get it. I just don't get it. There hasn't been a storm. There hasn't been a storm!' he yells up at the sky, like he's hollering at the weather gods.

'Can someone please help me?' Belle calls.

I wipe the tears from my eyes and clamber to my feet. We'd told Belle to wait by the trees but she's stumbling blindly down the beach toward us.

'I'll go get her,' the Flea says.

I nod. Dan and Cruz begin inspecting what's left of the boat. For a second, fear has me frozen to the spot. I don't know if I want to see any more. I force myself to walk over to them. The sea water feels icy against my warm feet and sends an instant chill through my body.

'How — how bad is it?' I ask them from the other side of the boat.

'It's bad,' Dan replies. I've never heard him so serious.

I look at Cruz and he shakes his head.

Bile burns at the back of my throat and I fight the urge to retch. As I walk round the battered hull, water sloshes up to my knees.

The inside of the boat is an empty shell. The deck has been ripped out and only the floorboards of the hold remain. I look at Cruz frantically. 'How did this happen? Is it storm damage? I don't understand.'

Cruz frowns. 'I do not know. They could have been caught in a storm but I don't see how we wouldn't have known about it. They would not have got that far from here with no engine. And for the boat to be so badly damaged . . .' He crouches down and examines the hole in the hull. 'It looks like it is caused by rocks. But how?'

We all look at each other blankly.

'Well, the life jackets are gone so they must be wearing them, right?' I look at Dan hopefully, like he'll know exactly what's happened.

But Dan's looking past me, at the sea. 'Uh-oh.'

'What?' I turn and follow his gaze.

Something square and white is bobbing towards us. We watch as a wave rolls in and deposits it on the sand, as if to say, *You think the boat's bad, look what I got for you this time.*

My heart plummets. It's a case – a vanity case. Jenna's vanity case. I stride back out of the water and grab the handle. Then I collapse down on to the ground, hugging the case to me as if it's Jenna herself.

'Why did you have to leave?' I cry. 'Why?'

In a flash Cruz, Dan, the Flea and Belle are surrounding me.

'It's okay,' Cruz says gently. 'You're right, there are no life jackets. They could have been rescued.'

'Yeah,' Dan says, 'for all we know they could have been picked up from the boat before it even got wrecked.'

'There's no way Jenna would go anywhere without her vanity case,' I sniff.

'True,' the Flea says. 'But hey, they might have been rescued in a hurry. She might not have had time to get it.'

I nod, desperately hoping that he's right.

'So, what do we do now?' the Flea says.

'What do you mean?' Belle asks nervously.

'Well, do we really want to go anywhere in a boat after this? I mean, hello, we don't even have any life jackets.'

We all look at Cruz. He frowns. 'The boat we found is in much better condition than this one though . . .'

'No kidding,' Dan says, looking at the wreck.

'No, I mean, even before they left, this boat was not truly seaworthy,' Cruz says. 'Why do you think I didn't already take you guys in it? There was a lot of structural damage after the storm. But the boat we have now,' he nods, 'it is in great condition.'

'But what if we get hit by a storm too?' the Flea says.

'We can't stay here!' Belle yells, making us all jump.

The Flea looks at her, concerned. 'We have to be careful, honey.'

'*We can't stay here!*' Belle's practically screaming now.

We all look at each other.

'It's okay,' I say. 'We're going to leave as soon as sun's up, right?' I call over to the others.

'Right,' Dan and Cruz say, followed by a slightly reluctant Flea.

I look at the silhouette of the volcano looming above the

rainforest. The sky behind it is turning purple. 'It won't be long now,' I say, taking hold of Belle's hands. They're still cold as ice. 'Come on, you're freezing, let's get back to the fire.'

Picking up Jenna's case, I lead Belle back to the fire and put some fresh sticks on it. The flames leap up hungrily.

'I have to get out of here, Grace,' Belle whispers. 'I have to get back to my mom.'

'I know. And you will.' I sit down next to her and put my arm around her. Then I look up the beach to the shadowy outline of the rainforest. My skin feels prickly with fear. *Are you there?* I say to Hortense in my head, but the only reply I get is the sudden squawk of a parrot.

'Cruz will get us all out of here,' I say firmly, trying to convince myself just as much as Belle. 'Listen, the birds are waking up. It'll soon be sunrise.'

'Come on, Beau-Belle, let's go get your stuff together,' the Flea says, coming over and helping her up.

Dan and Cruz start pulling the wreck of the boat further up the beach. I look down at Jenna's case and feel the sudden urge to open it. As I undo the zip, water trickles out on to my fingers. Inside is surprisingly messy for Jenna, but then I realise that she must have had to pack in a hurry once they decided to leave without us. Hurt crushes my heart. I guess years of friendship don't just disappear over night, no matter how bad things had become between us.

I think back to the last time I saw Jenna, looking down at me from the boat while I pleaded with her to stay. Will that be the last time I ever see her? I shove the thought from my mind and take her hair straighteners from the case. Just the very notion of hair straighteners seems crazy now. What does any of that stuff matter – hair straighteners, make-up, the latest look – when, at any moment, life can hurl you face to face with death?

I rummage further and feel the cover of a small, hardback book. I pull it out and open it. The first page is covered in Jenna's handwriting but the water has caused the ink to run so the words are just one long bumpy line. Is it her journal? I feel a weird mixture of guilt and longing. I know it's wrong to read another person's private thoughts but it might be the only way I get to hear Jenna's voice again. I carefully turn to an inside page. Once again most of the words have bled together, but one line remains unspoilt:

I can't believe I almost told G I slept with Todd, especially now we're stuck on this

What the hell? I hold the writing up to the firelight. But my eyes aren't playing tricks on me. It's there in black and white. Jenna slept with my boyfriend. But when did she sleep with him? My mind starts rewinding furiously. Was it here on the island? Or back at home? It can't have been here – it would have been physically impossible for them to sneak off without being noticed. So that means . . .

I feel sick as I think of how she questioned me over and over in the couple of weeks before we left about whether I was going to sleep with Todd on the cruise. My hands start shaking so hard I have to put the notebook down. I remember huddling next to Jenna in the hold of the boat after the storm hit. 'I have to tell you something, Grace,' she'd said, right after she asked me if we were going to die. Was that what she was going to tell me? Did she want to clear her conscience? I hug my knees to my chest and take a couple of slow, deep breaths. Even though Todd and I have broken up, it's like Jenna's reached out of her journal and socked me right in the stomach. I pick up the notebook and stumble to my feet. All that time I spent stressing about what *I'd* done to make her act so weird, and it was because *she'd* slept with my boyfriend. It was bad enough when I figured out she liked Todd, but this is the ultimate betrayal. So what if Todd and I weren't right for each other. She was supposed to be my best friend.

I start pacing round the fire. She can't have cared about me at all. She lied to me. She made me think she was the only person I could count on, and all the time . . . But she could be dead. The enormity of that realisation snuffs out my angry thoughts in an instant. I take one last look at the notebook then drop it on to the fire. A cloud of steam hisses up from it.

'Grace, honey, are you okay?' the Flea calls over from the cluster of trees where he's helping Belle to pack.

'I'm fine,' I mumble, sitting back down. I glance back into the case and notice a glint of silver. I look closer. 'Oh, no!'

'What is it?' The Flea starts walking over to me.

A silver chain is draped across Jenna's nail polish remover. I take it out and hold it up to the firelight. A pendant sways on the end. A pendant engraved with a snake above the letter H – for Hortense.

'The pendant!' The Flea exclaims.

I nod numbly.

The Flea frowns and scratches his head. 'How the heck did it get there? Where did you put it after we found it?'

I think back to when the pendant last appeared, by the HELP sign we'd made on the beach. Right after I'd seen someone trashing the sign. I'd taken it on to the boat – and flung it out to sea. So how had it ended up in Jenna's case? I remember Hortense whispering to me in the forest and telling me that every time Jenna had hurt me she'd done something to hurt her back. Was this her way of letting me know that she'd wrecked the boat? Had she *killed* Jenna for me? Then I think of how that one single line in the journal had remained legible. Had Hortense somehow managed to preserve it from water damage – so that I would see it? So that I would discover the truth?

'Where's Cruz?' I say, looking around frantically.

'He's right there, by the boat, honey.' The Flea takes hold of my arm. 'What's up?'

'Is everything okay, Grace?' Belle calls over from the trees.

'Yes, I'm fine,' I call back, but my voice is shrill. I turn to the Flea. 'How'd the necklace get in her case?' I whisper. 'I threw it into the sea.'

The Flea frowns. 'Why'd you do that?'

I start scuffing at the sand with my toe. 'I – it was making me uneasy, the way it kept turning up all the time.'

The Flea raises his eyebrows. 'Well, I guess it was washed up on the shore and Jenna took it. You know how mad she got when it went missing the first time.'

I nod and take a deep breath. I want to believe him. I really do. But fear keeps on clawing at my mind.

'Okay, guys, are you ready?' Cruz calls as he starts walking over from the boat.

I turn back to the fire and drop the pendant into the flames. *I don't care what Jenna did with Todd!* I yell at Hortense inside my head. *Just leave me alone. Leave us all alone!* I wait for her reply, for her soft sinister voice to echo back at me, but again there's nothing. All I hear are footsteps on the sand behind me. I turn and see Belle feeling around for my hand. I take hold of hers and grip it tight. Then I take a deep breath and look over at Cruz.

'Let's go,' I say. I don't care what kind of storms might be lurking out at sea. I have to get off this island. I have to get away from Hortense before she drives me insane.

Chapter Four

As the boat pulls away from the shore I start shivering uncontrollably. This is it. If Hortense is going to pull a stunt to get us to stay she's going to have to do it now. My throat feels so tight I can barely breathe. I close my eyes and think of Mom. Before Dad left and Mom's life collapsed in on itself like a burst balloon, she was a total yoga nut. One time, when I was freaking out about my mid-term math paper, she taught me how focusing on my breathing could help me stay calm. I imagine her thick southern drawl now, reminding me what to do: *In through the nose, honey, out through the mouth. In through the nose, and out through the mouth.*

I keep on doing this as Dan and Cruz hoist the sail. A sudden breeze causes the faded fabric to billow and the boat picks up speed. It's not until we've been going for a few minutes that

I allow myself to look back. The sunrise is making the peak of the volcano glow so red it looks like it's about to erupt. I look down at the beach. The pale sand is scarred with the scorched remains of our fires and, right in the middle, our HELP sign made of sticks. I think back to when we first arrived, and how beautiful and inviting the island had seemed after the terror of the storm. If only we'd known. I turn away and look out to sea. My heart is thumping like a bass drum. *Please, please let us get away*, I silently pray. At the other end of the boat, Cruz looks at me and smiles. But his eyes look anxious and I can tell he's thinking the same as me – is it really going to be this simple?

A sudden breeze spins the sail round and we all duck as it narrowly misses our heads.

'Shit!' Cruz grabs hold of the sail and tries to steer the boat back on course, but the wind is too strong.

'What is it? What's happening?' Belle asks.

'It's just getting a little breezy. No need to worry,' the Flea says, but his voice is tight.

'Help me,' Cruz calls.

All of us, apart from Belle, grab hold of the sail, but even four of us aren't strong enough to beat the force of the wind.

I look up at the sky, expecting to see storm clouds building, but it's vivid blue.

'At least we're not being blown back to the island,' the Flea says.

31

Cruz frowns as he continues to battle with the sail. 'We're not getting away from it either, though.'

We're speeding parallel to the island now, past the beach and the cove and on past a craggy wall of rainforest. It goes on and on. The island is way bigger than I'd imagined.

We all lean our weight into the sail, but it's no good. The wind is like a force field locking it into place. Then it suddenly changes direction. The sail swings round until the boat is facing the island.

'Oh no,' the Flea says.

'What is it?' Belle asks.

'Nothing,' the Flea and I chorus, exchanging worried glances.

'Come on!' Cruz yells and once again we try shifting the sail.

'Why's it so windy? Is there a storm coming?' Belle looks around blindly.

'No, honey, it's just a bit breezy now we're further out,' the Flea says. He turns to me and mouths the words, 'What the hell?'

I shrug. Fear takes root in the pit of my stomach.

The boat is cutting across the water like a speedboat now as it's sucked back in toward the island. But this time, there's no wide beach to land on. All I can see is a forbidding wall of rainforest.

'Shit. You think there's gonna be rocks up ahead?' Dan asks Cruz.

'I don't know,' Cruz replies.

'What are we going to do?' the Flea says.

'Will someone please tell me what's going on?' Belle sounds close to tears. I go sit down next to her.

'The wind is blowing us back inland,' I tell her.

'Back to the beach?' Belle's eyes dart from side to side. She looks terrified.

'No, we've come round to the other side of the island.'

'Hey, take a look at that,' Dan shouts, pointing straight ahead.

He's pointing to a small chink in the wall of green. As we get closer, the chink gets a little bigger.

'It's an inlet,' Cruz cries. 'Okay, we have to try and steer the boat toward it.'

But we don't have to steer at all. The boat is drawn to the narrow gap like a pea being sucked up by a straw. We all sigh with relief as we sail past jagged outcrops of rocks and into the opening.

'Holy moley!' the Flea exclaims. The inlet is so narrow the trees on either side meet overhead, forming a tunnel of green. A noisy chorus of squawks and screeches rings out around us, like a drunken band trumpeting our arrival. I look up and see two blood-red parrots watching us with beady black eyes. Their gnarled beaks are huge.

'What's happening now?' Belle whispers.

'We're going down the inlet,' I say.

Belle sighs and closes her eyes.

Dan takes his baseball cap off and gazes around. The Flea looks equally awestruck. Cruz stands at the prow of the boat, his shoulders broad and his back arrow-straight, as if he's preparing for battle.

My stomach churns as I wonder what might be waiting for us at the other end of the tunnel. I think of Hortense and how she looked when we came across her in the forest – her wizened skin and claw-like fingers, and the horrific rasping noise she'd made when she chased us.

'Look,' Cruz says, pointing ahead.

In the distance I can see a glimmer of light. The boat carries on sailing toward it. I look around at the others and a terrible thought enters my mind. *What if we're sailing towards our death?*

When we finally reach the end of the tunnel the inlet spills out into a huge lagoon. The water is bright turquoise, surrounded by a high wall of rainforest. It's like floating inside a huge green bowl and it's so breathtakingly beautiful that for a second I forget to be scared. I figure the others must be feeling the same, as they're all gazing around, open-mouthed. Only Belle still looks tense.

'Where are we?' she asks.

'I don't know, but it looks uncannily like paradise!' the Flea exclaims.

'We're in some kind of lagoon,' I tell Belle. I start looking round for signs of anything sinister. As the boat drifts toward the far side of the lagoon I notice something moving on the rocks at the water's edge.

'Look, there's someone there,' I whisper.

'Who is it?' Belle hisses.

'I'm not sure,' the Flea says, squinting toward the shore.

We all sit in silence as the boat glides closer and closer to the land. Whoever it is they are sitting cross-legged on the rocks, facing away from us. All I can make out is that they've got cropped white-blond hair and deeply tanned skin.

Dan looks at us. 'Should we call out to them?'

We all shrug, unsure what to do.

'Well, they're gonna see us soon enough,' the Flea says, 'so I guess it makes no difference.' He carefully gets to his feet. 'Hello!'

The figure jumps up and turns to face us. It's a girl. She's wearing a bright coral sundress.

The girl shields her eyes with a tanned hand and looks straight at us.

'Oh my freakin' God! I can't believe there's someone here!' the Flea exclaims, looking back at us.

'Yeah, and someone who doesn't look like they've just escaped from the set of *Dawn of the Dead*,' Dan says with a wry chuckle.

The girl starts running across the rocks toward us.

'Who do you think she is?' the Flea whispers.

'How the hell should we know?' Dan says, raising his eyebrows.

I look at Cruz. He shrugs.

'Hello!' the girl calls out as she reaches the water's edge.

'Hey!' the Flea cries excitedly. He turns back to us, his eyes wide. 'She speaks English!'

'Who are you?' the girl says in a clipped British accent. Then she starts to laugh. 'I'm sorry – that sounds really rude. But – where have you come from?'

'She doesn't just speak English – she *is* English!' the Flea whispers excitedly.

The girl starts wading through the water toward us. Her face is a perfect heart shape and she has the kind of welcoming eyes and wide smile that make you instantly feel at ease. As she gets closer I see a tiny silver nose stud glinting against her golden brown skin and a bright-blue butterfly tattooed on her wrist.

'Are you okay?' she asks, her eyes widening with concern as she gets closer to the boat.

'Yes, we're fine, thank you. Positively brilliant. Well, we are now we've found you!' the Flea exclaims in his best British accent. 'I'm Jimmy Patterson, but you can call me the Flea – everyone else does – and it is *very* nice to meet you!' He extends his thin arm over the side of the boat to shake her hand.

The girl laughs heartily as she takes it. 'I'm Lola. Very nice to meet you too.'

She grins at the rest of us. 'This is so cool!'

The way she says it, so excited and carefree, makes me want to cry. It feels so long since we experienced this kind of normality, I'm not exactly sure how to react.

Cruz nods at Lola, then he jumps down into the water and starts guiding the boat toward the sand. Dan quickly joins him.

Lola grabs hold of the side of the boat to help them. She looks at me and smiles. 'How did you guys get here?'

'Very long story,' I say.

'We were shipwrecked a few days ago,' the Flea explains. 'Over on the other side of the island.'

Lola shakes her head in disbelief. 'No way!'

The Flea nods proudly. 'Yes indeedy!'

'My name's Grace,' I say, climbing down into the water next to Lola. She takes hold of my arm to steady me. She's grinning like a Cheshire cat.

'This is brilliant. I mean, obviously it isn't brilliant that you've been shipwrecked, but it's so cool that you've turned up today. Ruby's last lot of guests have just left and I was thinking that it was going to be so boring until the next lot arrive.'

'Who's Ruby?' the Flea and Dan ask in unison.

Lola smiles at them. 'She runs the retreat.'

'The retreat?' Dan turns back to me and raises his eyebrows.

Lola nods. 'Yeah. It's where I'm staying. She set it up a couple of years ago, when she got sick of city life. Wait till you meet her. She's so calm and serene. She's like a walking advert for island living.'

The Flea leans close to me. 'Okay, tell me, am I dreaming right now?' he whispers.

'What's that?' Lola asks.

'Nothing,' the Flea says quickly. 'It just seems very different on this side of the island.'

'No kidding,' Dan mutters.

Lola stares at him, puzzled. Then she turns to look at Belle, who's still in the boat and staring ahead of her blankly. 'Is your friend okay?' she whispers to me.

'Yes, well, no – not exactly. She just lost her sight.'

Lola's huge eyes widen. 'That's terrible! What happened?'

'It's a very long story.'

'But how?'

I look at Lola and shake my head. If Belle hears us talking about her it'll only make her feel a million times worse.

Thankfully, Lola gets what I'm trying to say and nods. 'Okay, well let me take you guys up to the retreat. You look exhausted.'

The Flea and I help Belle from the boat.

'It's okay, Belle,' I whisper in her ear, 'she seems really nice.'

Belle nods and gives a tight little smile.

'Follow me,' Lola calls, before bounding across the rocks. We trail after her, the Flea arm in arm with Belle, and Dan right behind them. Cruz drops back and takes my hand.

'What do you reckon about all this?' I whisper.

He shrugs his shoulders. 'I don't know.'

'I can't believe we're back on the island.'

Cruz nods.

'Do you think it was Hortense?' I hardly dare look at him.

'I don't know. Sometimes you do get freak winds like that but . . .'

He doesn't need to continue. I know exactly what he's thinking because I'm thinking it too – Hortense was never going to let us get away that easily.

Once we get to the end of the rocks, Lola leads us through a cluster of trees. But it isn't like the rainforest on the other side of the island that's claustrophobically dense and seems to go on forever. These trees are a lot more spaced out and within a half a minute we've reached another huge clearing. It's cut through by a wide, green river, covered with plate-sized lily pads. A rickety wooden footbridge snakes across the water. 'We're almost there,' Lola calls back to us. 'Ruby isn't at the retreat right now. She went to the bay to see the last guests off.'

We all exchange glances again. After all this time feeling trapped on the island it's kind of freaky hearing her talk so casually about people leaving. Freaky, but unbelievably good. Maybe all isn't lost after all. Maybe we'll still be able to get out of here.

We make our way across the bridge. As it starts swaying wildly I'm too exhausted to even worry about what could be lurking in the water beneath. Once we're on the other side, Lola leads us through some more trees and then out into another huge clearing.

'Wowsers!' the Flea exclaims.

Several long cabins made from bamboo line the edges of the clearing. But my eyes are instantly drawn to the centre. There, looming above the cabins, is the strangest house I've ever seen. It's three storeys high and perched on wooden stilts so tall it's impossible to see inside from down on the ground. The walls are a light-and-dark patchwork of bamboo and logs, topped with a slightly lop-sided roof made from sheets of corrugated metal.

Lola sees us staring at it and starts to laugh. 'That's where Ruby lives. It's cool, isn't it? The retreat guests all stay in the cabins,' Lola points to one of them. 'There's plenty of room. Now the others have gone there's only me and Michael – my boyf— . . . *ex*-boyfriend, and Ruby here. The next guests are arriving in a few days – for the party.' She starts to grin. 'You'll be here for the party!'

'What party?' Dan asks, looking slightly shell-shocked.

'We can't stay for any party,' the Flea whispers. 'We need to get Belle to hospital.'

But before Lola can reply a guy comes out of one of the cabins, rubbing his eyes like he just woke up. He's broad shouldered and pale skinned, with copper-coloured wavy hair that almost reaches his shoulders. He's wearing long swimming shorts and has an elaborate tattoo of a dragon across one half of his chest.

When he sees Lola he starts to glare. 'Where have you been?' he asks. His accent is British too. Then he notices us. 'Who are these people?'

'This is Michael,' Lola says to us, her voice suddenly flat.

'Who are they?' Michael hisses at her. I take an instant dislike to him.

'I found them down at the lagoon,' Lola explains. 'They've been shipwrecked and they were –'

'And you brought them here?' Michael scowls at her.

'Well, yes. Obviously.'

'But what about Ruby?'

Lola stares at him. 'They've been shipwrecked!'

Ever the optimist, the Flea walks over to Michael, holding out his hand. 'I'm Jimmy the Flea, pleased to meet you,' he says cheerily. But Michael completely blanks him and continues staring at Lola.

'I'm sure Ruby won't mind,' Lola says, her cheeks

flushing. 'I couldn't exactly leave them there.'

Michael gives a sarcastic laugh. 'How compassionate of you.'

I feel my hackles rising. What the hell is this guy's problem? 'We've been shipwrecked,' I say. 'We need help getting back home.'

Michael looks at me blankly before turning back to Lola. 'Yeah well, it's your funeral.' Then he stomps back into the cabin.

Chapter Five

I stand, rooted to the spot. What's going on here? Why is Michael so concerned about Ruby's reaction? I look at Cruz questioningly. He shakes his head, clearly as bewildered as I am.

Lola turns and gives us a weak smile. 'I'm so sorry. Things are a little tense between us at the moment. We only just broke up. He isn't taking it very well.'

'No kidding,' Dan mutters, scowling after Michael.

I smile at Lola. 'It's okay.'

'He seemed a little worried about this Ruby . . .' Cruz says questioningly.

Lola glances up at the bizarre house on stilts. 'Ruby is very secretive about this place. She doesn't like people turning up uninvited.'

'Were you invited here then?' Cruz immediately asks.

Lola nods. 'Yes. When we were travelling in Central America we met some friends of Ruby's and they asked us to come here with them.' She lowers her voice. 'Michael wasn't all that keen. He thought it was a bit risky, coming away with a load of strangers to an island in the middle of nowhere.' She looks at me and smiles. 'But that's why you go travelling, right? To get away from the mundane and embrace the adventure.'

I smile and nod, but inside I literally ache for 'the mundane'. Since we set off for the cruise I've had enough adventure to last me several lifetimes.

'But don't worry,' Lola says quickly. 'I'm sure Ruby will be fine about you being here. She's really cool once you get to know her, and once she's certain she can trust you. Why don't you go and dump your stuff in there?' Lola points to one of the cabins. Thankfully it's not the one Michael stormed into.

I nod. 'Sure.'

We head over to the cabin, with the Flea carefully guiding Belle. Inside is sparse but clean. One wall is lined with a row of single beds. They're made from logs and covered in brightly coloured blankets. In the centre of the wooden floor is a coarsely woven, yellow and green mat. It's the kind of place I could picture Snow White's dwarves sleeping in.

'Oh man!' Dan exclaims, walking over to the nearest bed. 'Allow me to introduce myself,' he says to the bed, removing his cap with a flourish. 'I am Dan Charles and I've been dreaming of this moment *forever*!' He collapses down on to the bed, wraps himself in the blanket and gives a love-struck sigh.

The Flea laughs. Then he turns to Belle. 'There are beds, honey, actual beds! Obviously home-made, but full of rustic charm – think Pottery Barn meets *Jungle Book*.'

Belle nods.

'What do you guys make of all this?' I whisper, as I put my bag down in the corner.

'Well, clearly our friend Michael has a few issues,' the Flea whispers back, 'and I can't say I'm looking forward to meeting Ruby. But Lola is adorable and, compared to the other islanders we've met, even Michael seems downright charming.'

'Well, if this Ruby chick does get all heavy about us being here, we can just ask her to help us leave,' Dan says, his eyes closed and body spread, starfish-style across the bed.

The Flea nods. 'Absolutely. I mean, it's not as if we want to stick around, and if she's that uptight about keeping this place a secret we can just sign disclaimers and never talk about it again. I don't care. Quite honestly, after the things we've seen, I'll do anything to get out of here.'

'Are you guys hungry?' Lola calls from outside. 'Would you like me to make you some pancakes?'

'What the hell?' Dan is off the bed in a second.

The Flea grins manically and even Belle smiles.

'Did she just say *pancakes?*' Dan whispers, his eyes saucer-wide.

'I do believe she did,' the Flea replies.

'You bet,' Dan hollers.

'Okay – coming right up,' Lola calls back.

'Do you think we should tell her what happened to us?' I whisper. 'You know, about Belle and what happened in the forest?'

Dan shrugs. 'Dunno.'

'Maybe we should just play it by ear,' Cruz says. 'Figure out what's going on here first. And see what this Ruby person is like.'

We all nod. Then the others head out. Cruz and I hang back.

'We need to be careful,' he whispers, taking my hand.

I nod. It's exactly what I was thinking. It seems impossible to believe that, after everything we went through on the other side of the island, this side should be completely unaffected by Hortense. And not only unaffected, but some kind of peace-out, hippy retreat. It doesn't make sense.

'Do you think – do you think Hortense is still watching us somehow?'

Cruz frowns. 'I don't know.'

I force myself to be more positive. 'But if it is all okay over here, and people are coming and going then . . .'

Cruz smiles at me. 'I know. Then we will be able to leave

46

too.' His eyes start to twinkle. 'And I will have saved your life all over again.'

I frown. 'Oh really? And how'd you figure that one out?'

'Well, I brought you to this side of the island.'

I raise my eyebrows. 'That's funny. I could have sworn it was a gale that brought us here.'

Cruz shakes his head. 'Yeah well, that was just – what do you say? A minor detail.'

I start to laugh. 'Hmm.'

He pulls me close and kisses me lightly on the forehead.

I grin up at him. 'Come on, let's go get some pancakes.'

When we get outside, the others are gathered in the doorway of another of the cabins. It's smaller than the one we've just been in and, once we get there, I see that it's obviously the kitchen. The walls are lined with uneven shelves and I can't stop my mouth from falling open when I see the piles of exotic-looking fruit and vegetables on them. The others are all looking similarly awestruck. Lola takes a clay pot from a cupboard and tips a pale yellow powder from it into a large bowl.

'Corn flour,' she says when she sees the Flea staring at it. 'Ruby has a great farm here. It's amazing. She grows all kinds of things. Even coffee.'

'Coffee!' the Flea exclaims. 'Oh my, what I would do for a skinny French vanilla latte right now.'

Lola laughs. 'Well, you might not be able to get one of

those, but trust me, Ruby's coffee is divine.'

'I wonder if it is as good as the Costa Rican coffee,' Cruz says.

Lola looks at him. 'Are you from Costa Rica?'

Cruz nods. 'Yes. Do you know it?'

Lola grins. 'Of course. It's where Michael and I were before we came here. We did some voluntary work in San José. It's a beautiful country.'

'It's where you were before here?' Cruz repeats.

Lola nods. 'So, how do you guys all know each other?' she asks, bending down to fetch a cloth-covered jug from under a counter.

'We go to the same school in LA,' the Flea says. 'We're dance students.'

Lola looks up at him. 'Really?'

The Flea nods. 'Yes, apart from Cruz here. He was sailing the boat we were in when the storm hit.'

'So, you didn't know each other before?' Lola looks directly at Cruz and me.

I shake my head, aware that my cheeks are flushing. From the way Cruz has his arm round my shoulders it's obvious we're a couple. I had gotten so used to our insular world I hadn't really thought about what Cruz and I getting together must look like to someone from the outside. But if it bothers Lola she doesn't show it. She just smiles at me, then reaches under the counter again and brings out a basket of eggs.

48

'Holy omelettes!' the Flea exclaims.

'Eggs!' Dan gasps, in the exact same lovesick voice he used to address the bed.

'You have chooks here?' I say, as the vision of a golden omelette appears in my head, complete with a jaunty sprig of parsley. I am suddenly so hungry even my fingertips feel like they're screaming, '*feed me!*'

Lola nods. 'Yes. Right behind the vegetable garden.'

'The vegetable garden.' The Flea repeats her words with such heartfelt emotion it's like he's reciting a love poem.

'I can't imagine what it must be like to be shipwrecked,' Lola says, cracking the eggs one by one into the bowl.

I watch her, completely mesmerised.

'It must have been so scary.'

'Not nearly as scary as some of the shit that's happened since,' Dan mutters.

'What's that?' Lola stops what she's doing and looks at him.

'Nothin'.' Dan quickly looks away.

Lola takes the cloth from the jug and pours what looks suspiciously like milk into the bowl.

'Excuse me, but is that . . .' the Flea breaks off, clearly speechless . . . 'is that *milk*? Like, from a *cow*?'

'Yes.' Lola laughs. Then her face goes deadly serious 'When was the last time you guys had a proper meal?'

'About a year ago,' the Flea says, gazing dreamily at the

bowl. 'At least it feels that long. We've been living off coconuts, mostly. And the occasional fish.'

'And cold hot dogs,' Dan adds.

Lola looks at him. 'Hot dogs?'

'Yeah, they were in the boat we found.'

We all frown at him and he looks away, embarrassed.

Lola looks at the Flea. 'You found a boat?'

'Yes, the one you saw us in,' the Flea replies. 'We just found it randomly one day,' he adds quickly, sounding about as convincing as a little kid saying it wasn't him who drew on the wall in crayon.

Lola raises her eyebrows. 'Wow, that was lucky.'

The Flea nods and looks away. 'Yeah.'

Lola lifts up spoonfuls of the pancake mix, checking for lumps. My mouth, which has felt as dry as desert sand for most of the morning, starts producing saliva like it's a magical spring. Lola takes an ancient-looking iron skillet from a hook on the wall and leads us back outside. In the centre of the clearing are the remains of a large fire. Lola puts some dried leaves on top and stokes the flames back into life, then she places the skillet on a frame over the fire and ladles some batter into it. We all sit in a circle and watch, silenced by a mixture of hunger and longing.

'O.M. effing G! Is that what I think it is?' the Flea suddenly exclaims. We all follow his gaze off to the side of the clearing.

There, in the shade of some huge trees, is a round construction made from large clay bricks. Two wooden poles stand either side of it, with a beam running across the top. A rope hangs down from the beam, disappearing inside the bricks.

'Is it a — *well*?' I whisper — hardly daring say the word out loud.

Lola nods casually, like having a source of fresh water is the most natural thing in the world.

'And does it actually — work?' The Flea gazes at her hopefully.

'Of course.' Lola shifts the pan slightly and the batter sizzles.

Dan lets out a whoop and the Flea starts to laugh.

'I have a feeling this is going to be my best breakfast ever,' he says, putting his arm around Belle. 'See, Belle, I told you everything was gonna be okay. There's even a well — with, you know, *water*!'

Belle nods but she still looks real tense. I can't begin to imagine what it must feel like to suddenly go blind. It must be so scary.

'I'm just going to get some plates,' Lola says. 'Can you guys keep an eye on the pancake for me?'

'Oh don't worry, I won't be lookin' at nothing else,' Dan says, gazing at the batter as it bubbles gently in the pan.

Lola laughs and heads off to the kitchen.

'I think it's okay here,' the Flea whispers as soon as she's gone. 'I really don't think we've got anything to worry about.'

I don't know if it's the heavenly smell of the pancake cooking lulling me into a false sense of security, but even I'm starting to agree with him. I look at Cruz to try and figure out what he's thinking, but he's looking at the floor, his face expressionless.

'Do y'all think they've got some maple syrup?' Dan says dreamily.

'Oh my God, then I really will have died and gone to heaven!' the Flea exclaims.

Dan rubs his hands together. 'Or how about some chocolate syrup? Or —'

'What's going on?' A woman's voice echoes around the clearing, deep and stern. From somewhere inside the forest there's the sound of flapping wings.

We all look around, trying to find the source of the voice.

'I said, what's going on?'

I see a slight movement out of the corner of my eye and turn toward it. A woman is standing at an entrance to the clearing. She's wearing an over-sized, faded T-shirt as a dress, with a wide black-leather belt fastened tightly around the middle. Her Afro hair fans from her head like a dark halo and her brown skin gleams like a coffee bean in the sunlight. Her legs and arms are long and slim and she's standing bolt upright. She looks like an Amazonian queen. All that's missing is the spear.

The Flea jumps to his feet. 'Are you Ruby?'

The woman starts striding toward us. 'Who the hell wants to know?' Her accent is American. It sounds southern. As she gets closer I see that she actually isn't that old – early twenties max. It's her height and the way she carries herself that make her seem older.

'We've been shipwrecked,' I say, scrambling to my feet.

Ruby stares at me. Her eyes are pale blue and incredibly piercing against her brown skin.

I instinctively look down at my feet. 'We were trying to –'

'Grace!'

My skin erupts in goose bumps and I stare frantically into the dark of the rainforest. Maybe I was hearing things. Maybe it wasn't her . . .

'Grace, is that you?'

I watch, my heart pounding, as Jenna stumbles out of the forest behind Ruby.

Chapter Six

'I thought I'd never see you again!' Jenna runs across the clearing toward me and hugs me tight. Her pale blonde hair is as brittle as straw, and what's left of her make up has smudged into dark rings beneath her eyes.

I'm so numb with shock I can't speak. Over Jenna's shoulder I see Todd make his way into the clearing. Cariss is right behind him. Their clothes are soaking and tattered and they all look totally shell-shocked. I watch the gap in the trees, waiting for Ron to appear.

'Grace, what's happened?'

I look down at Belle. She's staring up at me, her eyes filled with panic.

'It's okay. It's the others.' My mouth is suddenly so dry I can barely get the words out. 'They – they're here.' I look back at Jenna – and grip her arms real tight to make sure she's not an illusion.

'Are these the friends y'all were telling me about?' Ruby asks Jenna. 'The ones you were shipwrecked with?'

Jenna nods, still staring at me. Her eyes are shiny with tears.

I swallow hard. They're alive. Relief surges through me, making my body tremble. I look back at the trees, but there's still no sign of Ron.

Everyone apart from Belle is standing now, and for a moment we're all silent. I guess no one knows quite how to act, or what to say. It's like everyone's waiting for someone else to take the lead.

Ruby stands motionless, watching.

'What happened to you guys?' the Flea asks, finally breaking the stunned silence. 'The boat washed up on the beach, totally trashed.'

'We hit some rocks,' Jenna mumbles. 'We had to swim back to the island.'

I look at Todd. He's staring at the ground. I notice that his hands are trembling.

'How did you find the retreat?' Ruby says to the Flea, her voice as icy as her pale eyes.

'Lola brought us,' the Flea says. 'She found us down by '

'Ruby!' We all turn at the sound of Lola's voice. She's standing in the doorway of the kitchen, holding a pile of plates.

When she sees the others her mouth falls open in shock. 'Oh. Who are —?'

'These are our friends,' the Flea says. 'The ones we —'

'I found them at the bay,' Ruby says curtly. 'Can I have a word with you please, Lola? In the house.'

'Of course.' As Lola walks past me she nods. 'Don't worry,' she whispers. 'I'll sort it out.'

I smile gratefully.

Lola hands the Flea the plates, then she follows Ruby over to her house and up the ladder inside.

I wait, half-expecting to hear raised voices, but it stays ominously quiet.

We all look at each other again. All apart from Todd, who keeps on staring at the ground.

The Flea goes over to the fire and grabs hold of the skillet. 'The others are safe, Beau-Belle. Isn't that great?'

Belle nods and gives a tight smile. I guess that given the hell Jenna and Cariss put her through before she's hardly going to be throwing a party.

'Where's Ron?' I whisper to Jenna.

Her eyes fill with tears again and she looks away.

I turn to Todd. 'Todd — what happened to Ron?'

Todd starts shaking his head.

My stomach lurches.

Dan goes over to Todd and places one of his huge hands

on his shoulder. 'What happened, bro?'

'We lost . . .' Jenna starts to cry. 'We lost him.'

Todd lets out a weird whimpering sound and covers his face with his hands.

'You lost him?' The Flea puts the skillet down and stares at Jenna, his mouth open in horror. 'But where?'

Jenna's now crying too hard to answer. We all turn to Cariss.

'In the sea,' she mutters. Then she starts crying too and sinks to the ground, hugging her knees to her chest.

I let out a gasp of shock. Cruz is over in an instant and takes hold of my hand.

Dan puts his arm round Todd's shoulders. 'Oh, man!'

'He might be okay,' Cariss stammers between sobs.

'He's not okay!' We all turn to face Todd as he finally speaks. Tears are streaming down his face. 'He was so out of it from that stuff he drank from the bottle in the forest. I tried to keep hold of him, but I lost my grip. I saw him get swept away. I saw him . . .' Todd chokes on his tears . . . 'I saw him go under.'

Cruz lets go of my hand and strides over to him. 'It is not your fault,' he says softly. 'The sea, it is too powerful. You did everything you could. You mustn't blame yourself.'

Todd wipes his eyes and stares at Cruz. I think of the tension between them before and for a horrible moment I think Todd might lose it with Cruz again. But then he starts nodding his head real slowly.

'Thanks,' he whispers.

Cruz places his hand on his arm. 'No problem.'

'Did Ron die?' Belle asks suddenly, causing us all to jump.

The Flea goes and crouches down beside her. 'It looks that way, yes.' I've never heard him so serious.

Jenna wipes her eyes and stares at Belle. 'What's up with her,' she whispers to me. 'Why is she staring like that?'

I move closer to her so I can whisper. 'She's gone blind.'

Jenna steps back in shock. 'What?'

I shake my head and put my finger to my lips.

'What's up?' Cariss says immediately.

'Nothing,' Jenna says quickly. Then she turns back to me. 'But how?' she whispers. 'What happened to her? Where did you find her?'

'I'll tell you later,' I whisper back.

Jenna nods and gives me a weak smile.

We all fall silent again.

'So, how did you guys end up here?' Cariss asks, eventually.

'We sailed,' the Flea replies.

'You *sailed*?' Cariss stares at him.

'But how?' Jenna looks at me, then immediately looks at the ground, her cheeks flushing.

Seeing her look so embarrassed makes me think of her journal and its shock revelation. I wait for anger to hit me, but all I feel is exhaustion, and overwhelming relief that they're still alive.

'Would anyone like a pancake?' the Flea asks hesitantly.

'Pancake?' Cariss says. Her voice is as timid and weak as a little girl's and nothing like the super-bitch she was before.

'Yes. We were just about to have some when you guys arrived.' The Flea replies, nodding toward the skillet.

'Yes please,' Cariss says meekly.

'We found another boat,' I say to Jenna. 'It was —'

'What's happened to Belle?' Cariss interrupts.

I glance down at Belle. She's feeling around in the sand for something.

'Belle, are you okay?' I say, going over to her.

'I dropped my mom's necklace,' she mutters.

I see it glinting in the sand by her foot and place it in her hand.

She breathes a sigh of relief. 'Thank you, Grace.'

'No problem.'

'What's wrong with her?' Cariss says.

'Belle's lost her sight,' the Flea says quickly as he flips the pancake over. I catch a waft and, despite all the trauma, my stomach lets out a rumble of hunger.

'What? How?' Cariss asks, but her eyes are now glued to the pancake.

'We don't know,' the Flea says. 'But I'm sure it will all be fine once we get back home and get her to a hospital.'

I go to give Belle's hand a squeeze. It's clenched into a tight fist.

'Okay, I say Beau-Belle gets first pancake,' the Flea says, quickly plating it up and passing it to her.

Belle feels around for the pancake. As she brings it to her mouth I swear every one of us mimes taking a bite.

Another awkward silence falls, broken only by the sizzle as the Flea pours some more batter on to the skillet.

Todd turns to Cruz.

'I owe you an apology,' he mumbles. 'We should never have taken your boat. I'm sorry.'

Everyone watches Cruz. He looks at Todd for a second, then he puts his arm round his shoulders and gives him a hug. 'No problem. Let's forget about it.'

The rest of us all sigh with relief.

'Cool,' Todd says, and he flashes me a glance.

I nod at him. Unspoken apology accepted.

'Let's just make a line under what happened before,' Cruz says, looking around the group. 'We need to work together now to get out of here.'

'Amen to that!' Dan says.

Jenna gives me a small, hopeful smile. I smile back. After everything that has happened, it really does feel right to let go of all the crap that happened before.

'I'm confused about Belle,' Cariss says loudly.

I want to groan.

Belle stops eating.

'I told you – it will all be fine once we get her to a hospital,' the Flea says, curtly.

'But a person doesn't just go blind for no reason.' Cariss comes and stands right in front of Belle, staring down at her like she's an exhibit in a freak show.

Belle starts to scowl.

'Where's Lola?'

We all turn to see Michael standing in the doorway of his cabin, arms folded.

'She's up in the house. With Ruby,' the Flea replies, a little frostily.

Michael looks up at the house, and for all his swagger, I see a definite look of fear cross his face.

'Who's he?' Cariss asks.

'He's called Michael and he's Lola's *friend*,' the Flea says pointedly, as he flips the pancake.

Michael looks visibly wounded. Then he looks back at the house anxiously. I wonder why he seems so uneasy at any mention of Ruby. Maybe it would be worth trying to make conversation with him to find out.

'So, how long have you and Lola been here?' I call over to him.

Michael waits for a moment, as if weighing up whether or not he should waste any energy speaking to me.

'About a month,' he says finally. 'Although it feels a lot longer,' he mutters.

I shoot a look at Cruz. He instantly meets my gaze, no doubt thinking the same thing. Is Michael acting so angry because of his break-up with Lola, or is it something else?

But before I have the chance to say anything, Lola climbs back down the ladder out of the house.

'Great news,' she says, jumping the final three rungs on to the sand. 'Ruby says you can stay.'

'But we don't want to stay,' Cariss says immediately.

Lola looks at her and smiles. 'I don't mean stay forever. Just for the party. Then you can leave on the boat with the other guests.'

'What party?' Jenna says.

Lola makes her way back over to us. 'Ruby's having a party at the end of the week. A lot of people are coming here specially for it. It's going to be amazing.'

We all exchange anxious glances. The thought of partying after what's happened to Ron seems horrific.

'Hmm,' Michael says pointedly, and for a second Lola's smile disappears. She frowns at him, then looks back at us and her smile returns.

'I don't think any of us are really in the mood to party to

be honest with you,' I say, looking round at the others. They all start nodding. 'One of our friends . . .' I break off, unable to actually say it.

'One of our friends just died,' Cariss says to Lola.

Lola's face falls. 'Oh my God! I'm so sorry. What happened?'

'It was when their boat hit the rocks,' I tell her quietly. 'So it would be great if we could just get out of here as soon as possible. We've been missing for days now – our folks are going to be going out of their minds with worry.'

Lola nods. 'Of course. But I'm afraid that won't be possible until the weekend, after the party.'

'What?' Cariss exclaims with one of her trademark pouts. 'Why not?'

Lola looks up at the house. I follow her gaze and I'm sure I see a shadow flit across one of the windows.

'Ruby doesn't have a boat,' Lola explains quietly. 'That was the whole point of her coming here – to be completely cut off from the outside world. The only time there's a boat here is when guests come to stay.'

Cariss frowns. 'How does she arrange for guests to come to stay if she's totally cut off?'

'She pre-arranges it with her friend Carlos. He brings them over on set dates.'

'But what if there's an emergency?' Cariss says. 'What if she needed to get off the island?'

Lola shrugs. 'It's the way she likes it.'

Michael mutters something under his breath and Lola shoots him a death stare.

Jenna turns to me. 'You said that you guys sailed here. Couldn't we use the boat that you found?'

I shake my head. 'That's what we'd been planning to do, but it isn't big enough for all of us.'

'Well, maybe some of us could go first and send for help,' Cariss says.

'What, like before?' Dan glares at her. 'I don't think so. Next time we leave, we all leave together.'

'Will the boat that's bringing the guests be big enough to take us all back as well?' I say. Everyone looks at Lola anxiously.

Lola nods. 'Oh yes. Carlos's boat is more than big enough, isn't it, Michael?'

Michael nods grudgingly.

'Ruby's friend Carlos brings her guests over from the mainland,' Lola explains.

'The mainland?' the Flea says.

Lola nods.

'What is this mainland?' Cruz asks immediately.

Lola laughs. 'Costa Rica of course.'

'Costa Rica?' Cruz looks shell-shocked.

Seeing his expression, Lola frowns. 'Yes, I —'

'How far are we from Costa Rica?' Cruz cuts in.

We all stare at Lola. 'I don't know exactly.' She looks at Michael. 'How far would you say, Michael?'

Michael shrugs. 'Don't know. It took us a few hours to get here.'

I glance at Cruz. He looks like someone who just got told the moon is actually made of cheese. I guess he must be shocked that Ile de Sang is so close to his home.

'We may as well just wait a few more days then,' the Flea says, plating up another pancake.

I take a moment to try and process this latest development. Finding the retreat, only to find that we're still trapped on the island is filling me with unease – especially given what's happened to Ron and to Belle. Pressure starts building in my head. Instead of escaping from Hortense, I can't help feeling that her net is tightening.

Chapter Seven

My pancake, when it finally arrives, brings some comfort at least.

'Oh, this is so good!' I murmur through a mouthful.

'Amen, sister!' Dan exclaims, licking the last trace of his from his lips.

Lola turns to me and smiles. 'Well, there are plenty more where that came from.'

'Now those are about the greatest words I think I've ever heard,' the Flea sighs.

I start feeling really confused. Lola seems so normal – and so nice. Surely she wouldn't be so happy if there was anything wrong with the retreat. Maybe Ruby's just hard to get to know. Maybe everything *is* cool here. And if it is, we only have to make it through a few more days before we can finally leave.

The warmth from the pancake starts spreading through my

body. I yawn so hard I don't think I'm ever going to be able to stop.

Lola looks at us, her green eyes wide with concern. 'You guys look so tired. Why don't you get some rest and I'll show you round the retreat later.'

'Sleep,' the Flea murmurs.

'In a bed,' Dan adds dreamily.

'With an actual pillow,' the Flea continues.

'And real live blankets,' Dan adds.

Lola gets to her feet. 'Go right ahead,' she says. 'The boys' cabin is that one over there.' She points to the cabin that Michael has once again retreated to in a sulk. 'And the girls' cabin is where you left your things before.'

Cruz and I look at each other and smile wistfully. It had been awesome to fall asleep in his arms these past couple of nights. But right now, I'm so bone-tired, I don't really care. All I can think about is lying down on a proper bed.

I go over to Belle and take her hand. 'Come on, Belle, I'll help you.'

She smiles up at me gratefully. 'Thanks, Grace.'

We all trudge over to the girls' cabin, including Dan, Cruz and the Flea, as they have to fetch their bags. I glance at Jenna. She's staring down at the floor, ashen-faced. I think of how she and Ron pretty much grew up together and how he idolised her. Although the feeling definitely wasn't reciprocated, his loss will have really hit her hard.

Inside the cabin, I help Belle into the bed closest to the door. Then I turn and see Cruz right behind me. He takes my hand and laces his fingers in mine.

'See you later,' he whispers.

I nod. 'Sleep well.'

'You too.' He kisses me quickly and I feel a pang of longing as I watch him head out the door.

After the boys have gone I go fetch my bag and bring it over to the bed next to Belle's. Jenna is sitting on the bed on the other side of mine and Cariss is already lying down at the far end of the cabin. I go over to Belle and hunker down next to her. She's curled up tightly on her side.

'Are you okay?' I whisper.

'Uh-huh.'

I stroke her hair. 'Just think, soon we'll be out of here for good. And at least now we've got proper food and shelter.'

I take hold of her hands and give them a squeeze. They're still icy cold.

I go back to my own bed and pull back the sheet. I can't quite believe I'm face-to-face with a pillow. Part of me doesn't want to reach out and touch it, just in case it's some kind of shipwreck-induced optical illusion. Jenna is still sitting up, staring down at her lap. I slide into the bed and sigh at the coolness of the cotton sheet on the backs of my warm legs.

Then, slowly, I lie down. I can practically hear every muscle in my body giving a grateful cheer.

'Wow!' I whisper, staring up at the ceiling. Even though the air in the cabin is almost as humid as the air outside, it feels so damn good to be lying on something comfortable it more than makes up for it.

'Grace,' Jenna whispers.

I roll on to my side and look at her. 'Yes?'

'I'm so sorry.' Tears are spilling down her face, leaving spidery black mascara trails. She looks so far from the flawless, ice-cool Jenna of before, it's scary. I reach out my hand to her. As she leans across the gap between our beds to take it I see that her hand's trembling.

'I thought we were all going to die,' she whispers, her voice choked with tears. 'I thought I'd never get the chance to see you again and –'

'What's going on?' Cariss says loudly.

Belle sits bolt upright. 'What's happened?' she says, her eyes darting round the cabin.

I quickly get up and go to her. 'It's okay. Jenna was just telling me something. Try and get to sleep.'

Belle eases herself back down but her eyes stay open. 'Can you stay here for a moment?' she whispers.

'Sure,' I say and I start stroking her hair again. Eventually she closes her eyes and lets out a sigh.

I go back to my own bed and see that Jenna has lain down on her side, facing away from me.

I lie back down. 'Jenna,' I whisper. But she doesn't turn round.

When I wake up later, the air is porridge-thick with humidity and beads of sweat are trickling down the side of my face like hot tears. For a moment I have no idea where I am. My mouth is as dry as cinder and my entire body's throbbing. I feel just like I did the one and only time I had a hangover. It was after a sleepover at Jenna's when her mom had left us home-alone to go on a date and we'd decided to make some cocktails. We were only about thirteen at the time, so our knowledge of cocktail making wasn't exactly the greatest. Basically we thought you put a whole bunch of pretty-coloured liquor into a shaker – we had no idea that specific measurements and ingredients were involved. Boy, did we pay the price the following day. It was the only time in my life my puke's been electric blue.

I turn over. Jenna is on her side facing me now, fast asleep. Her face is shiny with sweat and strands of her hair are plastered across her forehead. I think back again to that sleepover, and how much fun it had been. If someone had told me then how complicated and dark our friendship was going to become I never would've believed them. I wonder if Jenna was going to tell me about her and Todd before she fell asleep. The thought of having to broach that whole subject makes me feel very uneasy.

I turn on to my other side. Belle is fast asleep too, her breath coming in quiet little gasps. I ease myself into a seated position and see Cariss spread-eagled on her stomach on her bed. The heat's making me feel really dizzy. Very slowly, so I don't wake the others, I get up and creep over to the door. I'm just about to open it when I spot a framed picture hanging on the back. At least, I think it's a picture, but when I rub my fingers across the glass to remove the dirt I see that's it actually a mirror. I rub it some more and gradually a face appears, staring back at me, shell-shocked. My face is as brown as a berry, as my grandpa would say, and my cheekbones seem larger. But then I realise that it's actually my cheeks that have shrunk, hollowed out slightly, as if someone has been chiselling my face away.

I hurriedly look away and ease the door open. The clearing outside is deserted and the sun is beating down in white-hot rays. I walk over to the kitchen. The minute I get inside, my eyes are drawn to a pile of mangoes on one of the shelves. I carefully take one, fetch a knife from a hook on the wall and slice off the top. I'm so desperate to quench my thirst I dig out a huge chunk of the bright-orange flesh and shove it into my mouth. As the juice explodes over my parched tongue my knees actually quiver. I feel better instantly. I quickly eat the rest of the mango, then lick every last bit of juice from my fingers. I'm just about to go back outside when I hear voices.

'For God's sake, stop being so naive!' a male voice says in a British accent. Michael.

'I'm not being naive,' I hear Lola reply.

'Do you fancy her? Is that what this is about?' Michael hisses. He sounds real close to the kitchen now. I huddle back into the corner.

'Oh, stop being so immature,' Lola snaps. It's weird hearing her normally cheery voice sounding so mad. 'Just because I've ended it with you it does not mean that I've become gay. You're being ridiculous.'

'*I'm* being ridiculous?' Michael is practically yelling now.

'Shh, you'll wake the others.'

'Like I care!' Michael gives a sarcastic laugh. 'God, just when I think this place can't get any worse, we're invaded by a load of shipwrecked yanks.'

My skin prickles with anger. If I wasn't still feeling so light-headed from the heat I'd go right out there and set him straight.

'Michael!' Lola sighs.

'What?'

'Look, I know it's difficult, but we're only going to be here for a few more days. As soon as the party's over we'll be going back home. Can you at least try and be civil till then?'

'Me?' Michael gives a derisive snort. 'I'm not the one who dragged you half way round the world just to dump you.'

'That's not fair, I —'

'Not fair? I'll tell you what's not fair. Dumping your boyfriend so you can become some crazy chick's lapdog.'

'Ruby's not crazy, and I'm not her lapdog.' Lola's voice has gone back to being angry and tense.

Michael laughs. 'Oh no? You even got all your hair cut off for her.'

I hear footsteps marching away across the clearing and breathe a sigh of relief. But just as I'm about to go over to the door, Lola steps into the kitchen. She stares at me, shocked.

'I'm so sorry,' I say, my face flushing with embarrassment.

Lola sighs. She looks pretty shaken up. 'It's okay. I suppose you heard all that?'

I nod. 'I was really thirsty and I couldn't see anyone about so I thought I'd come and get something from here. I just had a mango. I hope you don't mind.'

Lola shakes her head. 'Of course I don't mind. Help yourself. I'm just sorry you had to hear us fighting. He can be so . . .' she breaks off and looks away.

'I'm sorry. Do you want to be left alone?'

'No.' She looks back at me and shakes her head. 'Actually, I could really do with a chat. Would you mind?'

'Of course not.'

Lola gives me a grateful smile. 'Let's go to the garden. It'll be a little cooler there.'

I follow her out of the kitchen. There's no sign of Michael. Lola leads me across the clearing towards a narrow pathway, which seems to lead straight into the rainforest.

'It's just through here,' she says. 'Ruby planted it all herself. It's like being in paradise.'

As soon as we get to the garden I see what she means. Tropical plants and flowers fill every available space with bright splashes of colour. It reminds me of my mom's paint palette when she's doing one of her abstract pieces.

We go sit down on a wooden bench beneath a huge palm tree. Its fronds fan out above us, forming a giant canopy and welcome shade from the sun. I wonder whether I ought to ask Lola about what just happened, but she beats me to it.

'Michael can be a bit of a control freak,' she says, looking straight ahead of her. 'It never used to bother me when were at home. We had our separate lives and our own friends. But when we went travelling and it was just me and him, twenty-four seven, it started driving me nuts.'

I nod.

'I'd decided a while ago that I wanted to break up with him, but I thought it would be best to leave it till we got back home. But then we came here . . .' Lola breaks off and looks around dreamily.

'Ruby's so inspiring,' she says, turning to me, her green

eyes wide. 'She's one of those people who makes you want to become a better person just by being around her. Do you know what I mean?'

'Uh-huh,' I do know what she means – it's how I always thought of my mom – until Dad left and she went to pieces.

'But Michael got so jealous,' Lola continues.

'Of Ruby?'

Lola nods. 'I think he'd got used to me going along with whatever he said. He didn't like it when I started to express my own opinion.' She looks at me and smiles. 'I know Ruby seems a bit stand-offish at first, but once you get to know her you'll see what an amazing woman she is. And she's been through so much. Her coming here to follow her dream and set up the retreat – it's made me realise that life's way too short to stay anywhere or with anyone that makes you unhappy.'

'Oh, I hear you,' I say. 'Getting shipwrecked's really taught me that one.'

Lola looks at me questioningly.

I take a deep breath. I guess it wouldn't do any harm to confide in her a little, since she's been so open with me. 'You know the blond guy, Todd, who was with the others that Ruby found?'

Lola nods.

'Well, he and I were dating when we first got to the island.'

I watch as Lola does the math, then looks at me, puzzled.

'We'd only been together a few weeks,' I say quickly. 'And I really wasn't sure if we were right for each other. Then I met Cruz.'

Lola nods. 'The Costa Rican?'

'Uh-huh.'

'He seems like a nice guy.'

My cheeks instantly, and annoyingly, turn love-struck pink. 'He is. Right from the first moment we spoke we just clicked, you know? It's like he gets me – and I get him. When I'm with him I don't have to put on any kind of act, I can just be me.'

Lola nods, but she looks sad and I realise that it's probably not too tactful to go waxing lyrical about true love with someone who's just had a massive bust up with their control-freak ex.

'Sorry. I guess I must sound like I'm sponsored by Hallmark.'

Lola shakes her head. 'No, not at all. It's nice to hear about something going well. But how did you break it off with Todd and get together with Cruz? That must've been pretty awkward.'

I nod. 'For sure. But it seems to be okay now. I think the shock of getting shipwrecked and – and losing our friend Ron – seems to have shifted everyone's perspectives.'

Lola nods. 'It's bound to.' She looks down at her lap. 'I was so sorry to hear about your friend. You guys really have been through hell, haven't you?'

I think about everything else that's happened – all the things I haven't told her, about Hortense. Hell pretty much covers it.

I sigh. 'Yeah, we sure have.'

'Well, I know that we've only just met but if you ever need to talk . . .'

I look at her and smile. 'Thank you.'

'As soon as I saw you I felt like we were going to be friends,' Lola says.

'Really?'

She looks away, embarrassed. 'Yeah. I got the same feeling when I first met Ruby. Like I just knew she was going to be an important person in my life.'

'Wow. Well, thank you. I really liked you too. And not just because you were the first person we'd seen since being shipwrecked!'

We both laugh and it feels so good to be doing something as normal as having a heart-to-heart with another girl.

'So, where's Ruby from?' I ask, deciding that now would be the perfect time to find out more.

But before Lola can reply I hear the sound of leaves rustling behind me and quickly look over my shoulder. Ruby is standing by the archway, her hands on her hips.

'She's from Louisiana,' Ruby says coldly.

Chapter Eight

'Sorry, I . . .' As I scramble to my feet my mind goes into overdrive. Ruby's from Louisiana. New Orleans is in Louisiana. New Orleans – where Hortense was from – and where my dad bought me the antique bowl that, it turned out, had once belonged to Hortense and had somehow brought us all here. It's a coincidence. It has to be. But why does it have to be? What if it's exactly as sinister as it sounds?

'So, where are *you*'all from?' Ruby asks as she makes her way over to us. She walks with the grace and poise of someone who's done ballet their entire life.

'I . . .' My mouth is suddenly dry again. 'Los Angeles.'

'Ah, yes, of course.'

What did she mean, of course? Did she know already? *How* did she know already?

'The others told me when I found them at the bay.' Ruby says, as if reading my mind.

'I was just showing Grace the garden,' Lola says. 'I hope you don't mind?'

Ruby carries on staring at me with her piercing blue eyes. I look away, willing my heart to calm down.

'She overheard Michael and me having an argument and she was very kindly providing me with a shoulder to cry on.' Lola gives me a reassuring smile, as if to say, *Don't worry, I'll make her be nice to you*.

Ruby looks at Lola and I'm surprised to see her gaze soften. She actually looks concerned. 'What's he done this time?'

'Oh, you know, more of the same . . .' Lola looks away, biting her lip as if she's fighting back tears.

Ruby sighs. 'It is a truth universally acknowledged that men will always be drawn to strong women. But the instant they fall in love with that strength, they feel the overwhelming urge to destroy it.'

Lola nods fervently. I think of Cruz and the way we spark off each other. I can't imagine him ever wanting to 'destroy' my strength. Why would he need to?

'Yes, men can be very weak,' Ruby says, coming to sit cross-legged on the ground in front of us. I sit back down on the bench. 'When they feel their power is being threatened their first instinct is always to lash out.' She takes a small, battered tin from a pouch on her belt, opens it with her long elegant fingers and takes out a hand-rolled cigarette and a silver lighter.

'That's exactly what's happened,' Lola says. 'Michael was so angry. He said the most ridiculous things.'

Ruby nods as she lights her cigarette. 'So predictable.' She blows a thin stream of smoke from her mouth. I watch as it spirals out into the hot air.

'Are you in a relationship, Grace?' Ruby says, looking at me suddenly.

I instinctively look away. Her freakish eyes are so intense it's like they can see right inside my brain, to my innermost thoughts. 'Uh – well, yes, I guess.'

'Uh – well, yes, I guess?' Ruby raises her thin eyebrows.

'Oh, wait till you hear what happened to Grace,' Lola says breathlessly, like she's about to divulge the latest happenings from *Gossip Girl*. 'It's such an amazing story.'

My face starts to burn. 'Well, I don't know if it's –'

'What happened?' Ruby cuts in curtly.

I fantasise about grabbing one of the vines hanging across the garden, and swinging out of there, Tarzan-style. But before I can do a thing, Lola is regaling Ruby with a blow-by-blow account of my private life.

'. . . And then she met Cruz,' she says, after what is probably only a minute but feels like forever.

Ruby frowns. 'Cruz?'

'The Costa Rican guy – with the curly dark hair.'

Ruby nods. 'Ah, yes.'

'And it was love at first sight.'

'Well, I don't know about that,' I say quickly. Jeez, could this get any more cringeworthy?

Lola smiles at me. 'Oh, come on, I've seen the way you guys are together. It's obvious.'

My face automatically grins – even though part of me still wants to kill her.

'How *romantic*,' Ruby says in the kind of disdainful tone you would normally reserve for a word like 'putrid'.

I decide that I've had enough of this particular girl chat and start getting to my feet. 'I think I'll head on back – see if the others are awake yet.'

'Why had your group split up?' Ruby asks, blowing a perfect smoke-ring into the air. We all watch it drift up and away.

'What do you mean?' I say, knowing full well what she means, but wanting to buy a bit more time so I can figure out what to say.

'Why had you split up?' Ruby says again, impatiently, like she's talking to a little kid.

'The others were worried about Ron,' I say, hovering somewhere between sitting and standing. 'He'd been acting real strange and they wanted to get him to a doctor.' Thinking of Ron makes my heart sink and I sit back down. Much as he used to annoy the hell out of me, the thought of him actually being dead floors me all over again.

'So y'all agreed that they should take the boat?' Ruby asks.

'Yes.' I stare right back at her. If I look away first she'll know I'm lying.

'I see.' Ruby blows a jet of smoke straight at me. I still don't flinch. 'So, where did you get the boat that brought you here?'

'We found it.'

'On the island?'

'Yes.' I wait for her to ask where. But she doesn't, she just looks at me for a while. But her stare has lost some of its hardness. Now she's looking at me like I might be interesting after all.

'Right.' She gets to her feet. 'I have to go see to the cows,' she says to Lola. 'See you guys later.'

I watch her glide out, speechless.

'She's amazing isn't she,' Lola says, grinning.

'Hmm, I guess.' I stand up. I need to see Cruz to talk through what just happened. 'Shall we go back?'

Lola nods and gets up. 'Sure. And thanks, Grace – for before. It was so nice to be able to talk to you about Michael.' She stares at me, her eyes wide. 'You have to follow your heart, don't you? You have to leave if something doesn't feel right any more.'

I smile at her and nod. 'You sure do.'

When we get back to the camp I see the Flea standing in front of the boys' cabin, stretching. When he sees us he waves and smiles.

'I'm going to fix some fruit juice for everyone,' Lola says, before heading off to the kitchen.

'Gracie, where you been?' the Flea asks, bounding over.

'Ruby's secret garden,' I say.

'You're kidding.' The Flea puts his hands on his hips, mock outraged. 'OMG, I have total garden envy. What's it like? Does it have borders and decking and a water feature?'

I shake my head and grin. 'No. To be honest, I didn't pay it too much attention, I was too busy talking to Lola about Michael – and then Ruby turned up.'

'Ruby? As in she of the mess-with-me-and-I'll-kill-you eyes?' The Flea's mouth drops open in shock. 'Did you, like, actually *talk* to her?'

'Kind of.' Now I'm back with the Flea I start feeling a bit more chilled about the whole Ruby encounter.

He stares at me. 'What happened? What was she like?'

'Not exactly what you'd call *warm*. And I don't think she likes men all that much.'

The Flea instantly looks dejected.

'Straight men, anyways,' I add quickly. 'You might be okay.'

'Yay!' The Flea grins. 'Cos with that fabulous 'fro goin' on, she is my kinda fag hag!'

83

'Yeah, well, I wouldn't go getting your hopes up too high.' I quickly look around to make sure Ruby's not about to make another surprise appearance.

'Jimmy!' We jump as Belle's cry echoes around the clearing. Somewhere in the rainforest a parrot squawks as if he's mimicking her. 'Jimmy! Grace! Where are you?'

I look at the Flea. 'Come on, quick.'

We run over to the girls' cabin. Belle is sitting up in bed. Her face and hair are drenched in sweat. Jenna is also sitting up, looking blank-faced from sleep.

'Jimmy,' Belle gasps.

'It's okay, hon, I'm here,' the Flea says, rushing over to sit next to her.

I go sit on the other side of her bed. 'Are you all right?'

Belle turns to me. 'I had a nightmare.'

I take her hand. 'It's okay. You're awake now. We're here.'

'Could you all please keep the noise down,' Cariss snaps from the other end of the cabin. I glance over at her. She's lying on her stomach with a pillow over her head. I look at Jenna and she smiles at me apologetically. I smile back. It feels so weird, this cautious dance we're doing with each other – but I guess it's better than how things were before.

'Okay, Belle, how about you and I go get something to drink? You're burning up,' the Flea says.

Belle stays still for a moment, then nods.

I watch, helpless, as the Flea ushers her out of the cabin.

'What happened to her when she went missing?' Jenna whispers.

I turn to face her. She's sitting with her knees tucked up to her chest. She looks so childlike. And so afraid.

I go over and sit on my own bed, facing her. 'I'm not sure. We found her in a cave.'

'A cave?' Jenna's eyes widen in shock.

'Uh-huh. Inside the volcano.'

Jenna shakes her head in disbelief. 'You guys went to the volcano?'

I nod.

'What was she doing there?'

'She was unconscious and . . .' I break off, not sure if I should mention the weird altar that we found her on.

'What?' Jenna stares at me.

'She'd been put on some kind of altar.' I guess Jenna would hear it from one of the others eventually.

Jenna looks horrified. 'What? Like a human sacrifice?'

'I'm not sure.'

'Was there anyone else there?'

'Yes.' I think of the pounding footsteps we heard when we got to the cave. 'But whoever it was ran away when we got there.'

'And when she came round she was blind?'

'Yes. No – not straight away. She was blind when she woke up this morning.'

'Oh my God – poor Belle.'

I study Jenna's face to check for any sign that she's being insincere, but she looks genuinely horrified.

'And her mom . . .' Jenna breaks off and starts to cry. 'I can't believe Ron's dead, Grace. I can't believe he's gone.'

I go over to her bed and put my arm round her shoulders. It feels weird though. Just like when you watch a movie and discover that a character you thought was one of the good guys was actually the killer, I feel like I don't know who Jenna is any more.

'I'm sorry,' she gasps into my shoulder. 'I'm so sorry.'

'Hey,' I say softly.

'I've been such a bitch.'

'It's okay.'

'No, it's not. You don't understand.' She looks at me, her eyes brimming with tears. 'I was a real bitch to Ron and now he's – he's dead and I'll never have the chance to make things right. But I can with you.'

I feel sudden dread at what she's about to say.

'I've been a terrible friend.'

I wait.

'I did something. Before we came away. Something truly terrible.'

My ribcage seems to tighten around my heart like a corset. 'What?'

'I slept with Todd.'

I look at her, and take a deep breath. 'I know.'

Chapter Nine

Jenna stares at me, her eyes glassy with tears. 'You know?'

'Yes.'

'But how?'

I look away. 'It doesn't matter.'

'Did Todd tell you?'

I shake my head.

Jenna frowns. 'But no one else knows.'

'Hey guys, do you fancy a drink?'

We turn and see Lola standing in the doorway. She looks so daisy-fresh and untroubled. She makes me feel about eighty.

'Sure – we'll be out in a minute,' I say.

Lola looks at us for a moment, puzzled.

'I'm just gonna get changed,' I tell her.

'Ah, okay.' Lola gives me a quick smile then goes back outside.

'Did she say something about a drink?' Cariss says, sitting up suddenly.

I look at her and nod.

Cariss gets up and marches over to the door. But when she gets there she lets out a piercing scream.

I leap to my feet. 'What is it?'

'Oh. My. God.' Cariss starts backing away from the door, her hands clamped to her mouth.

Jenna wipes her eyes and stands. 'What's up?'

Cariss points a trembling finger at the door. 'A mirror,' she gasps. Then she turns to us, her mouth hanging open. 'I look hideous!' She looks around the cabin in despair, then turns her gaze on me. 'Is there some place we can go to freshen up?' she asks. 'Like, now?'

'I don't know,' I say, then, seeing her look of horror, quickly add, 'there must be.'

'Why don't you go ask the British girl,' Jenna says.

'Okay,' Cariss replies, before racing out.

'I'm so sorry,' Jenna whispers as soon as she's gone.

I sit down on my bed. Jenna sits on hers and starts fiddling with the frayed edge of her blanket. 'I was jealous,' she says quietly.

'Of what?'

'You.'

I look at her to check she isn't kidding about.

Jenna pulls a thread from her blanket and starts twining it round and round her finger. 'I'd liked Todd for so long – and when he asked you out I couldn't believe it.' She continues playing with the thread. 'It didn't make sense. People like you don't go out with guys like Todd.'

I instantly tense. 'What do you mean?'

'Well, you're so . . .' Jenna breaks off, clearly searching for a word that will adequately describe 'people like me', yet won't piss me off . . . 'intelligent. And thoughtful.'

Hmm, I'm such a geek in other words. I look at her, but she won't make eye contact.

'And he seemed so into you,' Jenna continues. 'It drove me crazy. Especially when you wouldn't, you know – sleep with him.'

I start to squirm. This conversation is the emotional equivalent of ripping off a bandaid and shaking salt all over the wound. 'Why don't we go get a drink? There's no point going over this right now, it –'

'But there is,' Jenna cuts in, 'I need to explain. Please, Grace.'

I sigh. 'Okay.' I look down at my lap, willing it to be over quickly.

'One night, just before we came away, I ran into Todd at the gas station. He was on his way back from yours. He was really uptight because you guys had just had a fight and I . . .'

'You offered him a shoulder to cry on,' I mutter. I know

the night she means. Todd had come over to do some extra work on our tango routine for school and ended up throwing in a few extra moves of his own – even though my mom was in the room right next door. When I told him to back off he accused me of being just like his sister Ingrid, always wanting everything my own way, and stormed off in a rage. He'd rung me later to apologise, sounding really choked. And I'd accepted his apology. I'd even felt sorry for him when he started talking about how hard it was living with Ingrid's anorexia. But he'd obviously just been using that as a sob story to cover his guilt.

Jenna starts crying again, but I stay right where I am. Hearing the cold, hard details of her betrayal is making me feel sick. 'I'm so sorry,' she sobs. 'But if it's any consolation he only slept with me cos he was mad at you. The moment it was over, he was so cold. Like he'd realised he'd made a massive mistake. But that only made me even more jealous. Because you were the one he really wanted and I was just the one he could sleep with and cast aside. It was just like . . . it was just like . . .'

I look at her and nod, because I know what she wants to say. *It was just like her dad choosing Taylor over her all over again.*

At first I feel like yelling, *but you didn't have to sleep with him*, but then I look at her crying uncontrollably and my anger is replaced with a pang of sorrow. Our friendship can never be the same again – way too much has happened. But that doesn't mean it's the end of the world. Maybe sometimes we outgrow a friendship the same way we outgrow a favourite dress, and we just have to let it go.

I go over and put my arm around her. 'Come on, let's go. It's all gonna be okay.' And bizarrely enough, part of me truly believes that it is. Because it feels as if Jenna's been talking about another world, another lifetime. And she isn't the only one who's changed – I have too.

When we get outside, the others are sitting around the fire in the centre of the camp. They're drinking greedily from cups, which Lola is filling and refilling from a large earthenware jug. As we get closer Cariss puts her cup down.

'Can I please go freshen up now?' she says with a scowl.

Lola smiles at her patiently. 'Sure. As soon as you've all finished your drinks I'll take you to the spring. Hey, Grace, grab a cup.'

As soon as Cruz sees me he gets up and comes over and places his hand in the small of my back. Instantly my stress about Jenna and Todd fades. I look up at him and smile. I guess the good part of outgrowing something is that there's always the chance you'll grow into something way better. I grab a cup from Lola and tip the juice down my throat. It feels like liquid velvet on my tongue.

'So, tell us more about this spring,' the Flea says, looking at Lola hopefully.

Lola grins. There's a slight gap between her front teeth and, combined with her short hair, it makes her look like a cheeky little boy. 'It's amazing. It's like Mother Nature's very own power shower.'

'Oh, man, I need to get me some of that!' Dan says with a sigh.

Lola looks around at us. 'Would you like me to take you there now?'

A chorus of 'yes's rings out around the clearing. Todd is the only one who doesn't respond — he just stares at the ground despondently.

'Do you have any shampoo for dry hair?' Cariss immediately pipes up. 'Preferably with silk peptides.'

'Oh, here we go.' Dan says, rolling his eyes.

'You don't understand — my hair has been ruined!' Cariss hisses.

'Your hair has been ruined?' Todd scrambles to his feet. 'Your hair has been ruined?' he says again, staring down at Cariss.

She gets up. 'Well, yes — it's the sea and the sun, it's —'

'Ron's dead!' Todd yells. 'He's dead. And all you can think about is your damn hair!'

'I'm sorry.' Cariss stumbles back away from him. For once she actually looks genuinely remorseful.

I walk over to Todd, my heart pounding. I place my hand on his arm. He tears his gaze from Cariss and looks at me. His eyes are wild, crazed. It's terrifying seeing him like this.

'It's okay,' I say. Even though everything is about as far from okay as it's possible to be.

Todd stares at me. He's breathing fast, like he just ran a race.

'I'm going back to bed,' he finally says, before turning and heading back to the boys' cabin.

I look at the others, unsure of what to do.

'Should I go after him?' Dan asks.

Cruz shakes his head. 'No. I'd say leave him alone. He needs time – time to come to terms with what has happened.'

Dan nods.

We all stand in silence for a moment before peeling away one by one to go fetch our towels. When we get back Lola leads us along the pathway to the lagoon. We walk in silence and I know that Ron is on everyone's mind – a giant thought-bubble hanging over us like a dark cloud. Just before we get to the river, Lola takes us down a narrow passageway between the trees. An intricate network of vines hangs across the top, forming a web-like roof. Sunlight pierces through the gaps, falling, spear-like on the ground in front of us.

Cruz and I are at the end of the group. He grips my hand tightly, then leans in close. I think he's going to kiss me but instead he whispers in my ear. 'I need to talk to you.'

I nod. 'Me too.'

'Holy moley!' The Flea exclaims from up ahead. As soon as we reach the end of the pathway I see why. We are standing in front of a miniature version of the lagoon. On the far side, water cascades down a steep rocky wall, frothing white into a circular pool. It looks so inviting all I can do is gape. After we've recovered from our trance we race across the rocks, and start scrambling out of our clothes down to our underwear. Then, one by one, we drop down into the water.

'Wa-hey!' Dan exclaims, before diving beneath the foamy surface.

I sit down on one of the surrounding rocks and slide in. The cool water laps against my skin and bubbles like I'm in a Jacuzzi. It feels awesome.

Slowly, the Flea guides Belle down into the pool. Her frown melts to a smile as she sinks into the water.

Cariss heads straight for the waterfall and stands directly beneath it. The force of the water flattens her hair against her head instantly.

Lola watches us all and laughs.

'Aren't you gonna come in?' the Flea calls out to her.

She shakes her head. 'No, I'm good, thanks. I was here this morning.' She bends down and hands me a plastic tub. 'Have some shampoo,' she says. 'Ruby makes it from shea butter – it's heavenly.'

I put the tub on the rock next to me and open it. It's full

of a creamy coloured lotion. I take some on my fingertips and smell it. Immediately I'm transported to my mom's bathroom – it smells just like one of her bath oils. I start to smile.

'Do you like it?' Lola asks.

I nod. 'Uh-huh.'

I dunk my head under the water then put some of the shampoo in my hair and start to lather it up. I close my eyes, breathe in the aroma, and imagine that I'm back at home with my mom, sitting on the edge of her bath, having one of our epic chats about life and the universe.

I feel someone move through the water behind me. 'I think you might need me to help you,' Cruz says softly in my ear.

I turn to look at him. His wet hair is hanging round his face in tight black curls. 'Oh, really?'

'Yes. Otherwise, how will you get the back done?' He starts massaging my head gently. It feels amazing.

'Wow, you save lives *and* wash hair! Do you have any other talents I should know about?' I joke.

'Well now, that would be telling,' he says, putting his arms around my waist and pulling me towards him.

I look over Cruz's shoulder and see Jenna staring at us. 'Let's go to the waterfall,' I say to Cruz. Then I take his hand and start splashing my way across the pool.

Lola was right – the waterfall rushes down over us like the ultimate power shower. Next to us, the Flea is carefully positioning Belle beneath the water. She tips back her head and lets out a gasp. On the other side of them, Cariss is scrubbing at her hair manically.

I shake my head and step out from under the water. Cruz looks at me and grins. 'You are so beautiful,' he whispers in my ear. And for the first time in my life, I actually feel like I could be.

We stay in the pool for so long that my fingertips go as shrivelled as raisins. It's as if the water has created a magical space where we can feel happy and relaxed and not have to worry about all of the bad stuff. I guess none of us wants to break the spell and step back into reality. Finally, when the sun has passed right over the pool and sunk in a blaze of gold behind the trees, we haul ourselves out of the water and get back into our clothes.

When we get back to the camp the fire is blazing, with a huge iron pot hanging over it. A delicious aroma of herbs and spices hangs in the air. Now the sun is setting it feels much less humid and our chatter rings around the clearing like birdsong. It's only when I make my way over to the girls' cabin to dump my towel that I notice Michael sitting cross-legged in the shadows. He's holding a large pad in his lap and different coloured pencils are scattered on the ground around him.

'Hey,' I say as I come level with him.

He nods, but carries on looking down at the pad.

I wonder if I ought to say something else, but figure it's probably best not to push it. As I walk past I glance down, and what I see makes me stop dead. Michael's drawn a picture of a stunningly beautiful girl. Skeins of wavy, princess-style hair cascade down around her shoulders, but from the cat-like eyes and wide smile it's clearly a picture of Lola. It must be what she used to look like before she cut her hair. I hurry on, so he won't catch me spying on him. He must still really care for her to want to draw her. And he's clearly a really gifted artist. Shame he has to be so darn rude.

After we've all gotten rid of our towels we gather in a circle around the fire. Dan has managed to get Todd to come join us and he's sitting cross-legged, staring down into his lap. Lola has taken over chef duties, kneeling over the delicious-smelling pot and stirring the contents. I guess Ruby must have started the cooking, but she's nowhere to be seen. I sit down next to Cruz. The Flea and Belle are sitting in between us and Dan. Jenna sits directly opposite me, next to Cariss.

'I have a question,' Cariss says suddenly.

We all look at her.

Cariss stares straight at Lola. 'How does this Ruby person invite guests to the retreat if she has no way of leaving the island or contacting anyone?'

Lola continues stirring the pot. 'She has friends on the

mainland. They invite people over on her behalf. That's how Michael and I ended up here. We met her friend Carlos in an internet café and he asked us to come.'

'What? Just out of the blue?' Cariss stares at her more intently.

For once I'm not bothered by her rudeness. I want to know too.

Lola sighs and stops stirring. 'We'd got talking to him about our travels and I said that I'd never seen such beautiful scenery as I had in Costa Rica and he said that it was nothing compared to this place.' Lola looks around dreamily. 'And he was right.'

'So he just invited you over?' Cariss says.

'Yes.'

Cariss frowns. 'Seems a bit random.'

'It might seem random, but I can assure you that it's not.' A voice – Ruby's voice – echoes around the clearing.

We all look round. Ruby comes striding out of the shadows toward us. She's wearing a long, tight-fitting dress, patterned in green and blue. As she gets closer to the fire the fabric shimmers so brightly she reminds me of a peacock.

'I trust Carlos implicitly,' Ruby says, staring right at Cariss. 'He's one of my closest friends – he knows exactly the type of people I want to come here. And that's exactly who he brings.'

'Really?' Cariss replies sullenly. 'So, what kind of people is that, then?'

'People who could benefit from a total retreat from the world. People who share my beliefs about life. People who don't annoy the hell out of me.' Ruby glares at Cariss. 'Do you understand what I'm saying?'

For once, Cariss is silent. She nods sullenly at Ruby, then looks away.

Chapter Ten

We all watch as Ruby sits down at what automatically becomes the 'head' of the circle, in between Michael and Lola. Michael shifts away slightly, fixing his gaze on the fire.

'The soup is just about ready,' Lola says, giving the pot a final stir.

Ruby nods, but doesn't say anything. I glance at Cruz. He shrugs and pulls a bemused face and I get the totally inappropriate urge to laugh.

Lola starts passing round the bowls of soup. It's a rich red colour and crammed full of sweetcorn, green peppers and black beans. I take a spoonful and the tang of chilli radiates through my body to the tips of my fingers and toes. A symphony of 'mmms' and 'ahhs' echoes around the darkness as we all start wolfing it down.

'I thought it would be good to have a sharing circle,' Ruby says after a while. She's the only one who isn't eating, she just watches us all through her pale-blue eyes, her back straight as a rule.

'A what?' the Flea asks, as he spoons some soup into Belle's mouth.

'A sharing circle,' Lola says, her eyes sparking with excitement. 'We did one when Michael and I first came to the retreat. It's a really cool way to get to know each other.'

'We already know each other,' Cariss mutters.

'But *we* don't know you,' Ruby says instantly. 'And I like to get to know everyone who stays here.'

Cariss sighs, but she doesn't say anything.

'So, how does it work?' the Flea asks.

'We each take it in turn to share something with the rest of the group,' Lola says, placing her empty bowl on the ground in front of her.

'Something personal,' Ruby adds, 'so we get to see the real you.'

'What, like truth or dare, but without the dares?' the Flea asks.

We all exchange uneasy glances. I don't think any of us are too keen to play truth or dare again anytime soon.

'Truth or dare is a child's game,' Ruby says dismissively. 'A sharing circle is for adults.' She takes her cigarette papers and tobacco from the pouch on her belt. 'I think this time we should have a theme.'

Lola looks at her questioningly. 'A theme?'

'Uh-huh.' Ruby places a pinch of tobacco on to a cigarette paper. 'So, we shall share our greatest inspirations.'

Michael gives a sarcastic snort and we all turn to look at him.

'Is everything okay, Michael?' Ruby asks, as she starts to roll her cigarette. The silver rings on each of her long, thin fingers glint in the firelight.

Lola glares at Michael and almost imperceptibly shakes her head.

'Oh, yes,' Michael says, all fake sincere, 'everything's just perfect!'

As I watch him staring sulkily at the ground, I wonder what the hell Lola ever saw in him – he's like a spoilt five-year-old.

'Good,' Ruby says. 'So, who would like to begin?'

'Do you mean a *person* who has inspired us, or could it be a thing, like a piece of art?' the Flea asks.

'Your greatest *inspiration*,' Ruby replies, with her bored face on.

'Right. Thanks.' The Flea throws me a glance of despair.

Cruz puts down his bowl and takes hold of my hand. He starts tracing circles in my palm with his thumb. My heart starts fluttering in response, but then I see Ruby watching us and it kills the feeling stone dead. For someone who's meant to be running a chilled-out hippy retreat, she sure has a knack of making you feel uptight.

'I'll go first,' Lola says eagerly. The rest of us breathe a collective sigh of relief. Lola sits up on to her knees and gazes into the firelight. The flickering light makes her cheekbones even more pronounced. She looks like a beautiful magical elf. 'Well, if you'd asked me who or what my inspiration was before I came here, I'd have said a woman called Jenny Thomson.'

Cariss gives an exaggerated yawn and gazes off into the rainforest.

'Jenny worked in the care home where I grew up,' Lola continues, oblivious.

'What's a care home?' Jenna asks.

'It's where kids in Britain live if they don't have any family,' Lola explains.

'What, like an orphanage?' the Flea says, his eyes wide.

Lola nods. 'Yes, kind of.' She looks down into her lap. 'My parents were killed in a car crash when I was seven. They'd had me really late in life so I didn't have any other living relatives. If it wasn't for Jenny I don't know what I'd have done.' Lola gives a wistful smile. 'She was one of those people who just radiates love and warmth, you know? She actually managed to make me feel safe, even though my whole world had ended. Or at least, that's what it felt like at the time.' Lola wipes a tear from her eye. It's horrible seeing her so sad. I want to tell her not to worry — that she's ended up just as loving and warm as this Jenny woman was.

'So, who would your inspiration be now?' the Flea asks gently.

Lola looks at him, confused.

'You said, if you'd been asked before you came here it would have been Jenny,' the Flea says. 'Who is it now?'

Michael gives a pointed cough.

Lola ignores him. 'Now, it would be Ruby.' She turns and smiles at Ruby. 'You've taught me so much, in such a short space of time. And you've really inspired me to become a better, stronger person.'

'Oh please!' Michael slams his bowl down, causing the spoon to clank against the side.

Lola frowns at him. 'What?'

'You're sounding like a bad episode of *Oprah*.'

'Why don't you tell us about *your* inspiration, Michael,' Ruby says, cigarette smoke coiling from her mouth.

Michael glares into the fire. 'Salvador Dali,' he finally mutters.

'Good choice,' Cruz says appreciatively. He lets go of my hand and turns to face Michael. 'I am a great fan of his work also. So, do you paint?'

Michael nods and actually makes eyes contact with Cruz. 'Yes, I do.'

'He's a very talented artist,' Lola says, and despite the fact that he's been acting like a total idiot toward her, she actually sounds proud. 'You should show them some of your work.'

Michael looks back at the fire. 'Hmm.'

'So, what is your favourite Dali painting?' Cruz asks.

'The Persistence of Memory,' Michael replies instantly.

'Ah, yes, the famous melting clocks,' Cruz says with a grin. 'I love that one too.'

Michael looks back at him and this time he actually cracks a smile. 'I remember the first time I saw it, when I was a kid. I was blown away by the fact that art didn't have to be about drawing bowls of fruit. Or if it did, you could at least melt the fruit.'

Cruz chuckles. 'Yes, or have a tiger exploding out of it — like in the one with the pomegranate.'

Michael is really grinning now and he looks like a different person — a *nice* person. I look at Cruz and smile, and feel insanely proud that he has been able to unearth this side of Michael.

'Thank you, Michael,' Ruby says curtly. 'So, who wants to go next?'

'I will,' Cariss says quickly. She sits up straight and clears her throat, as if preparing to address the nation. 'My greatest inspiration of all time is my daddy,' she says in a trembly little voice I've never heard her use before. I guess if she were reading from a script the direction would be *'filled with awe'*. Dan sighs and the Flea raises his eyebrows at me as if to say, 'bullshit alert'.

'My daddy is actually a Hollywood icon,' Cariss says, staring at Ruby defiantly. 'Isaac Swayne? I guess you've heard of him?'

Ruby looks blank.

'Rogue Cop Killers? Stab and I Shoot?' Cariss says, looking put-out when Ruby still doesn't react. Cariss clears her throat and shoots Dan a defiant look. 'Anyways, he's not just my inspiration because he's such a fine actor, but because he has such an awesome attitude to life too.'

Dan stares back at her. 'Oh yeah?'

'Yeah. One time, when he hadn't learnt all of his lines for *Death Vengeance 3*, he took himself off to our cabin in Aspen and spent Thanksgiving all on his own!'

Dan frowns. 'And that's inspiring, how?'

Cariss sighs. 'Because he won't let anything get in the way of his success, not even his own family.'

We all sit in stunned silence.

'He does loads for charity too,' Cariss says, sounding a little desperate now. 'And once he even gave half of his coffee to a homeless person. From *Afghanistan*.'

'Interesting,' Ruby says, sounding more bored than ever. Then suddenly she turns to me. 'How about you, Grace? Who or what is your greatest inspiration?'

Instantly, my skin prickles. Why is she asking me?

I take a deep breath to compose myself. 'I guess it would be my grandpa,' I say hesitantly. 'I mean, there are tons of famous people I admire but my grandpa is the one person who's always been there for me through thick and thin. And he has this knack of being able to give the best advice in just one sentence.' I start to smile as I picture my grandpa sitting on the jetty at the back of his house, casting a line out into the lake, his pipe clamped between his teeth.

'Can you give us an example?' Lola asks.

'Oh. Well – uh – there was the time when my mom and dad had just split up and I'd gone down to South Carolina to stay with my grandpa while they sorted out the house and stuff.' I feel a pang of sorrow as I think back to that time and how we had all stumbled around each other, dazed by grief. Cruz places his hand on my back and I take a deep breath. 'We'd gone fishing together, and I hadn't said a word about my parents, but I guess my grandpa could tell how upset I was because all of a sudden he says out of the blue: "Just cos the sun ain't shining, Gracie, don't mean it isn't there".' My face starts to burn with embarrassment. I shouldn't have shared this with everyone – it was too personal; it sounds dumb taken out of context.

'That's really lovely,' Lola says with a warm smile. The Flea and Dan nod and Cruz rubs my back. My embarrassment is replaced with a rush of gratitude.

'I don't get it,' says Cariss. 'If the sun isn't there, it isn't there.'

'Yes it is,' Jenna says. 'It's just behind a cloud.'

'But what about at night-time?' Cariss looks up at the dark night sky. 'The sun isn't shining now, is it? Because it isn't here – it's in, like, Japan or something.'

'I don't think he meant it to be taken so literally,' Ruby says, and then she actually smiles at me. 'Thank you, Grace. Okay, who's next?'

'I'll go,' Dan says with a grin.

The Flea nudges me and whispers, 'Whaddya reckon? Tupac, or Notorious B.I.G.?'

I grin and watch Dan. He's looking down at his lap, thoughtfully. 'I guess it would have to be Shakespeare,' he eventually says.

'Shake what?' the Flea splutters.

'Shake*speare*,' Dan retorts.

The Flea takes off his hat and stares at him. 'What, as in the legendary English playwright? As in, "Romeo, Romeo, wherefore art thou, Romeo?"'

'Uh-huh.'

Cariss shakes her head in apparent disbelief.

'And why Shakespeare?' Ruby asks, staring at Dan intently.

'Yeah, I felt sure you'd say one of your beloved rap artists,' the Flea says.

'Shakespeare *is* the world's greatest rap artist,' Dan

replies. 'There ain't nobody who can string words together like that dude.'

'"Shall I compare thee to a summer's day?"' Ruby says, still looking at Dan intently.

'"Thou art more lovely and more temperate",' Dan replies, then he grins at her. '"But thy eternal summer shall not fade".'

Ruby smiles and for a second it's like her mask has slipped. She looks younger, and more human.

'So, who else?' Ruby says, tearing her gaze from Dan and looking round the circle.

'I'll go,' the Flea says eagerly. He puts his hat back on, and cocks it at a jaunty angle. 'My inspiration has to be the legend that was Fred Astaire.' He gazes into the fire dreamily. 'The first time I saw *Easter Parade* my life changed forever. I was off school sick and my mom let me watch it for a treat – I wasn't normally allowed to watch TV,' he adds with a shrug. 'My parents thought it stunted the imagination.' He laughs. 'The irony is, watching that movie fired my imagination more than it had ever been fired before. Every day after that all I did was dream of being a dancer just like Fred Astaire.'

'And now you are,' I say with a smile.

'Well, yeah, kinda.' The Flea grins. 'I like this game. I like it a lot! How about you then, Beau-Belle? Who's your greatest inspiration?'

'My mom.' As soon as Belle says it she starts biting her

bottom lip. The Flea gives her shoulders a squeeze. 'And why's that?' he says softly.

'Cos she – she's always been my rock.' Belle closes her eyes and sighs.

Ruby raises her eyebrows. I can't tell if she's looking interested or amused.

Lola leans over and strokes Belle's hand.

Belle smiles gratefully.

Ruby gets to her feet and looks down at us. We all wait for her to say something.

'Time to sleep,' she announces. 'Retreat life starts early. Lola will show you what to do.' She turns to go, then looks back over her shoulder in Dan's direction. 'It's been interesting getting to know y'all,' she says.

'But you didn't tell us your inspiration,' Dan calls out after her.

'Mother Earth,' she calls back, before striding across the clearing and up the ladder, until she's swallowed up by her strange house.

Dan whistles through his teeth.

We all start scrambling to our feet.

'Chores begin at sun up,' Lola explains as she collects the bowls. 'Don't worry, I'll come and wake you.'

'Don't you sleep in the cabin with us?' I ask.

She shakes her head. 'No, I sleep in the house now.'

'Yeah, she sleeps with our leader,' Michael says sullenly.

Lola's face flushes in the firelight. 'Ruby asked me to stay there with her, after the other guests had gone,' she explains. 'So I wouldn't feel lonely.'

Michael mutters something under his breath and stomps off to the boys' cabin. I look at Cruz and he takes my hand and pulls me to one side.

'Meet me at the pool, when the others are asleep,' he whispers. 'I need to talk to you.'

Chapter Eleven

It's only when I'm lying on my bed, waiting for the others to fall asleep and willing myself not to, that I realise that Jenna didn't share her inspiration. It's weird thinking of how the old Jenna would have loved the opportunity to be centre stage. I start replaying the evening's events in my mind. Ruby might be the Queen of Random, but she sure knows how to get to the heart of people. It was really interesting finding out everyone's inspiration. Interesting, and in some cases downright surprising. Who'd have thought Dan would be such a Shakespeare fan.

When the others quit moving about and I hear their breathing level, I ease myself out of bed and tiptoe across the cabin. I nudge the door open and peer out. The clearing is steeped in darkness. I look up and see banks of heavy clouds covering the sky, snuffing out any starlight. I creep out of the cabin and peer up at Ruby's house. It looms over the clearing, teetering slightly to the right.

I tiptoe across the clearing, but when I get to the entrance leading to the spring I almost turn round. It's so dark in forest – I'm not sure I'll be able to find my way with no light. But the thought of some alone time with Cruz makes it worth the risk.

I get halfway along the track when I hear a twig crack behind me. 'Hello?' I whisper, turning around. There's no reply. Fear grips my body like a steel claw. A shadow scampers across the track. Whatever it is can only be about a foot tall. It must be a monkey. I take a deep breath and carry on. I hope Cruz is already at the pool – I don't much fancy hanging round in the dark on my own. I hear the rush of water and breathe a sigh of relief. I've come the right way. I follow the sound until I reach the clearing.

'Cruz?' I whisper. Not that he'd hear me over the noise of the water. I peer around in the darkness. I don't know what to do. Should I stay up here on the rocks or go wait for him in the pool? I decide to get in as I figure I'll feel a bit less exposed. I quickly slip out of my T-shirt and shorts and clamber across the rocks. I slide down into the water. In the relative coolness of the night its warmth feels even more soothing than before. I take a deep breath and dunk down beneath the surface. When I come back up again I feel a hand grip my shoulder. It takes every fibre in my body not to scream. I spin round and see Cruz's silhouette right behind me.

'You nearly gave me a heart attack!' I hiss.

'Come here,' he whispers.

'I am here,' I reply. He takes me in arms. Our lips touch, mingling with the warm water.

He holds me tightly. 'I've missed you,' he sighs in my ear. 'I do not like this stupid girl/boy cabin thing. I want you to sleep in my arms always.'

'I want that too,' I say. 'But what can we do?'

'I have so much to say to you.' He brushes my wet hair back from my face. 'I've been saving it up all day, but now I finally get you alone, all I want to do is kiss you.'

I nod. 'Me too. I know, why don't we take it in turns?'

'In turns?'

'Yes. First we say something, then we kiss. Then we say another thing, then have another kiss.'

Cruz chuckles. 'I like it. But how about we say something, then we have ten kisses. Then we say another thing, then we have twenty kisses?'

'You're on!' I look around the spring. 'So, what do you make of it here? What do you think about Ruby?'

Cruz shakes his head. 'That's two things.'

I laugh. 'Okay, so, what do you think about it here?'

Cruz sighs. 'I'm not sure. I mean, it is better than the other side of the island, that's for sure, but . . .'

'Something still doesn't feel right?' I finish for him.

'Yeah. Something still doesn't feel right. There is no way we should be so close to Costa Rica for a start.'

'What do you mean?'

Cruz stares at me intently. 'When Lola said that it was just a few hours away from here?'

'Uh-huh.'

'Well that shouldn't be. There's no way we should be so close. Unless . . .'

'Unless what?'

'Unless the storm that brought us to the island had some kind of strange power.'

I look down at the ground. 'Hortense.' My skin starts to prickle with goose bumps.

'Okay, now we must have our ten kisses,' Cruz says in a fake cheery voice, obviously trying to lighten the mood.

He starts kissing my neck, his lips planting a trail all the way up to my chin. They reach my mouth on six, and after that I stop counting. Finally he breaks away.

'So, what is the next thing you wanted to say?'

My brain feels drunk on kisses. I take a deep breath to try and sober up. 'Ruby. What do you think of her?' I whisper.

'She is another thing that doesn't feel right,' Cruz whispers back.

I nod. 'I found out that she's from Louisiana!'

He frowns. 'Louisiana?'

'Uh-huh. Home of New Orleans – and a certain psycho voodoo queen!' I try to stay cool. 'I know that it's probably just coincidence – but it just feels kind of weird.'

Cruz nods and tiny droplets of water spill from his hair down on to my face. 'Have you heard anything – from Hortense – since we've been here?'

'No, not a thing.'

'And the smell?'

'No – nothing.'

'Well, that's something.'

'Yeah, I guess. Do you think Ruby could be connected to Hortense in some way – coming from Louisiana?'

Cruz frowns. 'I don't know . . .'

'We need to find out more about her.'

'We do,' Cruz whispers. 'But first, we have some kissing to catch up on.' He puts his hands on my shoulders and slides my bra straps down. I feel an ache of longing so intense it seems to be eating me up from the inside.

'One,' Cruz murmurs, as he plants a kiss on my bare shoulder. Then he moves his hands round to the clasp on my bra. As I feel it come loose my heart starts to pound. 'Two,' he whispers as he kisses my other shoulder and gently unpeels my bra from my body. He leans over to place it on the side of the pool, then pulls me back toward him. The feeling of our bare chests pressing against each other is unbelievable. His mouth starts hungrily kissing mine. I grip on to his hair. There's an urge building inside of me so strong it makes me feel wild, like a tiger. Cruz traces his fingers over my naked breasts and it's all I can do to stop myself from roaring. He lifts me up and I wrap my legs around his body. All of my fear, all of my awkwardness, is trumped by my desire for him. I feel his hand move up my inner thigh towards my panties – and then I freeze.

'I can't,' I hear myself whispering, timid and scared, in his ear.

His hand immediately returns to my waist.

'I'm sorry.' I rest my head on his shoulder and wish that a whirlpool would appear and suck me right away from there.

'No, I'm sorry,' he whispers in my ear. 'I go too fast.'

I unwrap my legs from his waist and let my feet float down to the ground.

'Are you okay?' he asks, looking at me, concerned.

I nod, even though I feel mortified. And so confused. Just seconds ago I wanted Cruz with every cell in my body. Why did I have to freak out like that? But I don't have to think too hard to figure out why. I've never made love with anyone before. And I don't want anything to go wrong. I can't begin to imagine how excruciating it would be, not knowing what to do. Maybe I ought to tell him the truth.

'I'm not feeling so good,' I find myself saying.

'Oh, no!' Cruz strokes my hair. 'What is wrong?'

'I think I'm just over-tired,' I mutter. *Tell him the real reason!* my inner voice yells. But I ignore it. I have shrunk from tiger to mouse. 'Maybe we should go back,' I mumble, feeling totally dejected. All the stress of the last few days wells up inside of me, as if it's been waiting for a moment like this to pounce.

'Maybe we should . . . but maybe we shouldn't,' Cruz says. He takes hold of my hands under the water. 'Do you remember what I said to you? In the tunnel, when we found the boat?'

I nod, too scared to speak in case opening my mouth lets the sobs building in my throat escape.

'I love you,' he whispers, gripping my hands tighter. 'Do you know how many times I have said that to anyone other than my family?'

I shake my head.

'None,' he replies. 'I have never felt like this before. And I cannot explain it. And it frightens me and —'

'Why?' I'm so shocked at what he just said I forget to be embarrassed.

'Why, what?'

'Why does it frighten you?'

He looks away. 'Because you might not feel the same,' he finally says, so quietly I can barely hear him over the rushing water. But I do hear him, and it makes me want to cheer.

'But I do!' I exclaim, squeezing his hands for emphasis. 'I really, really do.'

Cruz starts grinning. 'You do?'

'Yes, you doofus! It's about the only thing I do feel certain about right now.'

He laughs. 'Me too.'

I take a deep breath. 'I'm sorry I freaked out on you, it's just that I've never . . . I've never made love with anyone before and I . . . I'm scared I'll do something wrong.'

I close my eyes, as if that might somehow lessen my embarrassment. It doesn't work. Even the inside of my eyelids feel like they're blushing. Cruz lets go of my hands and wraps his arms round me. 'You could never do something wrong,' he whispers. 'But it is too soon.' He kisses my mouth so gently it makes me want to cry out. 'We have plenty of time,' he says, hugging me to him.

I nod and close my eyes tight.

But do we really? my inner voice whispers.

Chapter Twelve

By the time I get back to the girls' cabin the sky is beginning its journey from black to blue, and in the rainforest the first of the parrots are beginning to squawk. Cruz and I found a cubbyhole in the rocks above the pool and ended up lying there for hours, just talking and kissing.

I look across to the boys' cabin and give Cruz a final wave. Then I slip through the door and creep over to my bed. I lie down and let out a sigh. But although my body is glad of the chance to rest, my mind starts to race. Why do I feel as if something bad is going to happen? Why can't I just accept the retreat at face value? Round and round my head the questions go, until they finally spin into a hot and hazy blur of sleep.

A little while later I'm woken by the sound of a cough. I open my eyes. Pale light is filtering in through the cracks in the bamboo walls. I hear another cough and turn to see Jenna lying on her back, staring up at the ceiling.

'You okay?' I whisper.

She turns to me and I see that her face is streaked with tears.

'Jen, what's up?' I lean up on to my arm.

She shakes her head as if to say, *don't come any closer*. 'I don't know who I am any more,' she whispers.

I frown. 'What do you mean?'

'It's like, before, everything made sense, now nothing does.'

'But we'll be back home soon and then everything can get back to normal.'

Jenna shakes her head. 'But what if I don't want it to go back to normal?'

'What do you mean?'

But before Jenna can answer, the door opens and Lola bounds in.

'Good morning!' she cries. She's wearing a tight crop top and low-rise cargo pants, showing her tanned stomach and slightly protruding hip bones. Her hair is covered by a blue-and-white bandana. She looks awesome – especially given that it's clearly still *silly* o'clock. 'Time to do the morning chores,' she says, smiling at me warmly. 'How did you sleep?'

'Great,' I say, and it's not exactly a lie – for the very short time that I did sleep, it was great.

Belle stirs and mutters something under her breath.

'You okay, Belle?' I say, quickly sitting up.

'What's happening?' Belle mutters.

I get up and go over to her. 'It's time to wake up,' I say softly.

'Can I get you guys something to drink before we get started?' Lola cuts in. 'Water? Juice?'

'Juice would be good,' I reply. 'How about some juice, Belle?'

Belle nods and sits up.

'I'll go and wake the boys,' Lola says, and she heads back to the door.

I go over to Cariss's bed. She's sleeping on her back with a sock over her face like an eye mask. 'Cariss, it's time to wake up.'

'You gotta be kidding!' she mutters.

''Fraid not. It's time to do the morning chores.'

'I don't do chores.'

I sigh. 'Okay, whatever.'

I go back over to my bed and root around in my bag for the least dirty and crumpled of my clothes. This turns out to be a University of South Carolina vest top and a pair of pale denim shorts.

'I don't suppose . . .' Jenna begins.

I turn to look at her and she immediately lowers her gaze. It's freaky seeing her so timid.

'Could I borrow something of yours to wear? I lost all of my stuff.'

'Sure.' I pull out my next least crumpled outfit – a powder-blue sundress with a pair of tiny lovebirds on the front.

'Hey, I remember when you got this,' Jenna says with a smile. 'It was the day we went to Brentwood.'

I laugh. 'Yeah, and I bought that really dorky blouse with the pink collar . . .'

I fall silent and Jenna looks away. She's remembered it too – I'd bought the really dorky blouse with the pink collar because I was meeting Todd's parents for the first time that night. I sigh. Is this what it's going to be like from now on? Todd-shaped landmines littering our conversations?

I turn to look at Belle. She's still sitting motionless on her bed. 'How are you doing, Belle? D'you need a hand?'

Belle nods and I go over to help her get dressed. Behind me, I hear Jenna choke back a sob.

When we've all gotten up and congregated by the remains of the fire, Lola pours us each a cup of juice. As I watch Cariss grab hers greedily I can't help smiling – clearly chronic thirst has helped her overcome her aversion to chores.

'Ruby wants to cook a gumbo later,' Lola says, turning to the boys. 'So she's asked if you guys will go and catch some shellfish.'

'Awesome!' Dan exclaims. 'I love gumbo!'

'Can Grace come too?' Cruz asks. 'She's a world champion

fisher.' He looks at me and I feel a surge of energy rush between us, connecting us like an invisible bond.

But Lola shakes her head. 'I'm sorry. Ruby wants us girls to go with her.'

Michael snorts. 'I bet she does.'

Lola's face creases into a frown. 'What do you mean?'

Michael scuffs his foot in the dirt, refusing to look at her. 'So she can preach her feminist bullshit to her latest band of gullible followers.'

'Michael!' Lola glances up at the house anxiously.

'Hey!' I turn and glare at him.

'What?' he eyeballs me right back.

I feel my face flushing with anger. 'You've no right to talk about us like that.'

Cruz places a hand on my shoulder.

Michael sighs. 'I'm sorry.' But he doesn't sound sorry at all.

'Michael, can you show the guys where the fishing gear is kept?' Lola says, remarkably sweetly given the circumstances.

'Come on then,' Michael grunts at the boys and starts leading them off to one of the smaller cabins. Cruz takes my hand and links his fingers with mine. 'I will see you later,' he whispers, kissing me lightly on the mouth. I nod and sigh, wishing that I could go with him – even though it would mean having to put up with Michael.

As soon as the boys have left the clearing, Ruby appears.

She's wearing track pants and a chequered shirt tied in a knot at the front over her taut brown stomach. Like Lola, she has a bandana pulled tightly over her hair. Without the Afro halo, her eyes look huge and her cheekbones razor sharp. 'Good,' is all she says when she sees us.

Cariss raises her eyebrows and sighs. Jenna looks at the floor. She has scraped her dried out hair into a ponytail and her make-up-free face is blotchy from crying. Next to me, Belle starts looking around blindly. I give her arm a reassuring squeeze.

'Okay, let's get going,' Ruby says abruptly.

We follow her down the pathway leading to the garden, but instead of turning off at the archway we continue on until the path opens out into a wide field.

'Wow!' Jenna exclaims.

Even Cariss looks surprised.

The field is dotted with a handful of cattle grazing lazily in the long grass. But even though it's pretty bizarre seeing cows in a place like this, my eyes are drawn upwards – to the volcano, looming craggy and red at the end of the field. I had no idea we were so close to it.

'Where are we?' Belle says to me.

'We're in a field,' I tell her. 'And there are some cows.' As if on cue, one of the cows raises its head and gives a long, deep moo.

'Is that volcano active?' Cariss asks.

'What volcano?' Belle's fingers dig into my arm.

'Not any more,' Ruby says.

'Are we by the volcano?' Belle asks, her voice shrill.

'Kind of,' I say. 'But we're on the other side of it now.' Like that's gonna make her feel any better.

'But it *was* active?' Cariss says.

'Of course it was.' Ruby looks at Cariss like she's an alien from the planet Dumb. 'All volcanoes were active at some point.'

'Who's going to do the milking and who's going to see to the hens?' Lola asks.

'Milking?' Cariss's mouth drops open in horror – which doesn't improve her dumb appearance any.

'I'll take these two to see to the cows,' Ruby says, gesturing at Jenna and Cariss. 'You and Grace and the other one see to the hens.'

'Cool!' Lola grins at me.

Cariss and Jenna look horrified.

'Come on,' Ruby says to them briskly.

'There is no way I am touching a cow's nipple,' Cariss says indignantly.

'Oh no?' Ruby stares at her.

And then something real strange happens – Cariss looks down at the ground and mumbles, 'Okay then.'

As Jenna and Cariss traipse after Ruby, Lola gestures at Belle and me to follow her over to a small and slightly ramshackle shed in the corner of the field. Like the cabins, it's made mostly from bamboo and as we get closer I hear the clucking of hens. I give Belle's arm a squeeze. 'Hear that, Belle? Sounds to me like an omelette in waiting.'

Belle nods but she still looks freaked out.

Lola heads up a short wooden ramp to the door of the shed. 'The eggs here are amazing – so full of flavour.' She unlatches the door and about a dozen feathery balls roll out. The hens take a moment to rearrange themselves, as if embarrassed by their somewhat undignified appearance, then they start strutting about, pecking at the ground. Lola fetches a pail of feed from behind the shed and scatters it in front of them. A feathery feeding frenzy ensues.

'Come on, let's see how many eggs they've got for us,' Lola says before going inside the shed.

'You wait here,' I say to Belle, helping her to a shady spot nearby, then I follow Lola up the ramp. Inside the shed the air is warm and pungent with the smell of stale straw.

'I'm so sorry about what Michael said earlier,' Lola says quietly, as soon as we're alone.

'Hey, it's not your fault,' I say. I start feeling around in the straw and almost instantly find an egg. It's still warm. Carefully, I pick it up and place it to one side. Then I turn to look at Lola. 'What did he mean by Ruby's feminist bullshit?'

Lola sighs. 'It's like Ruby said yesterday, some guys get really threatened by strong women.' Lola looks up at me, and although it's pretty dark in the shed, I can tell her cheeks are flushed. 'Ruby's helped me become a stronger person – a stronger woman – and Michael just can't handle that. He blames her entirely for our break-up, which is massively irritating because it's like he's saying I don't have a mind of my own. But I do, and like I told you, I'd already decided to end it with him. Ruby only made it happen sooner, that's all.'

I nod, and start searching the straw for more eggs. 'So, how long were you guys together?' I ask, trying to disguise my disbelief that she could have ever gone out with him in the first place.

'Four years,' Lola replies. 'He was my first ever boyfriend. We met at a summer camp when we were fourteen.' She says this real quick, like she's tired of talking about him. But I can't help wanting to know more.

'Four years is a long time.' I manage to stop myself adding, *for dating a total jerk.*

'Yes. I suppose. Damn!'

I turn to look at her. 'Are you okay?'

Lola holds her hand up. It's dripping with egg yolk. 'I broke one,' she says, sadly, before wiping her hand on the straw. I decide to hold fire on any more questions.

From the other end of the field there's a low moo, followed

by a shriek. I guess Cariss is having problems adjusting to her new role as milkmaid.

'How long have you known Jenna for?' Lola asks.

'Oh, ages. She's my . . .' I break off.

'What?'

'My best friend,' I say, even though it's no longer really true.

'Really?'

'Yes. Well, she was. Why do you sound so surprised?'

Lola looks at me, then looks away. 'Oh, nothing. You just don't seem that – close, that's all.'

I nod. 'Well, things have been a little difficult since we've been here.'

Lola looks at me questioningly, but I decide not to tell her any more. I can't really bring myself to say it.

After collecting all the eggs, we clean out the shed and fill it with fresh straw. It's strangely soothing working together like this. We've just finished when Ruby comes striding across the field towards us. She's holding a metal pail and Cariss and Jenna are trudging along behind her, heads down. I can't make out exactly what Cariss is saying, but from the high-pitched whine of her voice and the way she's gesticulating with her hands I'd say she wasn't too impressed with her first brush with a cow's nipples.

As Ruby gets closer she looks at Lola and raises her eyebrows.

'I just want to get the hell off this island,' Cariss says to Jenna. 'It's one nightmare after another and I don't think I can take any more.'

Ruby lets out a sigh. Then she puts her pail down and turns back to face them, hands on hips. 'Listen up. In two days' time my guests will be arriving for the dark of the moon party. In three days' time, most of them will be leaving – and you will be leaving with them, and your *nightmare* will be over. So until then, can y'all please quit moaning?'

Cariss starts to say something, but I don't hear what it is. My head is swimming and I feel sick. All I can hear are Ruby's words, 'dark of the moon' echoing round my mind . . . and all I can see is the matching inscription on Hortense's bowl.

Chapter Thirteen

I turn to face Belle so the others won't notice the shocked
expression on my face. In my mind I see myself in action
replay, in my bedroom the night before we left, setting fire to
my cosmic wish-list in the antique bowl my dad bought me in
New Orleans. And I hear myself reciting the inscription on the
rim of the bowl as the paper burnt and my burning wishes flew
up to the stars.

'*Vivre éternellement dans l'obscurité de la lune.*'

'*Live forever in the dark of the moon.*'

I think of the matching bowl I found inside the volcano,
and how I'd felt Hortense's presence so strongly and heard her
voice, louder than ever in my head. The inscription seemed to
have been an important clue, but Cruz and I couldn't figure

out why. Now it feels as if another piece of the jigsaw has slotted into place.

I become aware of Cariss whining and zone back in on the others' conversation.

'I think we should get back to the camp,' Lola is saying. Her voice is more tense than I've ever heard it before; clearly she's reaching the end of her rope with Cariss.

'But why do we have to stay for the stupid party?' Cariss moans. 'Why can't we leave in the boat the guests come in as soon as they arrive?'

'The guests are only staying for one night,' Ruby says tersely. 'I'm sure you can survive. And anyway it's way too far for Carlos to go back and forth so many times in one day.'

'What does dark of the moon mean?' I say, in what I hope is a laid-back voice, even though my heart is pounding like it's about to burst.

Ruby looks at me. Her face is its usual bored-looking mask, but she's fiddling with the ring on her thumb like crazy.

'It's a phase in the lunar cycle,' she replies. 'When the moon is completely absent from the night sky.' She picks up her pail and turns abruptly on her heel. 'Come on, let's get back.'

'And you're throwing a party because of it?' Cariss says snarkily.

'Shhh,' Jenna says, frowning at her.

'All the senses are heightened during the dark of the moon,' Ruby says, without looking back, 'which makes it the perfect time for a party. Now, can we please get back?'

We walk back to the camp in silence. I wish I could see Cruz right now, and tell him what's happened and try to make sense of it. I grip Belle's arm and focus on my steps and my breathing, trying to get them in synch to calm my pounding heart. If Ruby is in some way connected to Hortense, I can't let her know that I'm on to her – I have to play it cool.

When we get back to the clearing there's no sign of the boys.

'Can we get something to drink, please?' Jenna asks Ruby.

Ruby nods. She looks distracted. 'Sure. Help yourself.' She hands the pail of milk to Jenna. 'I'm just going to see to something up in the house. Lola, could you help me please?'

'I'll be right back,' Lola says to me. Then she follows Ruby up the ladder into the house.

Jenna and Cariss head to the kitchen. Belle and I are left standing on our own in the clearing.

'Are you okay, Grace?' Belle whispers.

'Sure. Why wouldn't I be?' I look at her, trying to read her expression.

Belle places her hand on mine. 'You seem tense. I mean, I know I can't *see* you but I can sense it. I could feel it in your body. Is something wrong?'

I sigh. 'Maybe. I don't know. I guess I won't feel totally happy till we're out of here.'

Belle nods. 'Me too.'

I put my arm round her shoulders. 'How about we get a drink?'

Belle nods and I start guiding her across the clearing. When we reach the kitchen Jenna and Cariss are standing staring at the pail of milk.

'There is no way I'm drinking a drop without it being, like, disinfected,' Cariss says. 'And anyway, dairy is not good for my sinuses.'

Jenna throws me a hopeful smile. I'm just about to explain to Cariss that milk this fresh doesn't need to be 'disinfected' when Lola appears in the doorway.

'Ruby would like us to do a group meditation together,' she says. 'She wants you to see that retreat life isn't all about doing chores.'

'Cool!' Cariss says with a beaming smile.

We all stare at her in amazement. She actually sounds thrilled. 'I love meditation,' she gushes. 'It's so good for the soul.'

'Didn't know you had one,' Belle mutters.

I cough and give her arm a squeeze.

I fill cups with the creamy milk for myself, Belle and Lola, and then we all go back outside.

Ruby is sitting bolt upright in the patch of shade beneath

her house. In front of her a ring of candles burns around an assortment of crystals, causing them to glimmer. We follow Lola over.

'Sit in a circle,' Ruby instructs, and as we do as she says, she closes her eyes and presses her thumbs and forefingers together, pointing them skyward.

Who are you? I think as I stare at her.

Ruby opens her eyes. 'I always like to start a meditation circle by asking the cards for guidance,' she says.

'What cards?' Cariss asks. It's weird seeing her so engaged for once. Weird, and kind of unsettling.

Ruby picks up a dark red, velvet drawstring bag from the floor beside her. She pulls it open and takes out a pack of ancient-looking cards. 'Tarot,' she replies.

Jenna shifts uncomfortably. I know why. Her mom is obsessed with getting readings and has often based key parental decisions around what the cards say.

Ruby closes her eyes and begins shuffling the pack. Finally, she pulls out a card and studies it. 'Interesting,' she murmurs.

'What is it?' Cariss asks.

Ruby places the card down on the ground in front of her. Although I'm sitting right across the circle from her, I can see a skull and the word DEATH across the top of the yellowing background.

'Oh my God, does that mean that someone is going to,

like, die?' Cariss asks, looking around fearfully.

'Maybe it's about Ron,' Jenna whispers.

Ruby sighs. 'The Death card doesn't mean somebody's physical death.'

'What does it mean then?' Cariss stares at her.

'It means the beginning of a new era – out with the old and in with the new.' Ruby looks at Lola pointedly and Lola smiles. I guess she's hoping it refers to her and Michael.

'So, would any of y'all like a reading?' Ruby asks, looking around the circle at us. Jenna looks straight down at her lap.

'Yes, please.' Cariss holds her hand out.

Ruby picks up the Death card and places it back in the pack. Then she gives the cards another shuffle and passes them to Cariss, who grabs them eagerly.

'Give them a shuffle and think of a question you want answered,' Ruby says in her deep drawl. She's watching Cariss with a mixture of amusement and scorn.

Cariss shuffles the cards with a look of deep concentration upon her face.

'Then, when you're ready, pick one card,' Ruby continues.

'Only one?' Cariss pouts.

'One will be plenty,' Ruby says, enigmatically.

Cariss spreads the deck of cards into a huge fan on the ground in front of her. Then she makes a major production of choosing one, almost going for a card, then shaking her head and pulling away at the last minute. Finally she chooses one and places it down on the ground in front of her. 'Ooh, look, I got a queen,' she says proudly as she turns it over.

I lean across and see the Queen of Swords.

'Hmm,' Ruby says.

'What? It's got to be a good thing, to get a queen, right?' Cariss looks around the circle hopefully.

'Not if it's in reverse,' Ruby says.

Cariss frowns. 'What do you mean, in reverse?'

'It's upside down,' Belle says quietly.

'Well, how do you know?' Cariss snaps. 'You can't even see.'

Belle sighs and closes her eyes. I place my hand over hers.

'She's right,' Ruby says. 'The card is upside down and therefore it's meaning is reversed.'

'So, what does it mean?' Cariss says.

'The Queen of Swords reversed indicates a mean-spirited person,' Ruby says. 'Someone deceitful and vengeful. So tell me, who was your question about?'

Cariss looks away, clearly put out. 'It doesn't matter.'

Ruby nods and gives a knowing smile.

I feel a knot of tension form in my stomach. Someone as self-obsessed as Cariss would clearly have asked a question about herself. Is that why Ruby is doing this — to play mind games and unsettle us?

'Would anyone else like a reading?' Ruby asks, looking right at me.

'Okay,' I say. I'm not scared of her and her stupid games – or at least I'm not going to show it. I take the cards and give them a shuffle. Then I pick one straight from the top and lay it on the ground in front of me. My heart skips a beat when I read the faded black writing at the top of the card.

'What did you get?' Belle asks.

'The Moon,' I reply.

Ruby looks at me, and smiles.

'What does it mean?' I say, my mouth suddenly going dry.

Ruby picks up the card and studies it for a moment. 'Somebody has recently deceived you,' she says softly, closing her eyes. 'Somebody close to you. Somebody you would least expect to betray you in this way.'

I can't help glancing at Jenna. She looks down at her lap.

'Sounds ominous,' Lola says with a nervous laugh.

'It's okay, I think I know what it means,' I say.

'Oh really, what?' Lola looks at me questioningly.

I shake my head. 'I don't want to talk about it.'

'Are you sure?' Ruby says, her pale eyes boring into me.

'Yes.' I reply firmly.

Ruby sighs. 'Would anyone else like a reading?' she asks, looking straight at Jenna.

Jenna shakes her head.

Ruby puts the cards back in the bag and draws the string tight. 'Okay, let's get on with our meditation, and those of you who did pick a card, use this time to contemplate whatever issues came up.' She looks at Cariss and smirks.

We all sit upright and I close my eyes.

'Meditation is a great way of letting go of stress,' Ruby says, her voice deep and melodic. 'It's also a great way of connecting with Mother Earth. Close your eyes and focus on your breathing. In through the nose and out through the mouth.'

Hearing these words, I instantly think of my mom and I'm side-swiped by a pang of grief. Why can't I be back at home with her, instead of stuck in the middle of the rainforest with this freaky woman who is making me feel more and more on edge? What if I never see my mom again? Panic starts to rise in me, hot and choking. I take a deep breath in through my nose. *Focus, Grace*, I tell myself. I breathe out through my mouth, trying to push my fear out with it.

'Now, become aware of the sounds around you,' Ruby says.

I hear the parrots squawking in the forest, the hum of an insect, Belle sighing next to me. And the constant chatter of my thoughts. I need find out if Ruby really is somehow connected to Hortense. But how?

I take another breath of humid air in through my nose. I hear a shriek, like laughter, from somewhere in the forest and somewhere far way, the piercing cry of a gull. I breathe out, and then it dawns on me. If Ruby is anything to do with Hortense there's bound to be some kind of evidence in her house. I think of the ladder just yards from where we're sitting and the darkened rooms it leads to. For all I know, Hortense herself could be up there right now, watching us and waiting. Waiting for me. Fear sweeps through my body like an icy draft. I open my eyes – and see Ruby staring straight at me.

Chapter Fourteen

One time, when Grandpa and I were trekking through the woods where he lives, we came across a stray dog. It was really old and mangy, and as soon as it laid eyes on us it started to snarl. My first instinct was to run and hide behind Grandpa's legs. This was before he'd started to get old and, to my six-year-old self, he'd seemed as strong and tall as a pine tree. 'Dogs smell fear the same way they smell a bone,' Grandpa said to me. 'So you gotta bluff 'em. You gotta make like you ain't scared one bit.'

As I look at Ruby now and think of Grandpa's words, it's like he's right there behind me, his weather-beaten hand resting on my shoulder. So I continue staring right at her and I make myself smile. But before I can say anything I hear the sound of Dan's voice — and the boys come bursting into the clearing. They're laden down with pots and nets. Instinctively, I look for

Cruz. He's talking to Michael right at the back.

'Ah, well, looks like this meditation's over before it even began,' Ruby says brightly, but I can tell from the way her lips are pursed that she's annoyed.

I grab hold of Belle's hand and help her to her feet. 'Come on, let's go see if Jimmy actually caught anything.'

'Hey!' the Flea calls out when he sees us. 'You are never going to believe what happened. I caught a crab – with my own bare hands!' He bounds over and flings his arm round Belle's shoulders. 'And I'm talking the Jaws of the crab world, here. Seriously, the thing's a monster.' He winks at me. 'You know, I think all this hanging around with Cruz and Dan might be turning me into an actual hunter-gatherer!'

Belle laughs and hugs him. I leave them together and go over to Cruz. He's still deep in conversation with Michael.

'That will be very good,' Cruz says to him, before turning to look at me. His face instantly breaks into a grin. 'Hey. How did the chores go?' He grabs hold of my hand.

Michael gives me a tense smile before heading off to the boys' cabin.

'It was good,' I say. Then I stand on tiptoes and give him a hug. 'Something happened,' I whisper in his ear. 'Something I need to tell you about.'

'Same,' he whispers back. 'Let's try and get a moment together.'

I nod, and then he kisses me on the side of my neck and for one brief moment the world is held in a freeze-frame.

'Grace, do you want to help me peel some potatoes for lunch?' Lola calls.

'Oh man!' I sigh into Cruz's chest.

'It is okay,' he says. 'I will see you soon.'

I nod, kiss him quickly, then turn back to Lola. She's standing by the fire, smiling at me.

'Sure,' I call back.

As I make my way over to her, Jenna joins us. 'Do you need any help?' she asks, almost shyly.

'Oh, I think we'll be okay,' Lola says.

I see Jenna's face fall. 'I'm sure we could use another pair of hands,' I say, looking at Lola pointedly.

She looks at me, then nods. 'Sure. I'll just go and get some veggies from the kitchen.'

As soon as she's gone, Jenna looks at me, and smiles. 'Thanks, Grace.'

I smile back. 'No problem.'

When Lola gets back we set about peeling a pile of potatoes.

Belle and the Flea are sitting in the shade of the girls' cabin. Judging from his wild hand gestures, he's still regaling her with tales of his crabbing glory.

Todd is pacing up and down by the kitchen and Dan and

Cruz are sitting by the boys' cabin, looking at their catch. Ruby is nowhere to be seen.

'So, what do you think your tarot card was about?' Lola asks me.

'Oh, I don't know,' I say quickly.

'But you said you did.' Lola looks at me concerned. 'I hope it was nothing serious.'

I shake my head. Out of the corner of my eye I see Jenna shifting uncomfortably. 'No, it's all okay. Anyway, I'm not so sure I believe in the tarot – I mean it's kind of like astrology isn't it? You just twist the reading to fit the facts.'

Lola smiles. 'Maybe. Or maybe you are drawn to pick the card that most fits your situation. Who knows?'

Jenna gets to her feet. 'I'm feeling a little tired. I think I might go have a lie down.'

'Oh, okay.' Lola smiles up at her.

Jenna marches off to the cabin and I let out a sigh.

'Is she all right?' Lola asks. 'She seems very tense.'

I look at her and sigh. 'If I tell you something do you promise not to mention it to anyone?'

Lola nods. 'Of course.'

'I found out that Jenna – well, she likes Todd. Or at least she did.'

Lola starts to frown. 'Oh.'

'And something happened between them – before we came away.'

'What, when you and he were together?' Lola stops what she's doing and stares at me.

'Yes.' I take a deep breath. 'But it's all cool now. I mean, I don't even like Todd any more and I'm with Cruz now. So none of it really matters.'

'But still.' Lola shakes her head. 'So, that was the betrayal that came up in the cards?'

I shrug. 'I guess.'

Lola places her hand on my arm. 'It must've been horrible though.'

I nod. 'Yeah, it sucked. The funny thing was, it wasn't his betrayal that hurt so much – it was *hers*. That hurt way more.'

Lola nods, grim-faced. 'I can imagine.'

I notice Ruby climbing down the ladder out of her house. 'Hey guys, I could use some help getting the cabins ready for the other guests,' she calls out to the boys.

Todd, Cruz and Dan head over to her and they all disappear off into one of the cabins at the far side of the camp.

Just then Michael appears from the boys' cabin. 'Lola, can I have a word?'

Lola looks over at him, but stays where she is. 'Sure.'

'In private.'

She looks at me, embarrassed.

I smile at her. 'Go ahead. I'll be fine here. It's pretty much done.'

'Okay, well I won't be long.' She gets up and follows Michael off down the pathway toward the pool.

I carry on peeling the potatoes, thinking how glad I am that I've met Lola. She has such a gentle energy, it's so easy to talk to her.

I'm about to close my eyes and try to relax for a moment when I notice a figure slipping behind the pile of firewood at the far end of the clearing and into the forest. My body tenses. It's Ruby. I wonder where she's going. I take a deep breath – there's only one way to find out. I get to my feet and start to follow her.

The forest at this end of the retreat is far more dense – it reminds me of the other side of the island, and instantly I'm hit by the old feelings of claustrophobia. I peer into the gloom and can just make out Ruby up ahead slipping through the trees like a shadow. I follow her, prickly vines clawing at my skin. Suddenly, she comes to a standstill. I crouch behind a bush and hardly dare to breathe. Then I hear her moving again. I come out from my hiding place and continue on. Unlike the forest leading to the garden or the lagoon, there's no clear path this way, so I start making a mental note of landmarks so I'll be able to find my way back. This is kind of hard, given that it all looks so alike. My eyes scan the wildlife either side of me and I see a clump of red-tinged ferns to my right. When I look up again I can no longer see Ruby. Shit. Which way should I go? I decide to make a right and continue on through the tangled undergrowth. What if I've gone the wrong way? What if I end up lost? How will I explain myself to the others? I carry on, trying to ignore my rising fear. Then, finally, I see a slight gap in the trees up ahead of me. I creep up and peer through it. I swallow hard. Through the trees is a small clearing. The ground is pale and dusty and worn smooth of grass. And then I see something that nearly makes my heart stop. On the far side of the clearing, straight across from where I'm crouched, is an altar. It's about the same size as the one in the volcano and it's draped in red velvet and laden with objects. From this distance I can't make out what they are. My stomach starts to churn as I try to figure out what to do. Is this where Ruby came? Should I go back to the camp before she sees me, or should I try to get a bit closer to the altar to see what's on it?

Whenever Mom and I watch a horror flick our main bugbear is that moment the heroine is all alone in a spooky house and she hears an intruder downstairs. 'Stay upstairs and call the cops!' we yell at the screen from behind our cushions. But every time, without fail, she goes downstairs, totally unarmed, in the pitch-dark, and meets some kind of gruesome end. I feel exactly like one of those heroines now as I start edging around the outside of the clearing. If Mom was watching me on a screen someplace she'd be yelling her head off.

My heart racing, I creep on through the forest, careful not to make a sound. Then, finally, I just make out the back of the altar through a thick wall of trees and vines. But before I can get any closer, I hear footsteps in the clearing and I duck down. I shut my eyes tightly, like a little kid hoping this will somehow make her invisible. I hear movement on the other side of the altar and the sound of a match being struck. Then a voice whispering, but it's too quiet to make out who it is or what they are saying. The footsteps retreat and fade into silence. And then I smell it. The sickly sweet scent that haunted me when we first got to the island — the scent that always let me know when Hortense was near.

Chapter Fifteen

I crouch down so small it feels as if my ribs are going to crack. I'm half expecting to hear Hortense's voice in my head, tauntingly whispering, 'I can see you.' But there's nothing. The smell is getting stronger though. Very slowly, I lean slightly to my left and inch toward a tiny gap in the leaves. I peer into the clearing. It's empty. But I can see a thin wisp of smoke curling around the side of the altar. The smell becomes even stronger and I realise that it must be some kind of incense. I feel dizzy and light-headed and the ground seems to tilt beneath me.

Very carefully, I start to back away.

Somehow I make it round the edge of the clearing and stumble into the forest. I have to get back before the others realise I'm missing — if it was Ruby lighting the candles I can't let her know that I was here. I hurry on, looking out for the landmarks I'd noted on my way there. I feel sick to my stomach. Even though I didn't actually see Ruby, there's a voodoo-style altar about half a mile from her retreat. There's no way she wouldn't know about it, so she has to be connected to Hortense, right? But how? And why? I see the cluster of red-tinged ferns and follow the trail back to the camp. When I get to the stack of firewood I peer through a gap in the logs. Belle and the Flea are still chatting over by the girls' cabin. Todd and Dan are lying in the shade of the boys' cabin. Cruz is standing in the centre of the clearing, frowning and looking all around. I feel a rush of relief as I realise he must be looking for me.

I give the retreat one last scan. There's no sign of Ruby. I slip out from behind the woodpile and skulk across to the kitchen. If I can get in there without anyone seeing me I can make out I've just been having a drink. I check to make sure no one's looking and dart in through the door.

'Grace, what can I get you?'

I don't know how I don't scream at the sound of Ruby's voice. She's standing at the far end of the kitchen, chopping some herbs, all calm and Zen, like she's been there for ages.

I stand gaping at her for a moment. 'I – uh . . . I f-felt like a snack.' I'm stammering badly. Thankfully she doesn't seem to realise, or chooses to ignore it.

'Apple?' she reaches up to a cupboard and brings out

an apple. It's shiny and red, like the kind that poisoned Snow White.

'Thank you.' I take it from her, and try to calm myself.

'No problem.' Ruby turns back to what she was doing.

'Okay. Well, I'd better get back to the others.'

Ruby nods. 'Sure.'

I back out of the kitchen, and right into Cruz. This time I do yelp in surprise.

'Where have you been?' he asks.

I take Cruz's hand and pull him away from the kitchen. 'I have to talk to you right now,' I hiss.

'Sure.' He nods.

'Hey, where are you guys going?' the Flea shouts as soon as he sees us.

'For a walk,' I say quickly.

'Ah, I see,' the Flea says with a wink. 'Well, don't do anything I wouldn't.' He frowns. 'Actually, scrap that, *do* do exactly what I wouldn't.' He starts cracking up and I force myself to grin.

'We will,' I call back, my voice squeaky with tension.

I lead Cruz along the passageway to the pool, figuring that the sound of the waterfall will lessen the chance of anyone overhearing us.

'What has happened?' Cruz says, as soon as we're half-way along the track.

I turn and gaze up at him. 'I found another altar,' I whisper breathlessly. 'About ten minutes from here.'

Cruz looks baffled. 'How did you find it?'

'I followed Ruby.'

'What?'

'I saw her slipping off into the forest, behind where all the firewood is kept. So I followed her and I found a clearing with an altar in it.'

Cruz's face goes deadly serious. 'And what was Ruby doing there?'

'I don't know. I was hiding. But I heard her. I mean, I didn't actually *see* her, but I'm sure it was her, lighting some incense.' I grip hold of Cruz's hands. 'It had the same smell I always notice when Hortense is around.'

Cruz frowns down at the ground, clearly trying to process everything I've just told him. 'What was on the altar?'

'I don't know. I couldn't get a good look. I didn't want her to see me. But it has to be connected to Hortense, right? *She* has to be connected to Hortense. Earlier she let slip that she's throwing a dark of the moon party. *Dark of the moon* – just like on the bowls. I mean, how many more coincidences can there be?'

Cruz nods. 'I was talking to Michael before.'

'Oh, yes.' I remember them coming back to the camp, deep in conversation. 'What did he say?'

'He thinks that Ruby has somehow, what is the word for it? Brain-bathed Lola.'

'Brain-bathed?' I stare at him blankly. 'Oh, you mean, brain-*washed*?'

Cruz nods and gives a lop-sided grin. 'It is the same thing, no?'

'Well, kind of.' I frown. 'I'm not so sure about that. I've gotten to know Lola pretty well and she doesn't seem brainwashed. She sure does admire Ruby, but I wouldn't go that far. I think maybe Michael's bitterness is clouding his judgement.'

Cruz looks undecided. 'Maybe, but he seemed more concerned, more worried, when I spoke with him.' Cruz takes my hand. 'He is actually okay, you know, once you get to talk to him. I think it is just this place and everything that's happened since he got here. It is making him so tense.'

I sigh. 'I can relate to that, I guess. So, what do we do now?'

Cruz takes my hand and pulls me down on to the rock. The water bubbles and froths in front of us.

'I say we need more evidence. More concrete proof that Ruby is connected to Hortense. If we can get that we can tell the others and then decide what to do.'

I nod, feeling sicker by the second. 'We need to go back to the altar – get a proper look at it, when we know she isn't around. And we need to get into the house.'

*

When we get back to the camp the others have congregated outside the boys' cabin.

'Cool, you're back,' Jenna says, with a shy smile. 'We're all going to the spring to freshen up before dinner.'

'Bring any clothes you want to wash too,' Lola says, coming over. She's holding a basket full of dirty laundry.

'I'll just go get my stuff.' I run to the girls' cabin and over to my bed.

'So, how's it going with you and Cruz?'

I turn and see Jenna standing in the doorway.

'Oh – er – good. Thanks.' Although she looks genuinely interested, all I can think of is how mean she was to Cruz when we were on the other side of the island and it instantly puts me on my guard.

Jenna comes over and sits on the edge of my bed. She starts picking at the remains of her nail polish. 'Grace, do you think . . .' she breaks off and looks away.

'What?'

'Do you think there's any way we could go back to how we used to be?'

I look at her and sigh. 'I don't know.'

She looks up at me. The shadowy light of the cabin makes the dark rings under her eyes even more pronounced. 'I miss you.'

I want to say 'I miss you too' but the truth is, I don't. Not in the way she wants me to. Jenna stares at me and I guess my silence must speak volumes because the old icy glaze returns to her eyes.

'Right then,' she says, in a small, tight voice. 'I'll get out of your way.'

As she turns and walks over to the door, pity wrenches at my heart. I'm just about to tell her to wait when she turns round.

'Your precious Lola isn't quite as wonderful as you think, you know,' she mutters, her thin lips tightly pursed.

I can't even hide my sigh of disappointment. To think I was about to trust her again. 'Really,' I say, turning back to my bag and pulling out my dirty clothes. I hear the door slam behind me.

Chapter Sixteen

All the time we're at the spring, Jenna studiously avoids me, choosing instead to talk super-animatedly to Cariss. But my head is too busy with thoughts about Ruby to be all that concerned. When we get back to the camp, Lola shows us where to hang our clothes to dry. Then we set about cooking the gumbo. Cruz builds the fire, while I chop the potatoes we peeled earlier and some bell peppers and onions. The Flea provides Belle with a running commentary.

'Here comes Dan with the shellfish,' he says, as Dan hefts the pot over. 'Oh my God, he's gonna kill Fred!' the Flea exclaims as Dan pulls a huge crab out.

Dan frowns at him. 'Who the hell's Fred?'

'Fred *Astaire* – my crab,' the Flea says, his eyes wide with horror.

'You named your crab?' Dan grins. 'You need help, boy.'

'Of course I named him.' The Flea sighs. 'Can't you at least do something to take away the pain before you boil him alive?'

Dan gestures at the rainforest. 'Dude, take a look around you. It's the law of the jungle here – dog eat dog – or man eat crab.' Dan chuckles and slaps the Flea on the shoulder. 'It's all right, bro, Fred won't feel a thing. Not for long anyways.'

As if he can hear what's being said, Fred's pincers start snapping.

'Oh God.' The Flea shudders and gets to his feet. He takes his hat off and crosses himself. 'And yea, though I walk through the valley of the shadow of death, I will fear no evil, for thou art –'

'What the hell are you doing?' Dan frowns up at him.

'Giving Fred a proper send-off.' The Flea places his hands together in prayer. 'It's the least I could do – given that I'm the one who got him into this mess.'

I look at Cruz and try real hard not to laugh.

Lola comes over from the kitchen with a plate of ingredients. Dan grabs the Flea's arm. 'Look!'

The Flea stares at the plate. 'What?'

Dan points to a gnarled looking root on the plate. 'Looks like we're gonna be eating Fred *and* Ginger.'

We all start cracking up, including the Flea, although he tries real hard to keep looking traumatised.

We're still laughing when Jenna and Cariss sashay over. They're arm in arm. My heart sinks.

By the time the gumbo's ready the sun has set and the sky is glowing with vivid brush-strokes of apricot and purple. In the rainforest, the cicadas have begun their whirring evening chorus. As if on cue – or as if she was watching us – Ruby comes out of the house and strides over. She's changed into another of her tribal-style dresses. This one is silver and makes her pale eyes look even more startling against her dark skin. We all watch as Lola begins ladling the gumbo into bowls.

'Okay, everyone, let's get started,' Ruby says, sitting cross-legged, her hands resting on her knees as if she's about to begin meditating.

The gumbo is so delicious it's like tasting everything for the very first time – the tang of the juicy tomatoes, the slight bitterness of the bell peppers, the spiciness of the onion.

'Oh man, I think I just ate a piece of Fred,' the Flea says, a thin trail of juice trickling down his chin. 'How can something so wrong, taste so good?'

I see Cariss look at Jenna and raise her eyebrows, and Jenna do the same back. I feel anger building in the pit of my stomach. Why does Jenna have to be such a brat? After everything she's done, how can she expect me to want to be best buddies? And how can she switch her loyalties so quickly?

I bring my attention back to the food, which I guess is what everyone else is doing as no one speaks again until every bowl is clean.

'Could we have another sharing circle?' the Flea says, looking at Ruby hopefully.

Ruby nods. 'Of course.' She looks at Dan. 'Could you help me with something?'

Dan leaps to his feet and gives Ruby one of his twinkly-eyed grins. 'Sure.'

I instinctively want to reach out and pull him back.

Ruby gets to her feet and stands up tall. 'Follow me.'

We all watch as she leads Dan over to one of the smaller cabins. They disappear inside. I shoot an anxious glance at Cruz. He's frowning after them. The next second, Dan lets out a whoop and bounds out of the cabin holding a set of bongo drums.

'Cool!' the Flea exclaims. Beside him, Todd sighs. I feel a pang of concern as I look at his hollowed eyes and straggly hair. Much as the old Todd used to annoy me when he showed off, it's horrible seeing him like this. It's like he's withering away before us.

Ruby comes out of the cabin after Dan, holding a guitar with a mother of pearl pick guard. 'I thought that with y'all being dance students you might care for a little music.' she calls over to us in her velvety drawl.

'If I ever die and come back as a woman I want a figure like that,' the Flea says dreamily as Ruby sashays over. There's no denying that with her tiny waist and wide hips, she's the definition of hourglass. My heart sinks. I wish Dan and the Flea weren't so taken with Ruby. If she is connected to Hortense it's going to be so hard breaking it to them.

Ruby and Dan sit back down.

'So maybe tonight we could all start by sharing a song that has meant something to us,' Ruby says, starting to tune up the guitar.

'Ooh, good idea!' Lola says, grinning.

Michael shakes his head.

'What, you mean you want us to sing it?' Cariss says with a frown.

Ruby shakes her head, making her huge silver hoop earrings dance. 'Not necessarily – you could just tell us what it is and why you love it.'

'Can I go first?' the Flea says, raising his hand like he's in kindergarten.

Ruby nods. 'Sure.'

The Flea sits up straight. 'My favourite song of all time has to be "Over the Rainbow".'

'Now there's a surprise,' Cariss says snarkily. Jenna laughs. My blood begins to simmer.

'Why's that?' Lola says, smiling at the Flea.

161

'Because he's always wanted to be Dorothy,' Cariss snips.

My blood reaches boiling point.

But before I can say anything the Flea treats Cariss to a dazzling grin. 'I sure have, honey, I mean who wouldn't want to own those shoes? I guess you always wanted to be the Tin Man.'

Cariss looks at him blankly.

'No heart,' the Flea explains, still smiling sweetly. Dan chokes back a laugh and even Belle smiles.

'*Anyways*,' the Flea continues, 'the real reason I love that song is because it's just so damn hopeful. I defy anyone to listen to it and not come away feeling all cosy inside.'

'Would you care to sing it for us?' Ruby asks, and I notice that her gaze has softened slightly. She's looking at the Flea like she might actually like him.

He nods and smiles. 'I would be delighted to. I'll sing you my shipwrecked remix. Could you give me a beat please, Dan?'

'Sure.' Dan places one of the bongos in front of him and starts tapping it really soft and slow.

'Somewhere, over the rainforest,' the Flea starts singing and we all laugh. But, by the time he's got to the bit about the dreams that you dare to dream coming true, we're all sitting in rapt silence. His singing voice is incredible, sweet and soulful. As he carries on I think of my own dreams, of making it home to Mom and Dad and Tigger, back to my normal life, and my eyes start swimming with tears. When the Flea finishes, there's a moment's silence and then we all burst into applause. Even Ruby.

The Flea looks around the circle, grinning like crazy. 'Wow, thanks, guys.'

'That was awesome,' Ruby says, and she sounds like she means it too.

The Flea's face flushes and he looks down into his lap. 'Thank you,' he murmurs. Next to him, Belle feels for his hand.

'Who next?' Ruby asks, looking round the circle. Her gaze stops on me.

'Oh, I don't sing,' I say hurriedly. 'And I'm not really sure what my favourite song is.'

'Oh, come on, you must have a song that you love,' the Flea says. 'Or one that brings back happy memories at least.'

My mind is a total blank and I'm about to tell Ruby to pick someone else, but then I have a flashback to when I was little and the rare occasions my dad was home from work in time to put me to bed.

'Well, there's a nursery rhyme that my dad used to sing to me . . .' I begin.

'Ooh, which one?' the Flea says, looking way too excited.

'"Twinkle, twinkle little star",' I mutter, embarrassed. 'Only he'd always change the words to make me laugh.'

I close my eyes and picture myself snuggling up to Dad and playing with his neck-tie while he sang. *Twinkle, twinkle, little*

Grace, how I love your freckly face. My eyes fill with tears as I think of the way his deep voice would vibrate through me. I open my eyes and wipe away the tears.

'I love that song too,' Lola says, looking down at the ground. 'One of the few things I can remember about my mum is her singing that to me.'

I lean over and stroke her arm just above the butterfly tattoo. She looks up and gives me a grateful smile. Her eyes are glassy with tears.

'Thank you, Grace,' Ruby says. 'So, who would like to share something next?'

I sit back and feel Cruz's hand on mine. And instantly I feel grounded.

'Why don't *you* share something?' Cariss says, staring at Ruby defiantly.

'Yeah,' Dan says enthusiastically, making Cariss glare.

Ruby gives Dan one of her weird half-smiles. 'What would you like?'

'What've you got?' Dan says with a grin. Shit, why does he have to keep flirting with her?

Ruby smiles at him. 'I'd like to sing y'all my favourite Billie Holiday song, "Strange Fruit".'

'Man, I love that song!' Dan exclaims. He leans over and picks up the guitar. 'Can I accompany you?'

Ruby nods.

'I didn't know you played guitar,' the Flea says to Dan.

Dan winks at him. 'Yeah well, you aren't the only one round here with hidden talents, bro.'

Dan strums a few chords introduction.

Ruby sways in time, staring into the fire. Then she starts to sing. Her voice is incredible. Deep and husky. She's so good I briefly forget my suspicions and just listen in awe.

I hadn't heard the song before but pretty soon I realise it's about the lynching of black people in the south. As she sings about the bodies hanging from the trees I can't help shivering. In the rainforest the screeching of the parrots seems to get louder, as if they're the crows she's singing about, ready to pluck at the bodies as if they were fruit.

Ruby gets to the end of the song and stares into the fire.

We all sit in silence. It feels as if Ruby's velvety voice is still reverberating through the air. Belle sniffs and the Flea puts his arm round her.

'It's okay,' he whispers.

I hear Lola sigh and I turn to look at her. Once again she has tears in her eyes. 'That was incredible,' she whispers.

'Oh, for God's sake!' Michael exclaims.

'What?' Lola stares at him.

'Don't you think you're being a little over the top?'

Lola frowns. 'What are you talking about?'

Across from us, Cariss and Jenna exchange amused grins.

Michael gets to his feet. 'I've had enough. I'm going to bed.'

Lola sits motionless, staring ahead of her.

No one says a word as Michael marches across to the boys' cabin and slams the door after him.

Ruby looks at Lola. 'Are you okay?'

Lola nods, her face still expressionless.

Todd leans across and touches Lola on the shoulder. 'You sure?'

Jenna glowers at him.

Dan puts the guitar down and looks at Ruby. 'Thank you,' he says seriously. 'That was awesome.'

'Yeah, that was something else,' the Flea says. 'Billie Holiday would've been proud.'

Cariss gives a loud sigh. 'Do you think maybe we could lighten things up a bit?'

Dan glares at her. 'So, I guess African-American history doesn't matter to you?'

'It's not like that any more,' Cariss says sulkily.

Dan glares at her. 'Oh no? Maybe not in your palace . . .'

'Why don't we all dance?' Lola says suddenly.

I look at her, surprised. She smiles at me.

'Sure,' I say, getting to my feet. It's good seeing her look happier.

'I'll play guitar,' the Flea says. 'Mind you, I only know the chords to "Blowing in the Wind" — that's as far as my dad got with me before giving up.'

The Flea starts strumming and Dan gets to his feet and holds his hand out to Ruby. To my surprise she actually accepts his offer and gets up. Cariss looks livid. I turn and look over at Cruz. He grins and gets to his feet. We all start dancing apart from Todd, who has closed his eyes and lain down. Cruz catches hold of my hand and pulls me toward him.

The beat suddenly gets harder and faster. I look down and see that Lola has started playing one of the drums. Her eyes are shut and she's hammering away — no doubt taking out her pent-up frustration with Michael. She's actually really good and pretty soon we're all dancing round the fire, eyes closed, lost in the rhythm. Cruz starts dancing right up behind me and it feels awesome. I open my eyes a fraction and see Ruby and Dan dancing together, totally lost in the music and each other. This jolts me back to reality and I turn to face Cruz. He pulls me into his arms and I feel his breath in my hair.

'We must meet tonight,' he whispers in my ear.

I nod and pull him tighter. 'By the firewood,' I whisper back. 'We need to check out the altar.'

The drumming slows. Lola's head is slumped forward and she's breathing heavily. The Flea slows his guitar playing and gradually everyone else comes back down to earth.

The Flea looks at Lola and grins. 'Wow, that was something else.'

Lola opens her eyes. She looks a whole lot better now, relaxed again.

While everyone else slumps down to the ground, out of breath, Ruby stands ruler straight, back to her usual composed self.

'I say we go to bed,' she says.

'Really?' Dan looks majorly disappointed.

Ruby nods. It's as if the dancing never happened. 'We've got a big day ahead of us, getting this place ready for the new guests.'

Cariss sighs. 'Well, just so you know, I'm not milking any more cows.'

Ruby looks at her. 'No problem. You can clean out the toilets instead.'

Ignoring Cariss's screech of disgust, Ruby picks up her guitar. 'See y'all in the morning.'

'Do you need a hand?' Dan says, jumping to his feet and picking up the bongos.

'Please,' Ruby says over her shoulder, and they both start walking back to the cabin.

As I watch them go I see Dan lean in close to Ruby and whisper something in her ear. Ruby throws her head back and she actually laughs. The sound chills me to the core.

Chapter Seventeen

Tonight, after we go to bed, Jenna doesn't stop tossing and turning. I know Cruz will be waiting for me, but what should I say to her? If I don't tell her anything and just disappear off she might raise the alarm. I get up and pull on a pair of sweat pants so my legs don't get torn to pieces in the forest.

As I put on my sneakers Jenna coughs pointedly.

'I'm going to see Cruz,' I whisper to her.

She doesn't reply, just rolls over away from me.

Outside it's a cloudless night and, although the moon is now just a sliver, the sky is covered in glittering stars. I tiptoe around the shadows at the edge of the clearing. When I get close to the woodpile I see Cruz crouched down beside it.

'Hey,' I whisper, as I reach him.

He grabs my hand. 'Hey.'

'I hope I can remember my way in the dark,' I say as we head off into the trees.

It's so noisy in the forest it feels as if hundreds of unseen creatures' eyes are boring into us, watching our every move. I grip Cruz's hand tighter. Our palms are clammy with sweat.

'You okay?' he whispers.

'Uh-huh.' I see the red ferns. 'Okay, up ahead is where I lost Ruby before. We need to go right.'

We battle our way through the vines. It takes even longer in the dark, but finally we get to the path leading to the clearing.

'We'd better be real quiet, just in case . . .' I break off, unable to speak my worst fears aloud. *Just in case Hortense is there.* My entire body goes slack with terror. Somehow I find the courage to keep going.

As we creep toward the clearing I see a chink of light through the undergrowth. Then another. We get to the gap in the trees and both take a breath. The altar is ablaze with candlelight. But there's no sign of anyone about.

I stand on tiptoe so I can whisper in Cruz's ear. 'Should we take a closer look?'

He nods and we start to edge our way round the outside. About half way round I smell the sickly sweet scent of the incense and immediately my skin crawls. Once again, I expect to hear Hortense's voice in my head. But once again, I hear nothing, apart from the creaks and hisses from the rainforest.

We stop when we get to the back of the altar. I peer through a gap in the leaves. The clearing is still empty. But *someone* lit the candles. What if they're lurking nearby? I glance at Cruz. His face is set in concentration.

'What do we do?' I whisper.

He nods toward the altar. 'We need to get a closer look.'

'But what if they come back?'

He frowns. 'One of us should keep watch while the other takes a look.'

I nod. 'Okay. I'll check – you keep watch.'

He grabs my hand. 'Are you sure?'

'Yes.' I take a deep breath. My heart is pounding so hard I can feel the blood surging in my ears. Very carefully, so I don't make too much noise, I part the leaves in front of me and squeeze into the clearing. I hear Cruz move in behind me. Thick wisps of incense are coiling round the side of the altar. The smell is choking. I follow the smoke round, taking one final glance over my shoulder to make sure the clearing's still empty. Then I turn back to the altar, blinking at the dazzling light. It's covered in tea lights, their tiny flames flickering pale gold.

Once my eyes have adjusted I see a Virgin Mary figurine, identical to the ones we saw in the volcano cave, with trails of red trickling from her eyes like tears of blood. A ring of tea lights has been placed around her, as if for protection. The rest of the altar is covered in a random assortment of things. A shiny red apple, a bunch of dried out herbs tied together with string, an old glass bottle filled with what looks like water, huge red candles, with trails of wax running down them like protruding veins. And there, at the very front of the altar, is a doll. It's similar to the one Jenna found hanging over her bed in that it's made from sticks and bound with cloth, but this doll has jet black hair rather than blonde. I pick it up. My hand is trembling. The doll's face is shiny and smooth and a mouth and nose have been drawn on the wood. But where the eyes should be are two jagged holes – like somebody gouged them out. Just as I'm about to take a closer look I hear a loud hissing. I see a sudden movement out of the corner of my eye. A huge snake is gliding out from under the altar. I take a step back, clutching the doll to me. The snake hisses again and its black forked tongue darts out. It starts pulling itself up until it's as high as my waist. I bite down hard on my bottom lip to stop myself screaming. Sweat beading on my skin, I stuff the doll into my pocket and start backing away. The snake hisses again, like it's guarding the altar. I dive back through the trees, and crash into Cruz.

'There's a snake!' I gasp. 'Under the altar.'

Cruz grabs my hands. 'Are you okay?'

'Yeah. Let's get out of here.'

We scramble through the forest, not talking at all, just

focusing on finding the way back. I don't think of anything else till we're finally by the woodpile. I lean against Cruz to catch my breath.

'I need to show you something,' I say.

Cruz nods and takes hold of my hand. 'Let's go to the pool so we do not get seen.'

We skulk across the shadows at the edge of the camp and along the path to the spring. As soon as I hear the roar of the water I feel reassured. It's like a blanket of noise, wrapping itself around us. We make our way over the rocks to the alcove above the pool.

Once we're safely inside, Cruz places his hand on my arm. 'So, what did you see?'

At last, my heart rate starts returning to normal. 'Well, there was one of those Virgin Mary statues with the blood coming from her eyes – you know, like in the cave?'

Cruz nods.

'And there was a bunch of ordinary stuff, like an apple and – and some dried herbs, and a jug of water. And there was this.' I reach into my pocket and pull out the doll. Away from the candlelight it's impossible to see what's happened to the eyes, so I take a hold of Cruz's finger and get him to feel the face. 'Can you feel it? The eyes have been cut out.'

Cruz yanks his hand away like he's been burnt.

'What is it?'

'Belle,' he whispers.

'Oh my God, do you think that's what made her blind?'

I stare down at the doll. 'It's got black hair, just like Belle. The other doll — the one above Jenna's bed, had blonde hair — just like Jenna.' I look at Cruz. 'Do you think Hortense has cast some kind of spell on her?'

Cruz shrugs, but from the way he's frowning I can tell that this is exactly what he's thinking.

'What should we do?'

'We need to break the spell.'

'But how?'

'We need to take the doll apart. That is how to get rid of the magic.'

'Are you sure?'

Cruz nods. 'I read it someplace — or heard it somewhere. I cannot remember.'

'But what if it hurts Belle?'

We look at each other, then down at the doll.

'I don't see how it can,' Cruz says. 'We are not the ones who cast the spell. Only the person who made the doll has that power over it.'

I nod. 'Okay then. I feel the silky material holding the stick body together. Eventually I find the end and pull it loose. Then, very carefully, I start to unwind the fabric, until the doll's body has gone and just the pieces of wood remain. They're held together in a cross-shape with twine. I pick at it till it comes loose. Then I pull off the black hair. It feels real. I get a sick feeling in my stomach. Is it Belle's? Hortense could have easily taken some when she abducted her. I put the hair in my pocket. Then I look at the assembled doll parts on the rock in front of us. 'What should we do with all this?' I say to Cruz.

Cruz picks up the sticks. 'Let's throw it in the water.'

I gather up the fabric and together we throw the remains of the doll into the pool.

We huddle back into the alcove. Cruz sits behind and wraps his arms around me.

'What are we going to do?' I ask him. 'I don't see how Ruby can't be involved in all of this. She's been here for two years. The altar's well hidden, but it's so close to the retreat. How could she not have stumbled across it, after all that time?'

I feel Cruz nodding behind me. 'I know. But we have to be careful. We don't know what she's capable of.'

I twist round and look at him. 'But we have to do something. If she is something to do with Hortense she'll know about the bowls – she'll know that Hortense wants me for something. What about the people she's got coming for her party? What if they're in on it too? Shouldn't we warn the others? Shouldn't we try to escape?' Panic builds inside of me.

Cruz grabs hold of my hands. 'I think we should warn Dan and the Flea, but I'm not so sure about the others. Think about it — if we tell them, what will they do?'

I picture Cariss freaking out. And Belle getting even more spooked. And the others thinking I've lost the plot. 'Yeah, I guess.'

Cruz cups my hands in his. 'The fact is, when we tried to leave before, on the sailing boat, we were sucked back in to the island. I think we need to accept that we are dealing with some sort of — some sort of supernatural power here. We have to find a way to beat Hortense at her own game — to break her magic.'

Fear prickles at my skin. 'What do you think she'll do when she sees the doll is missing?'

'Who knows? My guess is that she won't be happy. We should watch Ruby very closely tomorrow. See how she is acting. If she is connected to Hortense then she's going to be upset too, no?' Cruz kisses me lightly.

I'm about to answer when I hear the sound of someone coughing over the rushing water. We both tense and shrink back into the darkness of the alcove.

A figure is striding out of the forest, towards the pool. I recognise the silhouette immediately.

'It's Dan,' I say, relieved. 'Shall we go see him? We could warn him about Ruby right now.'

But just then I see another figure, following Dan, tall and majestic, hair fanned around her head like an aura.

I watch in horrified silence as Dan plunges into the water, then turns back, laughing and holding out his arms.

Ruby walks to the edge of the pool. She tips her head back for a second, gazing up at the moon, then, in one swift movement, she slides her dress down and steps, naked, into the water.

'What are we going to do?' I hiss at Cruz. 'We can't let Dan get it on with her!'

Cruz looks as panic-stricken as I feel. Then his eyes light up. 'There is only one thing we can do,' he hisses. To my horror, he stands up and goes to the edge of the alcove.

'Hey!' he yells to Dan and Ruby. Then he turns and beckons to me. I sheepishly join him. Ruby and Dan stand motionless in the middle of the pool, staring up at us. It's too dark to make out the expressions on their faces but I'm guessing they're not smiling.

'Can we join you?' Cruz yells, like he doesn't have a care in the world. Before they can answer, he's grabbed my hand and is pulling me down over the rocks toward the pool.

As we enter the water I hear Dan sigh.

'Great minds think alike, eh, bro?' He holds his hand up to Cruz for a reluctant high five.

Cruz grins and winks at him. I steal a glance at Ruby. She's staring right at me. Then she turns to Dan. 'You know what, I'm feeling kind of tired. I think I'm gonna go to bed.'

'But we only just got here . . .' Dan breaks off as Ruby makes her way back to the edge of the pool. 'You want me to walk you back?'

'No!' Ruby snaps.

I stare down into the water, reminding myself that no matter how awkward this scenario is right now, it's a darn sight better than Dan getting it on with someone who could actually be in cahoots with Hortense.

'I'll see you guys in the morning – early,' Ruby says, before gliding through the water and lifting herself out of the pool.

I watch Dan as he gazes at her. His eyes are saucer wide. 'Thanks, guys,' he whispers. 'I was about two seconds away from touchdown when you showed up.'

'Don't you think you ought to . . .' I break off, too embarrassed to finish the sentence.

'What? Wait till I'm married?' Dan raises one eyebrow. 'Gee, Miss Grace, never had you down as a prude.'

'I'm not, it's just –'

'And anyway, what were you two doing down here?' Dan interrupts. 'Don't you think you're being a bit hypocritical?'

My face is burning up. 'I'm not being a prude, it's just – well, you don't exactly know Ruby all that well, do you?' I cringe – I sound like I'm trying to be Dan's mom.

'Right, and you all knew Cruz *really* well when you got it together.' Dan shakes his head.

'We are just worried about this place,' Cruz says, putting his arm round my waist. 'You remember all the strange things we saw over on the other side. How do we know Ruby is not, well, not connected to it in some way?'

Dan stares at Cruz like he's a lunatic. 'What? You think Ruby could have something to do with that old crone we saw? Are you serious?'

I look at Cruz, panic rising in me. I see him think for a moment, then he starts to grin and slaps Dan on the shoulder.

'Hey, I am sorry. You're right. I'm just stressed from what happened before. I just feel like we should all be on our guard.'

Dan waits a beat then, to my relief, he starts to nod. 'Sure. I see what you're sayin', but seriously, there's nothing wrong with Ruby.' He grins. 'Nothing wrong with her at all.' He starts making his way over to the edge of the pool. 'I'm beat. I'll leave you lovebirds to it.'

'No, wait, we're coming back too.' I look at Cruz and he nods. From now on we're gonna have to stick to Dan like glue.

When I get back to the girls' cabin there's no sign of movement from Jenna's bed. I look down at Belle. Her hair is loose and spread all over her pillow around her head. I immediately think of the doll's hair in my pocket. I wonder if there's any way I'd be able to match the hair, to see if it is Belle's. I get into bed and pull my sheet up over me. It's not quite as humid as it has

179

been previous nights. My body feels exhausted, but the second I close my eyes I think of Mom. We've been missing for so long now – she must be going out of her mind. *I'm still alive, Mom*, I say to her in my head. *And I'm gonna make it back to you, I promise.*

When I finally do fall asleep I dream that I'm holding a baby. He's gazing up at me with big brown eyes and waving his chubby little hands in the air. Then, suddenly, he's gone, wrenched from my arms by some unseen person or force. I hear a girl crying – wailing – and I sit bolt upright.

'Jenna?' I stare into the darkness toward her bed. But there's still no sign of movement. I look over at Belle and she's sound asleep too. Same with Cariss. I must've dreamt it. But the crying felt so real, so raw. I lie back down and sigh. I think back over all that has happened. There must be a way to make sense of it all – to put all the pieces together. Then I think of the altar inside the volcano and my heart jolts. Hortense had led me there, using Belle as bait. Now I've found another altar right by the retreat. Does Hortense want me because she needs to kill me? Is that why she's brought me here? To be some kind of sacrifice?

Chapter Eighteen

I toss and turn for what feels like the entire night, but I must have fallen asleep at some point because I wake with a start at the sound of a bird screeching on the roof of the cabin.

'Grace.'

At the sound of Belle's whisper everything comes flooding back to me about the altar and the doll and I get a sickly feeling in the pit of my stomach. I roll on to my side. Belle is sat up in her bed staring blankly into space.

'You okay?' I say in what I hope is a calm voice. For one crazy moment I hope that us destroying the doll has given Belle her sight back. But she just carries on staring blindly as she nods.

I wipe the sweat from my forehead with the bottom of my T-shirt. Then I have an idea. 'Hey, do you want to go to the pool?'

Belle nods and smiles. From her flushed cheeks I can tell she's as hot as I am.

Very quietly, so I don't wake Cariss and Jenna, I gather our things together and help Belle from the cabin. Outside, the air is heavy with humidity. There's no sign of life in the house or the boys' cabin. I guide Belle over to the pathway leading to the pool. As we go, I take a good look at her hair. 'Can you hold on a sec,' I say, coming to a halt.

Belle nods. 'Sure. Is everything okay?'

'Yeah – I just need to check I brought some soap.' I fish around in my pocket for the hair from the doll. I pull it out and hold it up as close as I can to Belle's without touching her. Although there's no way for telling for sure without a forensic test, there's no doubt the hair *looks* identical. And Hortense would have had plenty of opportunity to take it when she had Belle captive inside the volcano.

Belle continues staring ahead blankly. 'Well?' she says.

'Well, what?'

'Did you bring the soap?'

'Oh – uh – yes.' I stuff the hair back in my pocket, take a hold of her arm and carry on walking.

The pool is glimmering in the early morning sun. It looks really beautiful but when I think back to seeing Ruby and Dan together in it last night, it makes me shudder.

'Are you okay?' Belle asks.

'Yeah. Come on, let's get in.'

I slide out of my clothes, help Belle out of her shorts and T-shirt and guide her down into the water. Holding on to her hand, I quickly dunk my head beneath the bubbling water. It feels awesome on my hot scalp and I instantly feel clearer headed.

Belle stands motionless in the water. I squeeze her hand.

'Do you want me to wash your hair?'

'Oh, yeah, please.' She nods gratefully.

'Okay, duck your head under and get your hair wet.'

Belle dunks down. She comes up laughing and gasping for air.

I squeeze some shampoo from the bottle. 'I'm just gonna go behind you. Hold on to this rock.' I guide her hands to the side of the pool. Belle holds on and I start lathering her hair up.

'This feels like being a kid again,' Belle says. 'I used to love when my mom washed my hair.'

'Me too,' I say. Bath times were my favourite time of the day when I was little as it always meant getting my mom's undivided attention – and one of her awesome made-up stories.

Belle leans back, closer to me. 'Tell me about your family, Grace.'

'Oh, well, it's a pretty small family, compared to yours. Just me, my mom and my dad. Only my dad doesn't live with us any more. He moved out almost a year ago.'

'Really? Why?'

'He met someone new. His allergist actually. He went to see her cos he thought he was allergic to wheat. Turns out he was allergic to Mom and me.' I don't even bother to laugh. This joke wasn't funny the first time I thought of it – now it seems kind of pathetic. Truth is, I'd give anything to see Dad right now.

Belle turns around. The white lather peaks on her head look like marshmallow topping. 'That sucks,' she says, really softly.

I feel a warm surge of gratitude. Finally I feel like Belle and I are proper friends. I nod, then remember that, even though she's staring right at me, she can't actually see me.

'Yeah. It wasn't the greatest of times. But hey, that's parents for you.'

Belle smiles. 'It must be nice having Cruz though.' She closes her eyes and I continue lathering her hair.

'It is – real nice. It's funny cos before I met him it was like my parents were the most important people in my life – I guess that's why it felt like my world had ended when my dad walked out. But since I met Cruz it's made me realise that actually it is possible to get that closeness with other people. It kind of takes the heat off my parents – if that makes sense?'

Belle nods and a blob of lather starts sliding down the side of her face. I wipe it away to stop it getting in her eye.

'But you've only known him a few days. Do you really feel that strongly already?'

'Uh-huh.' My face flushes and I'm glad Belle can't see it. 'I know it sounds nuts and I've gone over it in my head, wondering if it's something to do with the trauma of being shipwrecked and all of our emotions being heightened or something. But the truth is – I felt it before we even got hit by the storm – the second I saw him.' I look away, embarrassed, but I want to tell her – I *need* to tell her – to help me make sense of it myself. 'The first moment I saw him it was like there was this instant connection between us. And now I'm gonna shut up cos I'm starting to sound really cheesy.'

Belle shakes her head, and to my surprise I see that her eyes are full of tears. 'It's not cheesy at all. I understand.'

'Have you ever felt like that about someone?'

She nods. But she looks sad.

'Who was it?'

'Someone from my past. But it didn't work out.'

I feel really bad for bringing it up. 'Come on, let's go stand under the waterfall and wash the shampoo off.' I take hold of her hand. 'I'm so glad we're friends now.'

Belle squeezes my hand so tight it hurts. 'Me too, Grace.'

I'm just about to lead her away when I see something that makes my blood freeze. There, in the water bobbing straight toward Belle, is the head from the doll. It's floating with its gouged eyes facing upward. I hold my breath and watch as it drifts right by us, literally inches from Belle. She continues staring blankly down at the water.

'Are you okay?' she says after a moment.

The doll's head floats off and disappears among some rocks at the pool's edge. I take a deep breath.

'Yes, I'm fine,' I reply, but my heart is pounding like it's going to leap right on out of my ribcage.

When we get back to the camp Lola comes running over from the girls' cabin. She's wearing a faded T-shirt and baggy pyjama shorts.

'Where have you been?' she calls. She looks stressed.

'To the pool,' I call back. 'We both woke up really early and it was so hot – we thought we'd go freshen up. Is everything okay?'

Lola sighs. 'Yeah. I just panicked when I went to wake you and saw you were weren't there.'

I stare at Lola. Her eyes are puffy and her short blonde hair is standing up in clumps. She looks like she hardly got any sleep last night.

'Sorry, we didn't want to wake anyone.'

Lola visibly relaxes. 'No, I'm sorry, I didn't mean to get stroppy. It's just that Ruby's freaking out and we need to have breakfast and start getting things ready.'

I stare at her. 'Why's Ruby freaking out?'

'Oh, because she doesn't think the camp will be ready in time.'

I wonder if that's the real reason. Or has she already

discovered that the doll's gone missing?

'Good morning, ladies!'

We all turn to see the Flea emerging from the boys' cabin. He's wearing his pyjamas – and pork pie hat, which he doffs to us.

'Hey, Jimmy, we've been to the pool,' Belle says excitedly.

'Without me!' the Flea comes bounding over like a puppy. 'How very rude!'

Belle giggles as he gives her a hug.

I let go of her hand and turn to Lola. 'Do you want some help getting breakfast ready?'

Lola smiles at me. 'Please. I was going to make a fruit salad, as it's so hot.'

'Sure. Fruit salad's my speciality.' I link arms with her and we head over to the kitchen. As we go past the girls' cabin, Jenna emerges.

'Morning,' I say.

'Morning,' Jenna mutters and she turns to look over at the boys' cabin. Todd stumbles out, blinking in the bright sunlight.

'Any chance of some coffee?' he says when he sees us.

'Yes, if you fancy making some,' Lola calls back with a smile.

Todd trudges over. His hair is greasy at the roots and the shadows under his eyes seem even darker.

'How you doing?' I ask quietly.

He shrugs and his eyes fill with tears.

I take his arm. 'Come on.'

The three of us enter the kitchen. It's much cooler in here. I close my eyes and breathe in the comfortingly homely smell of herbs.

Lola starts piling mangoes and oranges and apples on to the counter. Then she pulls a real old-looking coffee grinder out of one of the cupboards. It's made of black wrought iron, mounted on a battered wooden base. 'The beans are in there,' she says to Todd, gesturing to an earthenware jar on the shelf in front of him.

'Jeez, where'd you guys get this thing?' Todd mutters. 'Off the Ark?'

I stare at the grinder and a shiver runs down my spine. I can tell from the chips on the wooden base and the places where the iron has worn smooth that it definitely isn't some kind of vintage replica. But why would Ruby have such an old grinder if she's only been here two years? Why wouldn't she have brought a new one with her?

'Ruby loves antique stuff,' Lola says, as if reading my mind. 'You should see the mangle she has up in the house.'

Todd studies the grinder. 'You're not kidding.' He takes the jar of beans down and scoops out a handful. As he puts them into the grinder the smell of coffee makes me drool.

'Mmm,' I say. 'Sure smells good.'

Todd nods. 'Uh-huh.'

Lola turns to us, frowning. 'Damn, I forgot to get some water.' She heads for the door. 'Back in a minute.'

'Sure.' I nod at her and smile.

She slips out and I realise that Todd and I are alone for the first time since I broke up with him. I start studiously chopping some apples.

Todd must be feeling equally awkward as he grinds the coffee so fast I think the handle might fall off. After a couple of minutes he stops and sighs. 'Man, they must have had strong arms in the olden days.'

I smile at him.

He looks deadly serious. 'Grace, can I ask you something?'

'Of course.'

'Do you think . . .' he breaks off and looks away.

'What?'

'Do you think Ron knew that he was about to die?' Todd's head slumps down and his shoulders start quivering.

'Oh, Todd.' I go over and take hold of his arm.

'I mean, he was so out of it from whatever was in that bottle. Maybe he didn't realise. Maybe he didn't feel anything?' Todd looks at me, his eyes wide with a mix of desperation and hope.

'I'm sure he didn't,' I say. 'I'm sure he didn't feel a thing.' I hug Todd to me and feel his tears hot and wet on my shoulder.

'I'm so sorry, Grace,' he sobs. 'I was a total tool to you before – I'm so sorry.'

'It's okay,' I say. 'Really.'

Todd pulls away from me and wipes his face with the back of his hand. 'I just want you to know that I'm fine about you and Cruz, you know?'

'Thank you,' I whisper. Then I step toward him and kiss him on the cheek.

Someone coughs behind us and I turn to see Jenna standing in the doorway. Her face is etched with shock and pain. But before I can say a word, she's turned on her heel and gone.

Chapter Nineteen

Once I've chopped all the fruit I put it in a large china bowl, cover it with a towel and take it outside. Dan and Cruz are up and standing by the remains of last night's fire. As soon as I see Cruz I get the urge to grin like an idiot. As if he can tell I'm thinking about him, he turns round, and his face breaks into a goofy grin too. Resisting the urge to actually gallop, I casually stroll over to him.

'Morning!' I place the bowl of fruit down on the ground.

'Morning,' Cruz says, putting his arm round me and pulling me in for a hug.

'Hey.' Dan grins at me. I'm relieved that we've been forgiven for last night. 'Watcha got in there?'

'Fruit salad. Lola thought it would be good, given that it's so damn hot already.'

Dan nods. Cruz looks down at me. 'How did you sleep?'

'Oh, you know – about my usual two hours.'

Cruz immediately looks concerned. 'Bad dreams?'

'No – not really.' My stomach churns as I think back to last night. Usually when I have bad thoughts in the middle of the night, they seem a whole lot less scary by daylight. But not this time.

Dan looks up at the house. I guess he's hoping for Ruby to make an appearance.

'I was thinking, you know, about what you were saying last night?' he begins.

I feel a glimmer of hope. Maybe he's realised that we shouldn't trust Ruby. 'Yeah?'

'Yeah. Maybe it's time we told Ruby and the others what we saw – in the rainforest, when we went looking for Belle.'

'Oh, I don't know . . .' I look at Cruz, panicked.

Cruz somehow manages to look totally unfazed. 'I think we should wait a bit longer,' he says calmly. 'If we tell the others they'll only start to freak out.'

Dan thinks about this and nods. 'I see what you're saying, but I think we should tell Ruby at least. I can't see anything making that chick panic. And if we're all going in a couple of days we can't leave her here knowing there's a crazy on the loose. Look at what happened to Belle . . .'

I turn and look at Belle, sitting by the girls' cabin with the

Flea. How can I tell Dan that I think Ruby might be connected to her abduction? He'll think I'm nuts.

Then I have an idea. It's not a great one, but at least it might buy us some more time.

'Listen, Lola told me that Ruby's real stressed about getting this place ready in time for the next lot of guests. So why don't we wait till this evening, when we'll have gotten everything done and she'll be a bit more chilled?'

To my massive relief, Dan starts to nod. 'Yeah, I guess that makes sense.'

Cruz squeezes my hand and I squeeze his back. Morse code for, *phew that was close.*

Lola comes up behind us, carrying a jug of water.

Dan smiles at her. 'Hey. Where's Ruby?'

'She's gone to check on the animals. She'll be back soon.'

Cruz and I exchange glances. I know he's thinking the same as me. Will Ruby have seen that the doll is missing?

Todd comes out of the kitchen. He smiles at me and nods.

I nod back and feel a surge of gratitude that everything is finally cool between us.

'Can you guys get a fire going?' Todd calls over. 'I want to brew us some coffee.'

'Sure thing,' Dan calls back. Then he turns to us. 'Good to see him looking a bit happier,' he whispers.

I smile in agreement.

'It is for sure,' Cruz says. 'Let's get some wood.'

Cruz, Dan and I go over to the woodpile. We gather up armfuls and start heading back. But just as I'm following them, I stumble and drop half my sticks. I crouch down to pick them up, and see someone walking out from behind the pile. I look up to see Ruby towering over me. She's wearing brown linen cargo pants and a bright orange vest top. Her hair is flattened under a black bandana.

'Oh – er – hi,' I stammer. 'I was just – just getting some firewood.'

She looks down at me, but it's like she's looking right through me.

She must know about the doll. What if she knows that I took it?

'Okay. Great,' she mutters.

'What?' my voice comes out like a squeak.

Ruby glares at me. 'It's great that y'all are getting some wood. Excuse me.'

I watch as she strides off. She mutters something to Lola then quickly scales the ladder and disappears into her house, completely blanking Dan, who's gazing at her like a love-sick puppy. I glance at Cruz. He looks at me and raises his eyebrows. I quickly gather up my firewood and head back over to them.

'Ruby's not feeling too good,' Lola says, as I reach them. 'She's gone to have a lie down.'

*

After breakfast, Lola runs through a list of all the different chores that need doing. Cruz and I choose to clean one of the cabins for the new arrivals. As soon as we're alone in there I turn to him.

'Do you think Ruby knows about the doll? Do you think that's why she's saying she's saying she's not feeling well? I saw her come out of the rainforest right behind the woodpile and she seemed really tense. She could have been coming back from the altar.'

Cruz nods his head slowly and thoughtfully. 'It could be. How about Belle? Does she seem any different today?'

I shake my head. 'No. But I'm sure the hair on the doll was hers. It looks identical.'

I put my sponge back into the pail of water and wring it out. Then I crouch down and start scrubbing the floorboards under one of the beds. As I do so, one of them comes loose. I bend down and press my hand on the end of the floorboard and the other end seesaws up. 'Wow, one of these boards is seriously loose,' I say. Then, instinctively, I grope around underneath it. My fingers feel a piece of paper. I pull it out and go stand by a gap in the bamboo wall where the light is filtering through.

The paper is jagged along one edge, like it's been ripped from a notebook. It has the word 'PELIGRO' written at the top of one side. The rest of it is covered in a faded pencil scrawl that I recognise immediately. 'Oh my God!' I look over at Cruz, busy making up one of the beds.

He immediately stops what he's doing and comes over. 'What is it? What have you got?'

I hold the page out to him, my hand trembling. 'It's the man's writing, isn't it? The man we found in the woods. The man who – who killed himself.'

Cruz nods, not saying a word. Then he takes the page from me and studies it.

'What does it say?' My voice is shrill. 'What does *peligro* mean?'

Cruz looks at me, his expression deadly serious. 'It means danger.'

My heart pounds as I watch Cruz read. Then he mutters something in Spanish under his breath. I can't understand what it is, but I can tell from the tone of his voice that it definitely isn't good. 'What's wrong?'

I've never seen Cruz look so panicked – not even when we found Belle on the altar and thought she was dead. He looks at the door anxiously, then back at the piece of paper.

'*I am writing this note in fear for my life,*' he begins reading quietly. '*And if you are reading it, I pray that it helps save yours. I came to this island alone, intrigued by the legend of the voodoo queen, Hortense, and determined to find out if Ile de Sang actually existed. I have found both – or they have found me. And now I don't know if I shall ever escape. Hortense doesn't know that I know her identity. Not yet. She thinks I landed here by accident. She thinks I believe her tales of a travellers' retreat. But last night I heard her talking to the other one, deciding which of us she was going to possess next. My name came up and she laughed, saying that she hadn't been a man for about fifty years and how it would be fun. Fun? She talks about other people as if they're just outfits to be tried on and discarded. But then she said, "I will be glad when the chosen one comes and I can end this charade." It's something to do with the bowl, I know that much, because she was holding it as she spoke. And then she read the writing from around the rim. I got a chance to look at it, after they'd gone. It's in French.'* Cruz looks at me, his eyes wide, then he continues reading. *'It means, "Live forever in the dark of the moon".'*

I gasp.

Cruz looks at me again. 'You okay?'

I nod. 'Carry on.'

Cruz looks back at the paper. *'Her magic seems to be connected to the moon's cycle. As she held the bowl she said, "this will bring them to me and then finally I can get off this island — I can be free." I don't know what all of this means. But I do know that I have to make my escape tonight. I've seen what happens to the people she possesses. I've seen their graves. I have to get out of here and warn people. If this spell works and she is able to leave here and live forever, who knows what evil she will do. But if I don't make it and you are reading this because you are now a guest in this place — and if you know nothing of voodoo queen Hortense – I beg you, to leave immediately. Your life is in grave danger.'*

Cruz stops reading and looks at me.

I sit down on the closest bed. My throat is tightening and I can barely breathe. 'It *is* the bowl,' I whisper.

'What?' Cruz comes over and sits down beside me.

'It *is* the bowl,' I repeat. I look down at my hands. They're shaking uncontrollably. 'So, I must be "the chosen one"?' I turn to Cruz, staring at him, willing him to tell me I'm being stupid. But he just puts his arm around me and holds me close.

'This doesn't feel real.' I look at Cruz in terror. 'Nothing feels real any more.'

Cruz takes hold of my trembling hand. He looks so sad. '*This* is real,' he says softly. 'Us – you and me – it is real.'

I lean into him, absorbing his strength. 'Thank you,' I whisper.

He lifts his hand up and cups my face, and kisses my mouth so gently I gasp.

'I love you, Grace,' he whispers.

'I love you too.' As I say the words, tears burn in my eyes. I love Cruz, but I hate this. I hate being stuck here not knowing what's going to happen next, or if we're even going to make it out of here alive.

'No,' Cruz says, bringing his thumb up to my face and wiping away the tears that are now spilling down my cheeks.

His face looks ashen, despite his tan. 'You mustn't cry.' He hugs me close to him. 'I have a plan,' he whispers in my ear. 'A way we can escape.'

'What? How?' I look up at him hopefully.

'When the guests arrive for the party, they will leave their boat in the bay. What if we sneak off and take it during the party?'

'But how can we do that without being noticed?'

'We have to tell the others to go to the bay, one by one.'

I start to frown. 'But won't we have to tell them why?'

'We will tell them when we get there.'

'What if they don't believe us?'

Cruz brushes his hair back from his face. 'Look, all of them are desperate to get back to their home, right?'

I nod.

'If they want to believe us, they come – if they don't . . .'

The silence is filled with the terrible alternative – we leave them here, with Hortense.

'But until then, we have to act like nothing's happened.'

I look at Cruz. 'That's going to be so hard.'

He shrugs. 'We have no choice.'

'Do you really think that Hortense is able to possess other people's bodies?'

Cruz sighs. 'If you had asked me if such a thing was possible before we came here I would have said, no way. But now . . .'

he breaks off and looks at the door. 'So many terrible things have happened. So many things that are impossible to explain.'

I nod. 'But then who was it that chased us through the forest? The man said it was Hortense.' I shudder as I think of her shrivelled skin and rasping breath and the way the man had cowered in terror.

Cruz looks thoughtful. 'That must be her actual body – her ancient body. But then she possesses other people whenever she feels like it.' He looks back at the tattered piece of paper. 'Like outfits to be tried on and discarded.'

I nod – and then I have a terrible thought. 'Oh my God, if Hortense is able to possess other people's bodies, do you think – do you think she could be in Ruby's right now?'

He frowns. 'I don't know.'

Fear bubbles up inside of me. 'Maybe that's why I haven't been hearing her voice any more. Maybe she doesn't need to talk to me in my head – because she can talk to me face to face.' I clutch my hands together to stop them from trembling.

Cruz takes hold of them. 'Are you okay?'

I nod. I mustn't show him how scared I am. I mustn't show anyone. I have to stay strong. I can't let Hortense know that I know anything – whoever and wherever Hortense may be.

Chapter Twenty

The rest of the morning takes on a weird, surreal feel. It's like my body is on autopilot while my mind goes into overdrive. After Cruz and I have cleaned out the cabin we go for a drink and some more fruit. The heat is almost unbearable now, which isn't helping any. The sunlight is casting a weird Instagram-style glow, making everything look faded and washed out.

I spot the Flea and Belle leaning against the wall of the girls' cabin. The Flea is fanning Belle with a huge palm leaf.

'I think we should tell Belle and the Flea what's happened,' I whisper to Cruz. 'They're the only ones who won't think we've gone crazy and I want to warn them.'

Cruz thinks for a moment, then nods. 'You're right.'

'Hey, young lovers!' the Flea calls out. 'Come sit with us in the shade.'

We go sit down next to them. I take hold of Belle's hand and give it a squeeze. She smiles up at me.

'Listen, we need to tell you something,' I whisper, glancing around the clearing to make sure there's no sign of Ruby.

'Did you get engaged?' the Flea yelps. 'Oh. My. Holy. God! That is so romantic. Getting engaged while shipwrecked! I feel as if I'm living in a Jackie Collins novel.'

My face flushes. 'No! We did not get engaged!'

The Flea sighs. 'Shame. This place could really do with a wedding.'

'Jimmy!' Belle exclaims. Then she turns to me. 'What is it, Grace?'

I glance round the clearing, then lean in closer to them. 'You have to promise not to breathe a word to anyone.'

'Of course,' Belle whispers.

I take a deep breath. 'We've found out who's behind all of the weird stuff that happened on the other side of the island. We think we know who took Belle before.'

The Flea takes his hat off and stares at me, deadly serious.

Belle immediately looks panic-stricken. 'Who?'

I look around the clearing again.

'You cannot say a word of this to any of the others,' Cruz says.

'We won't,' the Flea says. 'I know I kid around a lot, but I know when to keep my mouth shut.'

Cruz nods and they all turn to look at me.

'This is going to sound really nuts,' I begin.

The Flea shakes his head. 'Honey, I was there when we went looking for Belle. I saw what happened. I can handle nuts.'

'We think it's something to do with a voodoo queen,' I say, squirming slightly at how crazy it sounds. But the Flea and Belle aren't laughing, they're staring at me open-mouthed so I carry on. 'Her name is Hortense, and we think she's living here on the island.'

Belle lets out a frightened gasp.

'Holy crap!' the Flea exclaims. Then his eyes light up. 'So that would explain the voodoo Barbie we found hanging over Jenna's bed.'

I nod. 'Uh-huh.'

'And the altar we found Belle on. And all the spooky stuff in the cave.'

'That's right. And you know the pendant we keep on finding?'

The Flea nods.

'That's her symbol on it – the snake over the letter H.'

The Flea shakes his head. 'Oh boy!' Then he grasps my arm. 'Was that – was that her in the rainforest?'

I nod. 'I think so, yes. And it's really complicated, but I think she's after me for something.'

Belle frowns. 'What do you mean?'

'Well, from the moment we got here, I started hearing this weird whispering. Like a woman's voice, telling me to do things.'

The Flea frowns. 'You're kidding? Why didn't you say anything?'

I feel my face burn. 'Because I thought you'd think I was going nuts. *I* thought I was going nuts!'

The Flea shakes his head. 'Oh, honey, you should have told us. That must have been horrific. What was she saying to you?'

'All kinds of things. Telling me to come into the forest. Telling me that I had to help her.' My skin starts to crawl as I remember Hortense's low voice whispering in my head. The Flea tightens his grip on my arm. I give him a weak smile. 'And you know the bowl I found by the altar?'

The Flea nods. 'The one you thought was yours?'

'Yes. Well, obviously it can't have been mine, but it is identical to the one my dad got me. And he got it for me in New Orleans – which is where Hortense is from originally. We think there might be some kind of spell on the bowls, to bring me here.'

Cruz glances round the clearing, then he takes the crumpled piece of paper from his pocket. 'We just found a warning note from the dead guy, hidden under a floorboard,' he whispers, gesturing at the cabin. 'He had been staying here – at the retreat – and he was on to Hortense.'

Belle frowns. 'But didn't you say that guy was crazy?'

Cruz nods. 'He was – when we saw him. I guess by then he had been pursued by Hortense for so long, the fear had driven him mad. But what he writes here – it is completely different. He sounds totally sane.'

'Shit!' The Flea stares down at the piece of paper, shaking his head slowly. 'We should tell the others.'

Cruz stuffs the paper back into his pocket. 'No. Not yet.'

The Flea frowns. 'Why not? If there's some crazy voodoo chick on the loose and she's after Grace, we need to get out of here. We can get Ruby to . . .' he breaks off and looks at me. 'Oh, wait a sec – you don't think Ruby has something to do with this?'

I shrug. 'I think so – maybe – but we don't have any proof. That's why we can't say anything just yet, not until we're sure.'

The Flea nods. 'I guess that makes sense.' He turns to Belle. 'You okay, Beau-belle?'

Belle nods, but her face looks frozen with fear. I take hold of her hand and stroke it. 'It's okay, Belle, we've got a plan – we've figured out a way to escape.'

'You have?' the Flea blurts out. 'Sorry,' he whispers. 'What is it?'

'Hey, you guys!'

We all jump. Lola is walking into the clearing carrying a basket of eggs. She waves to us then heads into the kitchen.

'Hey!' the Flea calls back to her. Then he turns to me

and lowers his voice. 'Should we tell Lola?'

I shake my head. 'Not yet. She likes Ruby so much. I don't want to say anything until we've got absolute proof.'

'But how are you going to get that?' Belle asks. Her hand feels clammy in mine.

'We have to get into the house,' Cruz replies.

We all look at the house, looming over the clearing. No one says a word but I can bet we're all thinking the same thing – *How the hell are we going to do that?*

Lola emerges from the kitchen and comes bounding over. 'Are you okay? You all look so serious!'

'It's this heat, honey, it's totally draining my mojo,' the Flea says.

The rest of us hurriedly nod and murmur in agreement.

'Hmm, maybe we should all go for a swim in the lagoon, to cool off a bit,' Lola says. She glances over at the house. 'I'm sure Ruby won't mind.'

At that moment Dan and Todd appear from the cabin they've been cleaning.

'Whassup?' Dan calls across to us.

'We're thinking of going for a swim,' the Flea says.

'That's the best goddamn plan I've heard all day.' Dan pulls off his T-shirt and wipes the sweat from his face with it.

'When I grow up, I want a set of abs just like that,' the Flea sighs, gazing at Dan.

'Count me in, Todd calls.

Lola turns to me. 'Where are Cariss and Jenna?'

'I guess they're still on toilet duty,' the Flea says with a grin. 'Ah well . . .'

I get to my feet and take hold of both Belle's hands. 'Come on, Belle, let's go get our swimming stuff.'

As soon as we get into the girls' cabin Belle sits down on her bed and clasps her hands together. 'I think I'm gonna stay here,' she mutters. 'I'm not feeling so good.'

'Oh, Belle.' I sit down next to her and put my arm round her shoulders. 'It's going to be okay. We are going to get out of here, I promise.'

'But how?' Belle looks at me, her eyes blank.

'Cruz has a plan.' I look over at the door to make sure no one's coming, then I huddle closer to her. 'We're going to take the boat that the new guests arrive in tomorrow,' I whisper. 'We're going to escape during the party.'

Belle's eyes widen. 'How are we going to get away without being noticed?'

'I'm going to tell the others to sneak off to the bay one by one.'

'Are you guys ready?'

We both jump about a foot off the bed. Lola is standing in the doorway, holding a rolled up towel.

'Pretty much,' I turn back to Belle. 'Are you sure you don't want to come?'

Belle shakes her head. 'There's no point. I won't be able to swim.'

'But you could cool down in the water at least. I'll stay with you.'

Belle smiles. 'It's okay. I'm tired. I'll just stay here and try to get some sleep.'

I frown. 'I don't know. I don't feel good leaving you here on your own.'

'I'll be fine. Jenna and Cariss will be back soon.'

I take a deep breath and try to get grounded. Even if Ruby is Hortense, she's not going to do anything to Belle now. She's only ever used Belle as bait. Bait to reel *me* in. My stomach churns. I force myself to smile at Belle. Then remember that she can't see me so I take hold of her hand instead. 'Hmm. Well, if you're sure.'

Belle squeezes my hand tightly. 'I'm sure. Thanks, Grace,' she whispers.

I hug her to me. 'No problem.'

One of the things I hate the most about this island is the way it plays with your emotions like a fickle friend. The lagoon is so breathtakingly beautiful that for a moment all I can do is stand and stare at the clear turquoise water in awe. It's almost impossible to believe that something so beautiful could be home to such evil.

We all plunge into the cool water, gasping at the relief from the heat. While the others start fooling around having water fights I gesture at Cruz to follow me and start swimming across the lagoon. It feels so good to be thrashing my arms and legs against the water, to close my eyes and imagine that I'm powering my way to freedom.

But after about a minute I start feeling tired. I open my eyes and look ahead of me at the high wall of green. Cruz swims up behind me. I turn to face him.

'Our boat's gone,' he whispers in my ear.

My chest instantly feels tight. 'Oh well, I guess it doesn't matter,' I say, trying, and failing, to sound chilled. 'It's not like we were going to need it again.'

'True.'

I feel Cruz's hands spanning my waist under the water and I let my body float in toward his.

I glance over Cruz's shoulder and see Todd treading water and chatting to Lola. Michael is sitting on the rocks by the edge of the lagoon, glaring down at them. About midway between them and us, Dan and the Flea are swimming round in circles.

I look back at Cruz. Water is trickling down his tanned face. In any other circumstances I would be swooning over how cute he is. But not now. Now, fear is all I seem capable of feeling. 'So, what's the plan?'

Cruz brushes his wet hair from his eyes. 'This afternoon, if

Ruby goes anywhere, we have to try and get into the house.'

I nod. 'I guess I could ask Lola if she'd show me inside . . .'

Cruz frowns. 'Do you think she would let you? I think that Ruby will have told her no one's allowed up there.'

I nod. 'Good point. I guess I'll have to try and sneak up when no one else is around and you can keep watch. If I do find some proof that Ruby is connected to Hortense, can we tell Dan?'

Cruz nods. 'For sure.'

The Flea comes swimming over to us. 'Houston, I think we may have a problem,' he says, nodding his head toward Dan, who is still swimming in the centre of the lagoon.

My body tenses. 'What is it?'

'That boy is one smitten kitten,' the Flea says with a sigh. 'All he can talk about is Ruby, Ruby, Ruby. Are you sure we shouldn't warn him off her right now?'

I shake my head. 'We tried last night and he wouldn't listen. We need to get some proof.'

The Flea raises an eyebrow. 'Well, y'all had better hurry up, cos he's got all kinds of plans for her and I ain't talkin' crochet. Y'know what I'm sayin'?'

We both nod. I look over to Dan and see that he and Lola and Todd are heading out of the water to join Michael.

'Come on,' I say to the Flea and Cruz, and we start swimming back.

'Say tom-ay-to,' Dan is saying to Lola as we get out of the water.

'Tom-ah-to,' Lola says in her British accent.

Dan and Todd start chuckling.

'I know — say aluminum,' Todd says.

'Alumin-*i*-um,' Lola says.

Dan starts cracking up. 'That's so funny!'

'Why?' Michael snaps. He's lying on the ground, and with his sunglasses on it's impossible to tell if his eyes are open or not.

'Why, what?' Todd says with a frown.

Michael sits up. 'Why's it so funny?'

'Easy, bro,' Dan says. 'We're only messing.'

'You need to take a chill pill.' Todd glares at Michael.

Michael mutters something under his breath and starts getting to his feet.

'What did you say?' Todd's face hardens and he marches over to Michael.

'I said, you need to get lost,' Michael says, but his voice is wavering, like he might be about to burst into tears.

'Michael,' Lola says in a low, warning voice.

He turns to her, tearing off his sunglasses, his cheeks flushing an angry red. 'What?'

'Don't be rude.'

'Rude? Me?' Michael laughs, high-pitched and semi-hysterical. 'As if *I* would be rude.' He glares at Lola but his eyes

211

are glassy with tears. Lola opens her mouth to speak but before she can say anything, Todd comes and stands between them.

'Quit acting like a jerk,' Todd says, right in Michael's face. 'So she's dumped you? So what?'

'So what?' Michael splutters.

'Yeah, so what?' Todd replies.

They're eyeball to eyeball now. I take a step toward Todd but I'm too late.

Michael shoves him in the chest, sending him flying back into Lola, who ends up sprawled on the ground.

Michael stares down at Lola, horrified. 'Lola – I . . .'

I run over to her and help her sit up. 'You okay?'

Lola looks around, dazed. 'Yeah, I – I think . . .' she stammers.

'What did you do that for?' Todd yells at Michael.

Michael carries on looking at Lola. Todd marches back over to him.

'Shall we all just go back to camp?' the Flea says anxiously.

'She dumped you!' Todd yells.

Michael visibly winces.

Dan and Cruz both step toward Todd.

'But at least she didn't die!' All at once the fury drains from Todd and his face begins to crumple. 'At least she didn't die,' he gasps as he starts to cry.

'Okay, it's okay,' Cruz says, as he grabs Todd in a bear hug.

'Lola?' Michael says, looking at her pleadingly.

'Leave me alone,' Lola says, getting to her feet and rubbing her arm. Her voice is trembling.

Michael reaches out a hand to her.

'I mean it.' Lola's voice goes steely and she glares at him. 'Leave me alone!'

The tears in Michael's eyes spill down on to his face. 'Right – if that's what you really want?'

We all look at Lola. She nods, then turns away.

Michael leans down and picks up his sunglasses. 'Okay,' he says defiantly. 'I'll leave you alone. All of you.'

We watch in silence as he marches off into the rainforest.

Chapter Twenty-one

When we get back to the retreat Jenna and Cariss are sitting by the fire. Their sulky pouts are so pronounced, you can probably see them from space.

'Where have you been?' Cariss yells as soon as she sees us.

'To the lagoon,' the Flea replies.

'For a swim,' Dan adds.

'Oh my God! You've been swimming while we've been doing the most disgusting job ever!' Cariss turns to Jenna, her jaw hanging open. Jenna's frown deepens.

Todd puts his hand on Lola's back. 'You okay now?'

Lola gives him a weak smile. 'Yes. Thanks. Are you?'

Todd nods. 'I guess.'

'Did you guys see Michael?' the Flea asks.

Jenna and Cariss shake their heads.

'Where's Ruby?' Lola asks.

'Putting clean sheets in the girls' cabin.' Jenna mutters.

I immediately think of Belle on her own in there and I break out in a cold sweat.

'I'll just go put my stuff away.' I glance at Cruz and he nods, clearly thinking the same thing.

I walk as fast as I can to the cabin and push the door open.

Belle is curled on her side on her bed. Ruby is standing with her back to her, looking down at my bed – my bag is wide open in front of her.

I feel a rush of anger and fear. What's she doing? Taking a deep breath, I stride into the cabin. 'Can I help you with anything,' I say as sweetly and calmly as I can.

Ruby's shoulders jolt with shock. She spins round to face me. 'Oh – no – I was just – changing the sheet on your bed.'

'Oh – right – thanks.' I come over and stand next to her. I'm so close I can smell her perfume. It's a mix of patchouli and musk. Stuff is spilling out of my bag on to the bed. It looks as if someone's been going through it, but I'm not sure if that's how I left it after getting my swimming stuff. I see the shorts I was wearing before lying crumpled on the bed. The shorts with the doll's hair in the pocket. Has Ruby been through the pockets? Has she found the hair? I glance at her hands. They're empty. She picks up a pile of dirty sheets from the end of my bed.

'Well I guess it must be time for lunch,' she says, her voice way friendlier than usual.

'I guess.'

She turns and I watch her sashay out of the cabin. I feel sick. I pick up the shorts and feel inside the pocket. The hair is still there. But that doesn't really mean a whole lot – Ruby still could still have seen it. I start tidying my stuff up to try and calm myself down. As I fold the shorts and put them back in my bag I see the corner of my cellphone. I pull it out of my bag and press the 'on' button, desperate to see my wallpaper pic of Mom and Tigger. But the screen stays black. Sorrow rushes into my body, sucking the air from my lungs. I sink down on to my knees and start to cry.

'Is everything okay, Grace?' Belle whispers behind me.

'Oh, Belle, you're awake.' I wipe my face and go sit on the end of her bed.

'What is it? Why are you crying?'

I swallow hard. Now I've started crying it's real hard to stop. 'I just miss my mom so much.'

Belle leans forward and puts her arms round me.

'I'm sorry,' I sob into her chest. 'I know it must be even worse for you, what with your mom being sick and all, but I just – I just . . .'

'It's okay.' Belle starts stroking my hair. Her arms feel so strong around me as she starts rocking me gently from side to side. Within seconds I'm feeling better. I sit back and wipe my face.

'I'm sorry.'

'Stop apologising,' Belle says firmly.

'It's just this place,' I say.

Belle nods. 'I know. But hey, only one more day.' Her voice is artificially bright, like she's announcing the final day of a sale.

I force myself to smile. 'That's right. Only one more day.'

Belle gives a sad smile, and I can tell she knows it's not going to be that easy at all. 'Shall we go get some lunch?'

'Sure.'

Unfortunately, Ruby decides to join us for lunch. And, even more unfortunately, she decides to use it as an opportunity to flirt some more with Dan. I try to ignore his showing off and her throaty laugh and force down some fruit. I need to formulate a plan. I have to try and get into the house this afternoon and I have to find out exactly where the bay is. I look at Cariss and Jenna who are now sat by the girls' cabin, nibbling apples. There's no point asking them – either they'll completely blank me or they'll start asking a bunch of questions I won't be able to answer, so that only leaves Todd. As if on cue, Todd gets to his feet.

'Who's for some coffee?' he asks, looking around at us.

Everyone groans.

'It's too hot even for me,' the Flea says sadly, 'And I drink so much coffee my blood type's been re-classified Caffeine Positive.'

'I'll have some,' I say quickly.

Todd nods. 'Sure thing.' Then he turns to Lola. 'You want any, Lola?'

Lola shakes her head. She's still looking pretty shaken up from what happened with Michael before and a bruise is forming on her arm.,.

Todd starts making his way to the kitchen and I follow him.

'Do you need any help?' I ask as soon as we get there.

He smiles and shakes his head. 'No thanks, I'm good.'

'Are you okay? You know, after what happened with Michael?'

He nods. 'I shouldn't have lost it with him but it's just . . .' he breaks off and looks down at the counter.

'I know.'

My mom once said that you can tell you've really clicked with another person when you can be comfortable together in silence. When Todd and I were dating I used to hate it if we fell into silence, and always felt the need to fill it immediately with inane trivia. But now, in the silence of the kitchen, I feel completely at ease. Todd must feel it too because he looks at me and smiles.

'Thanks, Grace.'

'Uh-huh.'

I walk over to the shelf with the fruit and pretend to be choosing an apple.

'So, how far is the bay from here?' I ask, casually.

Todd looks at me, puzzled. 'The bay?'

'Yeah, the one you guys ended up on, after you hit the rocks.'

Todd shrugs. 'Oh. I don't know. I was kind of out of it – after – after what happened, you know?' His face clouds over. 'I remember Cariss moaning about how long it was taking us to get here, but then again, Cariss moans about pretty much anything, right?'

I smile. 'Right. So, did you have to go through the rainforest the whole way?'

Todd shakes his head. 'No, there's a path – right next to the pool – it leads round to the bay. It's pretty easy actually.'

I can hardly believe it. Finally, some good news. 'The path's right by the pool?'

Todd nods. 'Yep, just behind the waterfall. Why all the questions?'

I somehow stop myself from punching the air for joy. 'Oh, I was just thinking about when we leave, you know, how far we'll have to walk to get to the boat.'

'Oh. Right. No, it's not that far. But you know, even if it was?' He looks at me, deadly serious all of a sudden. 'I'd walk all day to get back home.'

I nod.

'I'm even missing my sister.' His eyes suddenly fill with tears.

'Oh, Todd.' I go over and put my hand on his arm. 'I know what you mean. I'm missing my dad's girlfriend – and I haven't even met her yet!'

Todd laughs and wipes his eyes with the back of his hand. 'Wow, that's bad!'

We turn at the sound of a cough. Jenna's standing in the doorway, hands on hips, staring at us.

'We were just talking,' I say, then immediately get mad at myself for feeling the need to justify anything to her – especially when it comes to Todd.

'Really?' Jenna says, frostily.

'Yes, really.' I walk past her and outside. I can't afford to get riled by her holier-than-thou routine. I have to stay focused.

'Hey, Grace,' Lola calls over to me. 'Do you fancy coming with me to pick some flowers?'

I don't know if it's her clipped British accent or her open smile, but there's something instantly calming about Lola. She's like camomile tea in human form.

I nod and smile. 'That sounds great.' Then I look over at the others. Dan is handing out the fishing gear to the Flea and Cruz and Ruby appears to be issuing them with instructions.

'They're going to get some more fish,' Lola explains. Then she looks worried. 'I hope you don't mind me volunteering you to come with me instead. Would you prefer to go fishing?'

I shake my head and smile. 'No, it's fine.' And I mean it. Staying close to the camp will hopefully give me the chance to get into the house. 'What about Belle though?'

'Oh, she's gone back to bed,' Lola says breezily. But I instantly feel a pang of unease. Belle is starting to act real depressed. I wonder if I ought to persuade her to come with us. But if I do it might make it harder for me to slip away to look inside the house and anyways, if our plan comes off, we'll be out of here tomorrow and Belle will be on her way back to her mom.

'Okay, let's go,' I say.

Lola and I call goodbye to the guys and head off for the garden. As soon as we get there my tension eases a little. Even in the parching sun the flowers still look lush. We pick a few armfuls and take them to the bench and Lola shows me how to weave them into garlands.

After a while I glance at her. 'Have you seen Michael since – you know?'

Lola shakes her head. 'No. He's probably gone off drawing somewhere. He always does that when he's sulking.' She looks at me, her eyes wide. 'I'm so sorry about how he behaved earlier. I don't know what's got into him lately. I mean, I know he's stressed about us breaking up, but I've never seen him be so rude.'

'Hey, you don't have to apologise for him.'

Lola gives a sad smile. 'I know. But I still feel partly responsible.' She gives a big sigh. 'So, how's it going with you and Cruz?'

I smile. 'Great. Well as great as can be expected, given the circumstances.'

Lola frowns. 'What do you mean?'

'Oh, you know, being here,' I say hastily. 'We're all getting homesick. It puts a bit of a strain on things.'

'But you guys will be going soon.' Lola says, looking surprised.

'Yeah.' I make myself smile. Maybe I should tell her about Hortense. But before I can say anything, Ruby appears at the entrance to the garden.

'I'm just going to check on the livestock with Jenna and Cariss,' she says to Lola.

'Okay,' Lola replies chirpily.

As Ruby strides off my heart starts to race. This is the opportunity I've been waiting for. With Ruby out of the way and the others all off doing chores I might be able to sneak into the house. But what shall I tell Lola? I get to my feet and say the first thing that comes into my head.

'I'm sorry – I've just got to go to the bathroom.'

'Sure,' Lola replies, not looking up from her flowers.

As soon as I'm out of the garden I start running back to the camp as fast as I can.

When I get there I take a quick look around. There's no sign of life. The heat is so intense now, even the parrots' squawks sound muted, like they're too hot to really be bothered. I head over to the fire, making out that I'm looking for something. Then I glance round one more time and quickly dart into the shadows beneath the house.

As I grab on to the ladder, I notice that my hands are trembling. *Come on, keep it together*, I tell myself. I put one foot on the bottom rung. *But what if Hortense is up there?* All of a sudden this doesn't seem like such a good idea. But then how else am I going to get proof that Ruby is connected to Hortense? I think of Dan flirting with Ruby. And I think of the dead guy's warning, and how Hortense's net is closing around me. If I can't prove that Ruby is connected to all this I won't be able to convince the others, and we'll never escape. I take a deep breath and start climbing up the ladder.

It's so dark when I get inside it takes my eyes a few seconds to adjust. Gradually objects start appearing out of the gloom – a tall, narrow bookshelf crammed with books, an oak sideboard, a sofa-bed, pulled out, with a higgledy heap of clothes on it. I see one of Lola's tops draped over the end. So this must be where she sleeps. I squint around in the semi-darkness. I'm in a large room that takes up the entire lower floor of the house. The walls are draped with thick cloth in rich, dark colours and the floor is polished wooden slats. Over in the far corner, another ladder leads to the floor above. I head over to the bookshelf in the corner. It's crammed with a weird mix of old, leather-bound volumes and teetering stacks of modern paperbacks. I'm about to reach for one of the older books when I hear a creak from above me. I freeze, my hand poised over the book. Was I imagining it? Or was it the wind? But then I hear another creak, and another, as if someone is walking across the floor above me and over to the corner by the ladder. I watch, frozen with fear as the ladder starts to move. Then some kind of survival instinct kicks in and I race across the room and practically hurl myself back down the ladder outside. I'm moving so fast I lose my footing on one of the bottom rungs and land in a heap on the floor. Adrenaline pumps through my body, sending every nerve ending on to high alert. I scramble to my feet and stumble over to the kitchen. Once I'm inside I peer through a gap in the wall at the house. Is whoever I heard about to come out? I watch with bated breath. But then I spot a movement in the corner of my eye. Ruby has entered the clearing and is striding back toward the house. I watch as she climbs the ladder and disappears inside. I wait. But there's no sound.

I grip on to the counter next to me as my mind processes

this latest development. There's someone in the house. And Ruby must know that they're there. But who can it be? My mind echoes with the only possible answer: *Hortense*.

Chapter Twenty-two

I'm still watching the house when Jenna and Cariss trudge back into the clearing, carrying pails of milk and looking majorly pissed off.

'I can't believe she just left us to do all the work,' Cariss mutters as they come into the kitchen. 'Oh, Grace, what are you doing here?'

I quickly grab a mango from the shelf. 'I was just getting a snack.'

Jenna doesn't even make eye contact with me.

I fetch a knife and start peeling the mango.

'Grace! What happened? I was worried.' I turn and see Lola standing in the kitchen doorway, her arms laden with flowers.

'I'm sorry. I was just –'

'She was just fixing herself a snack while the rest of us

worked our butts off,' Cariss says snippily.

I glower at her.

Lola looks back over her shoulder into the clearing. 'Oh, Belle, are you okay?'

I push past Cariss and Jenna and over to the door. Belle is standing in the middle of the clearing looking dazed.

'Where's Grace?' she calls out.

'I'm right here, honey,' I reply and run over to her.

'I had the strangest dream,' she says. 'About a fire.'

My stomach flips. 'Can you remember anything else?' I whisper, thinking of the dreams I'd been having before.

Belle shakes her head. 'Not really.' Then she frowns. 'Oh yes – there was a baby crying.'

I take a deep breath. 'Well, you're awake now and –'

Just then I hear the Flea's voice and turn to see the boys heading back into the clearing. I let out a sigh of relief. 'Come on, let's go see what they've caught us for dinner.'

As soon as the Flea has hijacked Belle and is telling her his latest tales of fishing glory I grab Cruz's arm and take him to one side.

'I've been in the house,' I hiss.

'What?' he stares at me. 'Without me to look out for you?'

'Yes. I had to – it was too good an opportunity to miss.'

Cruz sighs. 'And did you find anything?'

'No. I didn't get the chance. There was someone in there.'

227

'What? Who?'

'I don't know. All I do know is that it wasn't Ruby, and it wasn't any of us, which means . . .'

Cruz's eyes widen. 'It could have been Hortense.'

We both stare up at the house. But before we can say any more, Lola comes bounding over.

'Hey guys, shall we start making dinner,' she says with a smile.

'Sure,' I say. I look back at Cruz.

'Later,' he whispers.

Dinner is subdued to say the least.

'Do you think we ought to look for Michael?' Cruz asks, when we've all finished eating.

'I'm sure he's fine,' Lola says. 'He's probably gone into hiding to teach me a lesson.'

'He's the one who needs to be taught a lesson,' Ruby mutters. I look at her. She's staring into the fire, her gaze hardened. Then she looks at Lola. 'How's your arm now?'

'Okay.' Lola smiles but it looks forced.

'Men who are violent towards women deserve everything they've got coming to them,' Ruby says, staring round the circle at the guys ominously.

'Well, he wasn't exactly violent to her,' the Flea mutters.

'No, he was violent toward me,' Todd exclaims. 'The guy's

a jerk.' He looks at Lola. 'Sorry, but he is.'

'Can we change the subject?' Lola says, starting to look upset.

'I think maybe we should have an early night. We have a very long day ahead of us tomorrow with the party,' Ruby says.

I instantly feel sick. It's like she just announced my execution.

'I was wondering if maybe we could have a chat?' Dan says to Ruby.

Cruz and I look at each other in panic.

'I said we all need to have an early night,' Ruby snaps.

Dan raises his eyebrows, clearly annoyed. 'Okay, okay, no need to bite my head off.' He gets up and glares down at Ruby. 'Sweet dreams,' he says snarkily, before stomping off to the boys' cabin.

Ruby remains completely impassive, her gaze fixed on Lola.

I breathe a sigh of relief.

One by one, the others take their plates out to the kitchen and disappear off into the cabins. Only Cruz and I hang back.

'Shall we go to the pool?' he whispers.

I nod. We take our plates into the kitchen and I peer through a gap in the wall, watching as Ruby and Lola climb the ladder into the house. Is whoever I heard still in there? For a crazy moment I wonder if Lola actually knows about Hortense — she and Ruby are so close after all. I try to push the idea from my mind. But another one immediately rolls into its place,

229

making my skin crawl with dread. If Hortense is hiding in the house, wouldn't Ruby be worried that Lola would discover her? Why would she invite her to stay up there? It seems like such a risk. I take a deep breath and try to calm myself. The fact that Lola doesn't know anything about Hortense means that she wouldn't be looking for anything, and Ruby knows this so I guess she figures it's safe. My fearful feelings start to subside. It's so easy to get paranoid in this place.

'Is the coast clear?' Cruz whispers.

'Uh-huh.'

We sneak round the shadows at the edge of the clearing till we get to the path, then we make our way to the pool in complete silence.

'I'm worried about Michael,' Cruz says, as soon as we reach the safety of the alcove. The water cascades down below us.

I nod. 'Me too. Surely he wouldn't go off in a sulk for this long.'

Cruz frowns. 'If he isn't back in the morning I am going looking for him.'

'Okay.' I sigh. 'Do you really think our plan is going to work?'

'Yes,' Cruz says firmly. 'It *has* to work.'

I look up at the sky. The Milky Way is glowing band of white above us. I think back to the first time I saw it, when I was sitting on the beach with Cruz – when I realised that he could speak English.

'I feel like I've known you forever,' I whisper, snuggling in to him.

'Maybe you have,' he whispers back.

I turn to look at him. He's looking down at me, his dark curls tumbling down around his face and, even though it's dark, I can still make out his brown eyes twinkling.

'What do you mean?'

'Well, my mother, she has this theory . . .' Cruz looks away, like he's embarrassed.

'Uh-huh.'

'She believes in – you know – reincarnate?'

'Reincarnation?'

'Yes. And she thinks that every time we begin a new life on Earth, there are a handful of people that we always are destined to meet – in every lifetime. The people that we love the most.'

I lean back into his arms and let his words sink in. 'So you and I, we could have met before, in other lifetimes?'

Cruz nods. 'Exactly. We would have been different people each time, with very different lives, but each time we would love each other, we would be, you know, soulmates.'

'That's lovely.' I start to smile. 'And it would explain why we feel the way we do.'

'Yes, it would.' He pulls me close. 'And just think – I probably saved your life in all these other lifetimes too!'

'Oh no you don't!' I say, giving him a playful dig in the ribs.

'I bet I've saved your life way more times.'

Cruz cups my face in his hands. 'Just think how many times we must have kissed,' he whispers.

'It's gotta be in the millions,' I say.

He shakes his head. 'No, more. What comes after millions?'

'Billions, trillions, gazillions!' I say with a laugh.

'Gazillions,' he repeats. 'Yes, that sounds about right.' He plants a kiss on my mouth. 'Gazillion and one,' he murmurs.

'Gazillion and two,' I say, kissing him back.

And then we stop counting. And it's like all there has ever been and ever will be is Cruz and me kissing. The one certainty in this messed-up, stupid world. And as he peels my T-shirt off and begins running his fingers up and down my back all I can think of is his mom's theory. And it doesn't feel crazy at all.

Cruz goes to undo my bra, then pulls away.

'No,' I murmur.

'It's okay, I won't,' he whispers.

'No, I mean yes.' I stop kissing him and look into his eyes. 'I want you to. I want you.'

Cruz sighs and I feel him shiver.

'Are you sure?'

I nod and hold him as tightly as I can. I've never been more sure of anything in my entire life.

Cruz tears off his T-shirt and presses his body next to mine. 'I love you, Grace,' he whispers in my ear. 'I love you so much.'

His words are like tiny fireflies, glowing brightly as they fly through my ears, along my veins and into my heart.

'I love you too,' I say.

Cruz starts gently undressing me. And for one beautiful, blissful moment, I forget all about anything other than him and me, kissing our way through the centuries until time itself stands still.

Chapter Twenty-three

When the sky starts to lighten and the first of the birds begin to squawk I feel eaten up with despair. *Please, please, please* I silently beg. *Please let us have just another hour.*

I picture the actual hands of time, on a giant clock-face somewhere deep in the cosmos, and will them to stop moving. But of course they don't and time keeps on passing and the sky keeps on lightening and the birds get even noisier.

'We should go,' Cruz whispers in my ear.

Our arms and legs are so tightly entwined it feels as if we've actually become one.

I feel physically sick at the thought of letting go. Because letting go will mean that the next chapter of my battle with Hortense will officially be beginning. *The next and final chapter*, my inner voice can't help adding. I start to shiver uncontrollably.

'Hey, come on, you need to get some sleep,' Cruz says, hugging me even tighter.

I nod, unable to speak in case I actually start to cry.

Once we've gotten dressed we make our way back to the camp in silence.

'I love you,' Cruz whispers, as we reach the girls' cabin.

'I love you too,' I say. And I mean it with every fibre in my body.

As I turn away and head inside it literally feels as if I'm having a limb torn from me. I creep over to my bed and lie down. My mouth is stinging from a gazillion kisses and my body aches. But my skin is tingling – I picture trails of Cruz's fingerprints glowing like the stars in the Milky Way all over me.

And, for the first time in what feels like forever, something trumps my usual fearful thoughts of Hortense: I am no longer a virgin.

For so long, I'd dreaded losing my virginity   stressing about not knowing what to do; that I'd make a fool of myself; that it would hurt really bad. I think back to the time when Jenna and I were about ten years old and we found an adult magazine that belonged to one of Jenna's 'uncles' stuffed behind the dryer in the laundry room. We flicked through the dog-eared pages and their mind-boggling images in horrified silence, before Jenna went and fed it through the waste disposal unit. Afterward we solemnly vowed to each other that, whatever happened, we were going to adopt our kids. Five years later, Jenna overcame her horror and lost her virginity to a hotel porter in Orange County. And now, finally, it's happened to me. I feel a sudden pang of sorrow. This is one of those moments in life when you really need to have a heart to heart with a girlfriend and share what has happened. I gaze up at the ceiling and sigh.

'You okay?' Belle whispers in the dark.

I sit up. 'Oh, sorry, did I wake you?'

'No. I couldn't sleep.'

'Are you okay?'

'Yeah. I guess I shouldn't have spent so much time napping yesterday. Where have you been?'

I get up and creep over to her bed.

Belle shifts over and lifts her blanket for me to get in. I lie down next to her and turn to face her.

'I've been with Cruz, at the pool.'

'Ah.'

'We . . .' I break off, suddenly embarrassed.

'What?'

'I slept with him.'

There's a moment's silence and I instantly regret telling her. I haven't been friends with Belle long enough to justify such an intimate conversation. But then she feels for my hand. 'Really? What was it like?'

And that's all the encouragement I need. 'Oh, Belle, it was awesome. It was my first time, but it didn't feel like it was my first time. It felt so right. But then Cruz has this theory – well, his mom has this theory, but now I have it too – that we are reincarnated after we die and every time we come back to life we end up falling in love with the same people over and over again. Only they're not the exactly the same people – they're different in each lifetime, obviously, but they're the same at heart, just reincarnated into different bodies.' I take a pause for breath.

Belle squeezes my hand. 'You really love him, don't you?'

'Yes,' I whisper. 'I do.'

Belle grips my hand even tighter. 'Never forget how you're feeling right now.'

'I won't.'

Belle moves closer. 'I mean it,' she whispers in my ear. 'Never, ever forget. Love is the only thing that counts.'

I end up falling asleep in Belle's bed. When I wake up I'm curled on my side facing away from her. For a brief moment I can't figure out what I'm doing here – and then I remember – and think of Cruz. And suddenly I can't stop smiling.

'Grace?' Jenna's voice pierces my blissed-out haze.

I half open my eyes. Jenna's standing next to the bed, hands on hips and frowning. She's dressed in one of Dan's T-shirts and a pair of leggings. Her hair is hanging limply round her shoulders in dry clumps.

'Why are you in Belle's bed?'

I feel Belle stir beside me.

'We were chatting. I guess I fell asleep,' I mumble.

Jenna looks at me. For a second I see hurt flicker across her eyes, but almost immediately, the icy gaze is back.

'Yeah well, it's time for breakfast,' she mutters, before stomping outside.

I turn and look at Belle. Her eyes are still shut but she's definitely grinning.

After I've helped Belle get dressed, I pull on a clean vest top and shorts and we head outside.

The boys are sat round the remains of the fire. They're chatting, but their voices are still subdued from sleep. My eyes become tracking devices for Cruz. As soon as they find him, excitement starts to dance inside of me. He's standing a bit apart from the others, looking over at our cabin like he's waiting for me. Like a reflex action, my mouth curls into a grin. Cruz smiles back, but I can tell it's forced – I can tell he's worried about something. Dread sweeps through my body. Now what?

I guide Belle over to Dan and the Flea, then head straight to Cruz.

'Are you okay?'

He takes my hand and pulls me close to him. 'Yes, yes,' he says, not sounding okay at all. Then he pulls me in for a hug. 'Michael still isn't back,' he whispers in my ear. 'And I do not think he can have gone to do his drawing because I found all of his art things under his bed. And I found something else as well.'

But before he can tell me what it is, Ruby and Lola start climbing down the ladder out of the house. They're both wearing bikinis.

'Hey!' Lola calls as she walks over to us. 'We're going to go swimming before breakfast. Do you guys fancy it?'

Everyone livens up at this, especially Dan and Todd, who are gazing at Lola and Ruby with their eyes on stalks.

'What should we do?' I hiss at Cruz.

'Make an excuse to stay back,' he whispers.

'I'll be along in a minute,' I call over. 'I'm just going to grab a mango from the kitchen.'

'I need to use the bathroom,' Cruz says.

Ruby stares at us for a moment, and her pale eyes make my heart race. But then she turns back to the others. 'Okay, let's go,' she says.

The others race off to get changed. I go into the kitchen and peer through a gap in the wall, waiting for them to leave. After a couple of minutes they all head off.

A few moments later Cruz appears. He strides into the

kitchen and pulls a piece of paper from his shorts pocket. I watch as he unfolds it.

On the paper there's a pencil sketch of a woman. I can tell immediately from the halo of hair and hourglass physique that it's Ruby. She's standing with her legs planted firmly on the ground like a warrior, looking up at the sky.

'Do you see it?' Cruz whispers.

'It's Ruby,' I say.

'Yes, but look – around her neck.'

I grab the page from Cruz and hold it up to the pale light filtering through the bamboo walls. Michael has drawn a pendant round Ruby's neck. The engraving on the pendant is sketched very lightly, but I recognise it immediately. A snake uncoiling upwards, over the letter H.

I turn back to Cruz. 'Hortense,' I whisper.

He nods.

'But I haven't seen her wearing the pendant. Have you?'

'No. But Michael must have. Before we got here, maybe?'

My hands become clammy. 'Do you think he knows about Hortense?'

Cruz frowns. 'I'm not sure. He might not have known what the pendant meant.'

'But he sure is suspicious of Ruby.'

Cruz takes the picture from me and puts it back in his pocket. 'I have to go and look for him.'

'I'm coming with you.'

Cruz shakes his head. 'No. If we both disappear Ruby will know something's up.'

I stare at him. 'But what if something happens? It isn't safe for you to go off on your own. Hortense could be out there somewhere.'

Cruz takes my hand. 'I'll be fine. I'll keep my eyes wide open. Can you try and get back inside the house? We have to get more proof that Ruby's involved with Hortense so that we can tell it to the others.'

I sigh. 'Okay then. But don't be gone too long.'

He nods. 'Of course. And you be very careful. Do not go into the house unless you feel certain Ruby won't find you. Okay?'

'Okay.' I stand on tiptoes and kiss Cruz on the mouth as hard as I can. It's like I'm trying to imbue him with some kind of superpower to keep him safe. He wraps his arms around me and kisses me back, slowly and passionately, like he wants it to really count. I fight the overwhelming urge to cry. After what happened last night, this shouldn't be happening. Today should be spent drifting around in a delicious afterglow. I should not be feeling terrified that I might never see him again – that Cruz might disappear like Michael. Anger fills me. I hate this island and I hate Hortense.

'I love you,' Cruz whispers.

I hug him to me. 'I love you too.'

Then I drag myself away from him and go over to the doorway and peer into the clearing. 'Coast's clear,' I whisper.

'Okay, see you later, alligator.'

I get the sudden urge to start laughing hysterically.

Cruz frowns at me. 'You have to say your bit.'

'All right, all right – in a while, crocodile.'

Cruz grins and plants a kiss on the top of my head. Then he darts out of the kitchen and skulks around the edge of the clearing, disappearing behind the woodpile. I feel sick. He must be going to the altar.

I take a moment to compose myself, then head back outside. I walk around to the cabin and see Belle sat leaning against the doorpost, her eyes closed, face tipped back in the sun.

'Hey, Belle, didn't you want to go to the pool?' I call over to her.

She starts and looks around blankly. 'Grace?'

'Uh-huh.' I hurry over to her, but as I do I hear the sound of movement behind me. I spin round and see Ruby standing by the ladder beneath her house. She's staring at me – her face completely expressionless. I fight to stay calm.

'Oh – I thought you'd gone for a swim.'

'I forgot my towel,' Ruby says, coldly.

Shit! Shit! Shit! She was in the house when Cruz left. What if she saw him?

'You coming?' she says to me, as she starts walking across the clearing.

'Oh, I don't know. Maybe I'll stay here and keep Belle company . . .'

'It's Okay,' Belle says. 'It's nice sitting in the sun – before it gets too hot.'

'Well, if you're sure.' My heart is now beating all kinds of crazy. I don't want to leave Belle on her own, but how can I say anything with Ruby right here.

'Where's Cruz?' Ruby asks, coming right up behind me.

'He had to go to the bathroom. He wasn't feeling so good,' I stammer. I take a deep breath. I mustn't let her know anything's up. I mustn't give anything away.

'I'll just go get changed,' I say. And I turn and smile at Ruby so hard it makes my jaw ache.

Chapter Twenty-four

All the way to the lagoon, Ruby and I don't exchange a single word. Inside my head, however, is noisy with accusations and thoughts of how much I hate her. As soon as we get to the lagoon I make myself greet the others and dive into the turquoise water as if I don't have a care in the world. Then I swim round and round in a circle. When I finally feel calmer I swim back to the water's edge. Jenna and Cariss are sitting on the rocks, huddled over in conversation.

'It just doesn't make sense,' I hear Cariss say.

I look over and catch her eye. She looks away.

Lola swims up behind me and pulls herself out of the water.

'I'm going to ask her,' Cariss says loudly. 'Hey, Lola?'

Lola turns to her and smiles. 'Yes?'

'How does Ruby know when her guests will be arriving?'

Lola grabs a towel from the rock and starts to dry herself. 'It was arranged in advance – with her friend Carlos who brings the guests in his boat.'

Cariss frowns. 'But what if there's some kind of problem? What if this Carlos can't make it? Or his boat breaks down? How does he let her know?'

Lola's smile starts to fade. 'He can't.'

'Don't you think it's a bit of a dumb system?' Jenna says, shielding her eyes from the sun as she looks up at Lola.

'No, actually, I don't,' Lola snaps. 'I think it's perfectly in keeping with the nature of the retreat – and being cut off from the rest of the world.'

Jenna and Cariss raise their eyebrows at each other. And although they're clearly pissing Lola off, I can't help feeling relieved that they're getting suspicious – it will make it a whole lot easier to tell them about the getaway plan later.

There's a loud splash and we all turn to look at the water. Dan's performing some kind of dolphin impression to try and impress Ruby.

'That woman is such a tease,' Cariss mutters.

'Don't bad mouth her,' Lola snaps. I look at her in surprise. She's looking really mad. Lola flings the towel down. 'You should be grateful for all she's done for you.'

'She's hardly been the hostess with the mostest,' Jenna mutters.

245

'Well, you two have hardly been the greatest guests,' Lola replies. Her face flushes an angry red beneath her tan.

'How dare you!' Cariss leaps to her feet and glares at Lola. 'You have no idea what we've been through. Has it ever occurred to you that maybe we just want to get the hell out of here and not be stuck here for days with your precious friend?'

I see Lola clench her fists and quickly pull myself out of the water. 'Are you okay?' I say, touching her on the shoulder.

She gives me a tense smile. 'I'm fine. I'm sorry.' She drops her voice to a whisper. 'I'm just a bit stressed about Michael that's all. I think I'll go back to camp.'

'Do you want me to come with you?'

'No, it's okay.' Lola gathers up her things and heads off toward the path.

'Gee, Grace, you sure know how to pick your friends,' Cariss snips.

I glare at her. 'What's that supposed to mean?'

'Well, first that piece of trailer trash, Belle, and now that stuck up British chick. What about your loyalty to Jenna?'

I look at Jenna. She looks away.

'Leave it, Cariss,' she mutters.

Cariss frowns at her. 'Why? I thought you guys were supposed to be best friends. Grace has been a complete bitch to you since we got here.' Cariss turns back to me. 'And as for the way you've treated Todd — running off with the help the second we got shipwrecked.'

'I said, leave it,' Jenna yells this time.

Cariss shakes her head and gives a theatrical sigh. 'Oh, whatever!' She stomps over to the edge of the rocks and dives into the water.

'I'm sorry,' Jenna mutters. Then she starts biting her lip the way she always does when she's trying not to cry.

'Are you okay?' I say softly.

'What do you care?' she mumbles. But there's something about the way she's looking at me that makes certain she wants me to tell her that I do care. She *needs* me to tell her that I care.

'Of course I care,' I say.

Jenna looks down at the water, like she's thinking of following Cariss, then she turns back to me. 'This place is driving me crazy,' she mutters. Her voice is tight and strained. 'Everything feels so out of control. I don't know how to handle it.' Her voice starts to wobble. 'I don't know what to do.'

I try to hug her. She stands statue-still in my arms. 'It's okay, I feel the same,' I whisper in her ear.

She pulls back and looks at me. Her eyes are filled with tears. 'You do?'

I nod. 'Yes. And you're not going crazy. There is something very wrong here, but I can't say anything about it right now.

Just try and keep it together and I'll talk to you later. There's something I need to tell you.'

'Is it to do with her?' Jenna nods down to the water where Ruby is splashing about with Dan.

'Yes,' I whisper. 'I'll tell you more later — when she isn't around.'

Jenna nods and she gives me a weak smile. 'Thanks, Grace.'

I nod and give her hand a quick squeeze. 'Why don't you have a swim? It might make you feel a bit better?'

Jenna nods. 'Okay. But we're definitely going to talk later?'

'Yes. Definitely.'

Jenna walks over to the edge of the rocks and eases herself down into the lagoon just as the Flea gets out.

'Hey, Gracie, everything all right?' He shakes the water from his hair and heads over.

'Yeah, I guess. Are you going back to the camp?'

'Sure am. Gotta check on Beau-Belle.'

'Great — I'll walk with you.'

As we walk, I link arms with him. 'Something's happened,' I whisper as soon as we get into the trees.

The Flea immediately stops walking and looks at me, concerned. 'What is it?'

'Cruz found Michael's art stuff — it was under his bed.'

'So he hasn't gone off painting?'

248

'No. And Cruz found something else – in his sketch pad.'

'What?'

I glance over my shoulder to make sure there's no one about. 'A picture of Ruby – and she's wearing a pendant just like the one we kept finding before.'

The Flea frowns. 'What – the one with the snake and the H.'

'Uh-huh.'

'Damn!'

'Exactly.'

We start walking again. The Flea looks around furtively. 'Where's Cruz?'

'He's gone looking for Michael.'

'On his own?' The Flea's obvious concern makes my stomach churn.

'Yeah – he didn't want Ruby to know.'

'But still. I don't think it's a great idea for any of us to go off on our own right now. Not with psycho voodoo queen on the loose.'

'I know. I told him not to go for long.'

The Flea nods. 'Okay, good – maybe he's back already.'

We walk into the clearing, but it's deserted. My heart sinks.

'I'll just go get changed.'

The Flea nods. 'Me too. See if Belle wants to come out to play.'

'Sure.' I run over to the girls' cabin.

Belle's lying on her bed, with her hands pressed together in prayer position, whispering something under her breath.

'Oh, sorry,' I say.

'Grace, is that you?'

'Yes. Sorry, I didn't mean to interrupt.'

'It's okay, I was just saying a prayer for my mom.'

I feel a wistful pang. I wish I had a faith I could believe in, something to give me some hope right now.

'Cruz came by,' Belle says, shifting into a seated position.

'He did?' My heart leaps. I go sit on the end of her bed. 'Where is he? What did he say?'

'He said to tell you he didn't have any luck so he's going to check down by the pool.' Belle frowns. 'He said you'd know what he meant.'

'Yes, yes, he – uh – lost something.' I can barely contain my relief. He made it back from the altar okay. I take Belle's hand. 'The Flea wants to know if you want to go hang with him for a bit.'

Belle nods and smiles. 'Sure.'

When we get outside the others are all arriving back from the pool. We join them by the fire. Ruby passes round a huge bowl of fruit.

'Where's Lola?' she says with a frown.

Cariss looks down at the ground.

'She came back early,' I say. 'I guess she's in the house.'

250

We all look up at the house. Its darkened windows stare back at us like the hollow eyes of a skull.

Ruby nods. 'Okay. I'll take her some food. And then I have to go to the bay to wait for the guests.' Her face lights up. It's weird seeing her look so excited, and it only adds to my sense of dread. I feel like a rabbit with my leg caught in a trap, waiting for my captor to arrive and finish the job.

'You want some company?' Dan asks, clearly over her snub from last night.

'No, it's okay,' Ruby says coolly.

Dan looks away, visibly wounded.

'I need you to go catch some fish for tonight,' Ruby says, her voice switching to silky-smooth.

Dan's expression instantly softens. 'Sure.'

Cariss sighs.

Ruby takes a banana from the fruit bowl and climbs the ladder up into her house. I think of Lola and her earlier outburst. I hope she's okay. I guess the pressure of Michael disappearing must finally be getting to her. I feel a nervous fluttering in my stomach as I think of Cruz wandering about the forest, searching for Michael. I sit on my hands to try and make myself feel less jittery. I wish he'd get back already.

All around me, the camp becomes a hive of activity. Dan and Todd fetch the fishing gear. Cariss and Jenna start doing a yoga workout over by the girls' cabin. The Flea clears up the breakfast dishes, while talking loudly to Belle about a show he once saw on the Reality Channel about a guy who drowned in his own dishwasher. But all I can think is: where the hell is Cruz?

As the boys head off fishing and the Flea leads Belle over to the kitchen, Lola comes stumbling out of the forest. She's still wearing her bikini and her arms and legs are covered in scratches.

I spring to my feet. 'Lola! What happened?'

Lola looks at me, her eyes wide and glassy with tears. 'I – I . . .'

'Lola!'

I jump at the sound of Ruby's voice. She's standing by the ladder to her house. She's changed out of her swimming gear and is now wearing flared linen pants and a fitted tee.

'Are you okay?' Ruby strides over to Lola and takes her by the arm.

'Yes. I – I – just went to check on the chooks.'

'In your bikini?' Ruby looks at Lola's scratches. 'Why didn't you get changed before you went into the forest?'

Lola looks at her blankly. 'I don't know. I wasn't thinking.'

'Damn right.' Ruby sighs. 'Come on, let's get some ointment on those scratches.'

I watch as she leads Lola up into the house, totally confused.

Why would Lola go check on the chickens without getting

changed first? Why is she so stressed? I sit back down, watch the house, and wait. Eventually Ruby and Lola reappear. Now Ruby's looking just as tense.

'I'll see you later,' she mutters as she strides past me.

Lola comes and sits down beside me. She's gotten changed into a pale-green T-shirt dress and the scratches on her arms and legs are covered in a white cream.

'You okay?' I say, looking at her curiously.

She nods and gives me a weak smile.

'Did you really go check on the chooks?'

'Yes.'

'Really?'

She looks down at the dusty ground. There's a long silence and then she shakes her head.

'So where did you go?'

'To look for Michael,' she whispers.

'Ah, I see.'

'Ruby's convinced that he's still off somewhere in a sulk, but I'm not so sure any more. He's been gone such a long time.' Lola looks really anxious. I touch her arm.

'It's okay, don't worry – Cruz has gone looking for him.'

Lola looks stunned. 'What?'

'I'm sure it's nothing to worry about, but he – he found all of Michael's art stuff under his bed, so he doesn't think he can have gone off painting.'

'But if he hasn't gone painting, what's he doing? Where's he gone?'

'I don't know. He's probably just hiding out somewhere — to let off steam. Cruz will find him. Don't worry.'

Lola frowns. 'I should let Ruby know.'

'No!' I can't keep the alarm from my voice.

'Why not?' Lola stares at me.

I quickly rack my brains for an answer that won't involve telling her my suspicions about Ruby. 'I don't want anyone panicking — especially not Ruby. Not with the other guests about to arrive. Hopefully Cruz will find him and they'll be back any minute now.'

Lola looks down into her lap. Then finally, she nods.

I put my hand on her arm. 'Are you okay?'

She nods again, then gets to her feet. 'I need to do something — to stop me stressing out. Shall we prepare the vegetables for the meal?'

'Sure.' I get up and follow her over to the kitchen.

The next couple of hours drag by, like time is stuck in treacle. With every agonising second that passes with no sign of Cruz I feel increasingly sick. Somehow, I manage to make polite conversation with Lola and the Flea and Belle, but all the while a voice in my head is yelling, *Cruz should've been back by now. Why isn't he back by now?* We finish the chores and wander outside to sit on the dusty ground by the fire. I'm just about to make an excuse and go looking for him, when the boys return from fishing.

'No guests yet?' Dan calls out, looking round the clearing hopefully.

'No, not yet,' Lola calls back.

Dan frowns. 'Where's Cruz?'

'Oh – er . . .' I look at Lola.

'Yeah, where's he got to?' Todd says, bringing a bucket of shellfish over to us. 'I haven't seen him since first thing.'

'That's right,' Dan says. 'Last time I saw him was before we went swimming.'

'He told me he was going to look for something by the pool,' Belle says. 'Grace knows about it, don't you, Grace?'

Everyone turns to me.

My face starts to flush. I have no choice but to tell them. 'He's gone to look for Michael,' I mutter.

'On his own?' Dan says.

I nod.

'Maybe we should go looking for them,' the Flea says, with a worried frown. 'They might have gotten lost in the rainforest.'

'What's going on?' Cariss calls, as she and Jenna come wandering over.

'Cruz has gone looking for Michael,' Todd tells her.

'And?' Cariss stares at him blankly.

'And he's been gone a long time so we're just wondering

255

whether we ought to go looking for them,' the Flea says.

We all fall silent for a moment.

'So, he said he was going to look down by the pool?' Dan asks Belle.

Belle nods.

Dan turns to the Flea. 'Come on, Jimmy, let's go check it out.'

'I'll come too,' Todd says.

As we watch the guys set off I feel a surge of relief. I pick up the bucket of fish and start heading over to the kitchen.

Cariss gives an exaggerated sigh. 'I don't know why they're bothering.'

I stop in my tracks and turn on her. 'Oh really? You'd just leave them would you?'

Cariss glares at me like I'm insane. 'Why not?'

'Are you kidding?' I gesture wildly at the rainforest, all of my pent up fear erupting into fury. 'Do you have any idea what's out there. Do you –'

But before I can say any more I'm interrupted by Jenna screaming. She's pointing a trembling finger at Belle who's still sitting cross-legged on the ground, staring blindly at the charred remains of the fire. Right behind her, a huge snake, identical to the one I saw by the altar, is gliding across the ground toward her. Its fangs are bared, ready to strike.

Chapter Twenty-five

For a second, fear holds us all statue-still.

'What's happened?' Belle says. 'Who screamed? Why have you all gone quiet?'

'There's a —'

'Shut up, Cariss!' I hiss, looking round desperately for a stick or something I could use to beat the snake back.

'It's okay,' Lola says, her voice super-calm.

Jenna and Cariss gasp as she takes a step towards Belle.

The snake extends itself and hisses.

Belle jumps. 'What was that?'

'It's nothing,' I say.

'Just take my hand,' Lola says, creeping forward and reaching her hand out to Belle.

'Why? What's going on?' Belle's voice wavers.

'It's okay, just do as she says,' I say.

Belle reaches out and Lola grabs both her hands. Then she pulls Belle to her feet. The snake is now just inches away from them. We all hold our breath. The squawking sounds from the forest seem to die down, like someone's put the parrots on mute. All I can hear is the blood pulsing in my head.

'Now just walk forward with me, really slowly,' Lola says, gently guiding Belle toward us.

Belle steps forward, lurching slightly. The snake pulls itself up even higher and hisses again.

'What's that noise?' Belle says.

None of us say a word.

Hardly daring to breathe, I watch as somehow Lola inches Belle across the ground and out of the snake's reach.

'We have to kill it!' Cariss says, suddenly brave as we stumble toward the kitchen.

'Kill what?' Belle says, looking terrified.

I go over and link arms with her. 'There was a snake,' I say as calmly as I can. 'It was right behind you. That's why Lola got you to move.'

'We have to kill it!' Cariss says, more insistent this time.

'No we don't,' Lola snaps. 'It hasn't hurt anyone.'

I'm trying to get my heart rate back under control when the sound of voices drifts through the forest. We all turn to see who's coming. At first I think – I *hope* – that it's Cruz and

Michael. But then I hear a girl's voice that I don't recognise.

'The guests must have arrived!' Lola exclaims. Belle grips my arm. She looks terrified. I grip her arm back, partly to reassure her, partly to reassure myself. If my suspicions are right; if these people are friends of Ruby's, then they could also be linked to Hortense.

Jenna looks back over her shoulder. 'Oh my God, the snake's gone!'

'Where?' Cariss shrieks.

The voices get louder. I start looking round frantically for the snake, but it's disappeared without trace.

'It must have gone back into the forest,' Lola says. She smooths down her hair and looks toward the sound of the voices. Ruby comes striding into the clearing. A group of about twenty people follow her, chatting and laughing and carrying backpacks. The second they spot us every one of them falls silent and looks at Ruby expectantly.

'Hey guys!' Ruby cries, a super-animated version of her usual self. 'Let me introduce you. This is Lola . . .' the guests all nod and grin at Lola, like they've already heard loads about her. 'And this is Belle,' Ruby continues, actually coming over and placing a hand on Belle's arm. 'And this is Grace.' She turns and gives me a beaming smile. The others all stare at me. I stare right on back, trying to spot any obvious sign that they might be connected to Hortense. But they all look surprisingly normal.

Most of them are pretty young – late teens, early twenties max, and they all have the tans, body piercings and tattoos of the seasoned backpacker. The only one who stands out is an older guy with dark curly hair and a swarthy complexion. I'm guessing he must be Carlos.

'I'm Cariss,' Cariss snaps, glaring at Ruby. 'And this is Jenna.'

But it's like none of the others really hear her, they just keep on staring at me, Belle and Lola, and smiling.

'Do you guys want to go freshen up in the lagoon?' Ruby says.

Her guests immediately start nodding and murmuring in agreement. It makes me wonder if they've been here before.

'Aren't you going to tell her about the snake?' Cariss mutters to Lola.

'What's that?' Ruby says.

'Oh, there was a snake, but it's gone now,' Lola says casually. I study Ruby's face for any flicker of reaction. But it remains blank.

'Ah. Okay,' she says. 'Side-effect of jungle life, I'm afraid.' Then she turns to the others. 'You guys, go make yourselves at home. You're in those cabins over there. Girls on the left, boys on the right.' She points to the cabins we prepared yesterday.

The guests file past us, and although I could just be being paranoid, I swear a couple of them glance at me as they go by.

A couple of minutes later they all reappear in their swimming gear.

'Let's go,' a tall blond guy wearing an array of friendship bracelets says. He heads straight toward the path leading to the lagoon. They *have* been here before.

Ruby looks at us. 'Do you guys want to come too?'

'Okay,' Lola says.

Belle squeezes my arm. 'Can we go? I could do with freshening up.'

My heart sinks. The last thing I feel like doing is going to the lagoon with Ruby and her friends. 'Oh, I don't know. I'm feeling kind of tired . . .'

'A swim might make you feel better,' Belle says.

'I don't think so.' Panic is rising inside of me. Time is running out. I have to go look for Cruz.

'I'll take you,' Lola says, taking Belle's arm.

Belle gives a forced smile. But right now I don't care. All I care about is finding Cruz.

'So, are you guys all from America?' Cariss says, remarkably chirpily. I glance at her and see that she's making eyes at a tall black guy standing at the back of the group.

'Sure are,' he replies. He has a deep southern accent, similar to Ruby's. I watch as he looks at Ruby and gives her a knowing smile.

Just go already! I feel like screaming.

Finally, they leave. I stand in the clearing looking around wildly. Which way should I go? But before I can decide, I hear the sound of the boys' voices. I turn and watch them come back into the clearing. When I see no Cruz or Michael with them my stomach lurches. Something bad has happened. I know it for sure.

The Flea looks at me and frowns. 'No sign of either of them,' he says.

'They must have both gotten lost,' Dan says. 'We need to tell Ruby.'

'She's just gone to the lagoon with the new guests,' I say flatly.

'Oh, they're here?' the Flea asks.

I nod.

He stares at me. 'What are they like?'

'Oh, you know . . .' I can barely bring myself to speak I feel so sick. I should never have let Cruz go off on his own. What was I thinking? 'I have to go look for them,' I say.

'No!' the Flea exclaims. 'You can't. What if you get lost too? We have to wait for Ruby to get back.'

'We can't wait for Ruby!' I practically yell.

'Why not?' Todd looks at me like I'm crazy.

'Because – because – we need to do something right now.'

'But we couldn't find them,' the Flea says gently.

'You guys only looked down by the pool, right?'

They both nod.

'Okay, well I'll go take a look that way.' I point to the other end of the clearing. 'Down in the field with the chooks and cows.'

'But what if you –' the Flea begins.

'I won't get lost,' I interrupt. I force myself to smile at him. 'I promise.'

'Do you want me to come with?' the Flea says.

I shake my head. 'It's okay. I'll be fine. I'll just go check the field then come straight back.'

'O-kay then,' the Flea looks really uncertain, but before he can change his mind I dart off across the clearing and into the forest.

Where are you? I say to Cruz inside my head, hoping that in some crazy, soulmate way he will somehow read my mind and be able to let me know. But all I hear is an ear-splitting shriek as a parrot swoops in front of me. My heart seems to jolt against my ribcage. *Okay, keep calm. In through the nose and out through the mouth*, I tell myself as I focus on my breathing.

When I get to the field, it's ominously quiet. At first I think the cows have strayed off, but then I see them, all lying in a cluster at the far end of the field. I look up at the volcano looming over them and instantly I'm transported back to the other side of the island and that terrible day we went looking for Belle.

Where are you? I say again in my head. But this time I'm talking to Hortense.

I turn to the chicken shed. The door is shut but there's no sound at all from inside. I walk over. The ramp leading up to the shed is littered with feathers. My mouth goes dry. Have the chooks been attacked in the night? But they can't have been – the door's still locked. I lift the latch and open the door. The warm stench of stale straw hits me. But the shed is totally empty. Where on earth have they gone? I look around the field and my head starts to hurt. What the hell is going on?

I sit down. Just when it feels like I'm going to be consumed by panic some kind of inner survival instinct kicks in. I can't fall apart now. I have to believe that I will find Cruz. I am not going to let Hortense beat me.

Atta girl, Gracie! I can just hear my grandpa say, as I get to my feet and take a deep breath.

I look up at the volcano and clench my fists tight.

'You're not going to win,' I hiss, staring up at its blood red peak. 'You're not going to win.'

A sudden gust of wind whips across the field, causing the long dry grass to sway back and forth. I stay standing bolt upright, staring at the volcano. The wind lashes against my face. I don't even blink.

Chapter Twenty-six

After about a minute, the wind drops as suddenly as it appeared. I feel strangely emboldened, as if I've somehow won a minor, but important, battle. And so, before heading back to the camp, I decide to take a look down by the bottom of the field. Being so close to the volcano causes a sinister montage of memories to start playing in my mind. I think of the strange drumming sound, the skulls with candles inside them, Belle stretched out on the altar, her skin icy and waxen. The cows moo angrily as I approach. I find myself saying, 'There's a good cow,' in the gentle, coaxing voice I use on my cat Tigger and the ludicrousness of the situation strikes me. How did I get here? How can any of this be real? *This is real – us – you and me.* I hear Cruz's voice in my head and I pull myself together again.

The bottom of the field is bordered by a thick wall of

bushes and trees. I look for a pathway but there's none and the branches are too dense to push my way through. I'm about to turn and go back when I spot a narrow gap between two trees. The undergrowth is flattened – like it's been trampled underfoot.

I stoop and peer into the gap. My skin erupts in goose bumps as I see that it opens into a narrow tunnel. Crouching down, I start shuffling my way through. I've only been going a few seconds when something tears my arm. I look down and see a long scratch snaking up from my elbow. Damn. I'm surrounded by some kind of brambles. Then I think of Lola and all the scratches on her arms and legs. Did she come here looking for Michael? Very slowly, I continue. It takes me about thirty seconds to get to the other side, but I manage to make it without getting scratched again. I stumble out and stand up straight. I've come out into another field right beneath the volcano. Then I look down and gasp in shock. The field is covered in mounds of earth, each bearing a wooden cross. My throat tightens and a cold sweat erupts on my skin. I'm standing in some kind of graveyard. But who do the graves belong to? I shiver as the obvious answer comes to me – Hortense's victims. And then I think of the man's note. What was it he'd said? *'I've seen what happens to the people she possesses. I've seen their graves.'* I feel sick with fear. And then a terrible thought hits me. Is this how I'm going to end up? Buried under a mound of earth on some hellish island, miles from home? I feel as if I can't breathe and for a second I think I might be about to have my first ever full-on panic attack. But then a memory of my grandpa pops into my head. It was when I was about eight and he'd taken me to the Memorial Day parade. 'Did you ever kill anyone when you were in the army, Paw-paw?' I asked him. He didn't answer, not directly. But he did say something that comes back to me with crystal clarity right now. *Sometimes, you have to kill to stop others from being killed, Gracie.*

A strange numbness wraps itself around me, like a suit of armour. I take one last look at the graves, then I turn and push my way back through the undergrowth.

When I get back to the retreat, the others have returned from their swim. On the surface, everything looks so fun, so innocent. Ruby's friends are all gathered round the kitchen, wet-haired and laughing. They look like they just stepped off Venice Beach – but they haven't – they're here to see Ruby. They're here for the dark of the moon party and therefore they have to be connected with Hortense.

'Grace!' Lola calls to me as she comes out of the kitchen and starts handing round a bowl of mangoes to the others. I pretend I haven't heard her, not sure I can even trust *her* any more.

I look around the camp. Todd and Dan are in deep

conversation over by the boys' cabin. Todd looks more relaxed than he has in days. It makes my heart sink. I feel like marching over and telling them my suspicions about Ruby. My heart starts pounding. I could show them the graves. How would Ruby be able to explain that?

'Are you okay?' I jump as Lola touches me on the back of my shoulder.

'Yes, of course. Why shouldn't I be?' My whole body is prickling with tension.

'It's nearly party time,' Lola says with a smile.

'Great,' I reply, but my voice is terse.

'Something's wrong, isn't it?' Lola says.

I take a deep breath. 'No – well – it's just with Cruz and Michael going missing, I'm not exactly in the party mood.'

Lola's smile instantly fades. 'I know but . . .'

'But what?'

'I'm sure they'll turn up soon – like Ruby says, it's not as if there's anywhere they can really go.'

'You told Ruby?'

Lola looks shocked. 'Well, yes, I thought she ought to know. I was worried.'

I break out in a cold sweat. 'What did you tell her?'

'That Cruz had gone looking for Michael.'

I clench my hands into fists, trying to keep my tension from showing on my face. 'And what did she say?'

'She said that Cruz was wasting his time.'

I clench my hands so hard my nails feel like blades digging into my palms. 'And what's that supposed to mean?'

Lola frowns. 'Grace, are you sure you're okay?'

'I'm fine!' I practically yell. 'What did Ruby mean, he's wasting his time?'

Lola gives me a patient smile – the kind of smile a mom would give a kid who just doesn't get what the adults are talking about. 'Because Michael is clearly having a strop with me. He'll be back when he's hungry.'

'But he's been gone for ages. He must be starving by now. You were really worried before.'

'Yes, but that was before I spoke to Ruby.'

I'm starting to understand why Michael had gotten so frustrated with Lola's infatuation with Ruby. 'So if Ruby says something's okay it just is?'

Lola's face flushes. 'No – but . . .' she looks away, hurt, and I feel a stab of guilt . . . 'she always makes thing seem better.'

'Right.' I sigh. Then I decide to take a gamble and tell Lola what I saw. 'Did you know that there's a graveyard on the island?'

For a split second I see a flicker of shock register on Lola's face, then, quick as a flash, it's gone and she's nodding and smiling calmly again.

'Yes.'

'You did?'

'Yes. Ruby showed me. But how do you know about it?'

My stomach sinks as she stares at me. 'I saw it earlier – when I was looking for Cruz,' I mutter.

'Oh.'

Silence.

I study her face. 'So, who do the graves belong to?'

Lola maintains her cool. 'The people who lived here before.'

'What people?'

She shrugs. 'I don't know. Ruby said there was a whole community that used to live here.'

'What, and they just upped and left?'

She looks down at her feet and starts scuffing at the ground with her toes. 'Yes.'

'Gracie!' We both turn at the sound of the Flea's voice. He and Belle are making their way over from the girls' cabin.

'Thank God you're back,' he says quietly as soon as they reach us. 'I don't think I could take it if anyone else went missing, especially you.' He gives me a hug but I don't relax into it – I can't. If I do I might weaken.

'I'm sure Cruz and Michael are fine,' Lola says to him. She's smiling but her voice is tight. 'They're probably just lost in the forest.'

It takes every ounce of my will power not to say, *Oh please!*

'Maybe once the party starts they'll hear the music and be

270

able to find their way back to us,' Belle says softly.

'Yes,' Lola says, almost defiantly. 'Oh look, Ruby's made the punch.'

We all watch as Carlos helps Ruby carry a huge cauldron-style pot to the centre of the clearing. Lola skips over to join them. Clearly she can't get away from me quick enough. I stare after her trying to figure out this latest turn of events. Is she really so in awe of Ruby that she can't see how weird it is that both Michael and Cruz should go missing?

Dusk is just starting to fall. One of the other guys lights a torch from the fire, then he starts going round the edge of the camp, lighting the other torches that have been put there.

'Looks like it's party time,' the Flea says dryly. 'But at least that means we're a step closer to getting out of this place,' he whispers.

'As long as Cruz turns up,' I reply. 'We're not leaving here without him.'

'Are we still planning on taking their boat?' Belle whispers.

'Uh-huh.' I look around to check no one's close enough to hear what I'm about to say, then I lean in closer to them. 'I just found a graveyard.'

'What?' The Flea's jaw drops.

Belle lets out a gasp.

I notice Lola saying something to Ruby and Ruby looks over to us.

'On the other side of the field where the cows are,' I whisper.

'Oh my God, do you think it's something to do with the voodoo queen?' the Flea asks.

I nod. 'Yes.'

Ruby calls Dan and Todd over to her. We watch as she tells them something, then they head off to the cabin where the musical instruments are kept.

'So, what's the plan?' the Flea asks. He's looking really serious now.

'Well, without Cruz and Michael we can't just leave. I'm going to have to confront Ruby instead – in front of everyone.'

'But what will you say?' Belle asks. 'You have no proof that she's connected to this Hortense person.'

'I'm going to have to sneak into her house. So I need you guys to help me.' I look at the Flea. 'Jimmy, can you make sure Ruby doesn't go up there while I'm gone?'

The Flea nods.

'Now, I need to go see Cariss and Jenna.'

'They're in the girls' cabin,' the Flea says.

'What are you going to tell them?' Belle asks.

'I'm just going to warn them that something's up. I need them to be prepared.'

The Flea nods. 'Good plan. What about Dan and Todd?'

We both look over to the centre of camp, where Dan and

Todd are putting some drums on the floor by Ruby.

'I think we're going to have to leave it for now. Dan's too besotted with Ruby. I'm gonna have to get some proof before I can tell him anything.'

The Flea nods. Then he grips hold of my arm. 'Good luck, Gracie.'

I swallow down the lump in my throat. 'Thank you.'

Belle looks at me blank-faced. I lean forward and kiss her on the cheek. 'Don't worry, Belle, we'll get you back to your mom real soon.'

Her eyes instantly fill with tears. 'I love you, Grace,' she whispers.

'I love you too,' I say.

Then, clenching my fists to stop myself from crying, I head over to the girls' cabin.

Inside, the air is musty and humid. Jenna and Cariss are both lying on their beds, staring up at the ceiling.

'Hi,' I say, slightly nervous.

'Hey, Grace,' Jenna says. Cariss remains silent.

'I just wanted to tell you that something's likely to happen tonight.'

Jenna sits up. Her eyes are red from crying. 'What do you mean?'

I go a bit closer and lower my voice. 'You know I said that something was wrong here?'

She nods. Now Cariss sits up. I think it must be the first time I've had her complete, undivided attention.

'Well, just be prepared.'

Cariss frowns. 'What do you mean?'

'I think something bad's happened to Michael and Cruz and I'm going to confront Ruby about it.'

'What is it?' Jenna says, her eyes wide with genuine concern.

'I'm not sure yet. I just need to get some proof.'

'Proof of what?' Cariss says.

I fight hard to stay calm. Falling out with Cariss now would be fatal. 'I don't know, but I think Ruby has something to do with it. I just wanted you guys to know, and to be ready.' I look at Cariss, praying she'll just accept what I'm saying.

Cariss continues to frown. Then she grabs her pillow and hugs it to her. 'I knew she was trouble,' she says quietly. But for once she doesn't look smug – she actually looks worried.

Jenna gets up from her bed.

'Be careful,' she says. With her make-up-free face and her messy hair she looks about ten years old. She looks just how I remember her when we were first friends – before any of the crap with her dad happened. Before she changed. I step forward and hug her tightly.

'Oh, Grace,' she whispers in my ear.

'It's okay,' I whisper back. 'It's all okay.' Then I take hold of her hand. 'Come on, let's go join the others – and remember, just act like everything's cool.' I turn to look at Cariss, to make sure I definitely have her on board. She nods curtly and springs from her bed.

Outside, the others have all gathered round Ruby. When she sees me approaching she smiles. It's the kind of smile I'd imagine a crocodile giving its victim right before swallowing it whole.

'Great. Now we're all together I guess the party can begin.'

One of her friends – a thin, pale guy with his hair in dreads, starts tapping out a beat on one of the drums.

'Y'all help yourselves to some punch,' Ruby says, pointing to the huge pot beside her.

Dan immediately grabs a cup and fills it from the pot. Todd swiftly follows him. The Flea and I exchange worried glances.

'Is it alcoholic?' the Flea asks, clearly thinking the same as me.

Ruby shakes her head.

'It's not?' Dan says, obviously disappointed.

'Alcohol is a false high,' Ruby says, enigmatically. 'And you won't be needing any false highs tonight, trust me.'

A murmur of agreement ripples through her friends.

Dan instantly grins and winks at Todd.

I breathe a sigh of relief.

Lola picks up a couple of cups. 'Do you want some, Grace?'

I shake my head. I'm so tense now I don't think I'd be able

to swallow a thing. Lola fills the cups and hands them to Jenna and Cariss.

I turn round and scour the edge of the camp. The torches are flickering brighter now darkness is descending. I think of Cruz still out there somewhere once it gets dark and the jungle really starts coming to life and it makes me feel sick. I take a deep breath to steady myself. I have to focus on what I need to do. I'm running out of time.

Chapter Twenty-seven

When I was little, before my mom and dad's marriage went into self-destruct, they would have house parties almost every weekend. It became a kind of tradition that I would sneak downstairs at the start of the party and everyone would make a huge fuss of me, pretending to be so surprised that I'd made an appearance. At first I'd love seeing the grown-ups all looking so happy. But there always came a point when, to my five-year-old self, they'd start becoming a little scary. As they got drunker and louder and more wild-eyed, I'd always end up sneaking back to the safety and comfort of my bed. Now the dark of the moon party is getting into full swing, everything starts taking on that same nightmarish quality. The music is too loud, the laughter too shrill, everyone's faces are hollowed out by shadows, and above us the sky is a black chasm, unbroken by a single star. But this time I have no cosy bedroom to escape to.

I'm not sure how long the party has been going before I finally get the chance to slip up into the house. Fear and tension have made time stretch and warp. Ruby and the others are all dancing together, their eyes closed. Some of them are pounding away on the drums, the others have their hands raised to the gaping darkness. The hypnotic rhythm seems to have sent them all into a trance. I look around for the Flea, then spot his hat in the middle of the crowd. Damn. Only Belle is apart from the others, sitting cross-legged by the fire, but I can hardly ask her to keep watch. I look at the house, looming over us. I decide to risk it. It may be the only chance I get. I slip around the edge of the clearing, then, taking one final glance over my shoulder, the others are all still lost in the dance. I start climbing the ladder.

Inside the house is strangely cool. Outside, the drums beat faster and faster, like the island is filled with hundreds of hearts all thumping as loud as mine. And then I remember hearing that sound before – back when we were searching for Belle, in the rainforest. 'Follow the sound of the drums,' Hortense had whispered to me. 'Follow the sound of the drums.' I check the room for any signs of life then make my way over to the ladder leading to the second floor. My throat is tight and my palms are sweating. What if Hortense is up there, waiting for me? But I have to do this. I have no choice. Panic threatens to overwhelm me, but I force my feet to climb the ladder, my clammy hands slipping on the wood. I peer through the hole in the floor and scan the room. It's surprisingly empty. All I can make out in the darkness is a single bed and an old bureau in the corner. I clamber up and creep over to the bureau. The lid's locked. Damn! I fumble about on top of it for a key. I don't find one, but I do find a thick, pillar candle and a book of matches. I tear a match from the book and light the candle. Amber light flickers about the room, causing shadows to dance all around me. The hairs on the back of my neck prickle as I look straight ahead. A huge portrait of a woman is hanging on the wall. At first I think it's Ruby. But, as I go closer and hold the candle up to the canvas, I see that it's someone different. Her hair is tightly braided into thin cornrows – just like the horrific woman who chased us through the forest. But unlike that wizened old crone, this woman is strikingly beautiful, with clear, brown skin and dark, almond-shaped eyes. Although she doesn't look at all menacing, I can't help feeling that I'm looking straight at Hortense. And she's looking straight back at me.

'Where are you?' I whisper.

I pick up the candle and head over to another ladder that leads to the next floor. Holding the candle in one hand and the ladder with the other, I start climbing up. I have to go real slowly as the ladder keeps wobbling, not helping my nerves any. When I reach the top, I place the candle down on the

279

floor and use both hands to pull myself up.

A huge, canopy style bed takes up the far corner of the room. It is shrouded in wispy drapes. I pick up the candle again and as I creep over to the bed a sickening feeling of dread weighs heavy in the pit of my stomach. Through the sheer drapes I can see the silhouette of a figure lying completely motionless on their back.

Hortense.

I feel bile burning at the back of my throat. I want to turn and run, but then I see something on the cabinet beside the bed that stops me dead. A tiny red light – blinking on and off. It looks like the notification light on a Blackberry cellphone. But how can it be? Summoning all my courage, I creep closer. The figure on the bed remains motionless. I hold the candle out and nearly drop it in shock. It's not a Blackberry, but a brick-sized cellphone with a long thick aerial. The red light in the top corner blinks again. How is this possible? How is there a phone up here? I feel sick as I realise the answer. Ruby was lying when she told us about being cut off from the rest of the world. I lean forward to pick up the phone and I don't know how I keep from screaming. As the candlelight shines through the drapes over the bed, I see grey braids splayed out across the pillow and that wizened face, the cheeks shrunken and hollow. Hortense is literally just a foot away from me. But her body remains completely still. She must be sleeping. But how can she not sense that I'm so close to her? I stare hard at the body on the bed. There's no sign of movement at all. Not even the slightest rise and fall of her chest from breathing. And then I remember the man's warning note and an awful realisation dawns on me. Maybe Hortense isn't really here after all. Maybe all I'm looking at is the empty shell of her ancient body. Maybe right now, she's in someone else's body.

In the corner of my eye I see the red light flash again. I grab the phone and move as quickly as I can toward the ladder.

Feeling almost drunk from fear and adrenaline I make it down to the second floor of the house. I have to try and use the phone. But how can it work? There's no reception on the island. Then I remember my dad telling me about satellite phones that work anywhere in the world, and how journalists use them to file reports from far-flung places. That would account for the size of the phone and the huge aerial I guess. But how does it stay charged? I look around the room and spot a familiar shape squatting in the shadows in the corner. A gas generator, just like the one my grandpa has in his cabin in the woods.

Hardly daring to believe that the phone might actually work, I automatically start entering my home number. As I press the first digit the screen lights up. It works! My fingers start trembling uncontrollably. I finish entering the number and bring the phone up to my ear. My hand is shaking so much I nearly drop it. Nothing happens and then, after what feels like the longest time, a high-pitched disconnected tone rings in my ear. I want to scream with frustration. But then I realise that in my panic, I hadn't used the international dialling code. What *is* the international dialling code? My mind feels as gloopy as porridge as I try desperately to remember. *Think, think, think!* Outside, I hear Ruby call, 'Where's Grace?'

Shit!

And then the numbers come to me. I enter the digits painfully slowly to make sure I don't mess it up. I bring the phone back to my ear and wait. And wait. I'm just about to give up when I hear the very faint purr of a ring tone. Oh my God! I picture the phone on the kitchen wall at home ringing. I will Mom to be home. I will her to be making her way over to the phone right now. It keeps ringing. Why didn't I call her cell phone? What if she's out? What if she's –'

'Hello?'

My legs buckle at the sound of Mom's voice and I lean against the bed for support. The voice is so distant, so faint, but so definitely hers.

'Hello?' she says again, slightly louder this time.

'M-mom?'

I hear a scream at the other end of the line. Tears start pouring down my face.

'Grace? Is that you? Oh my God! Where are you? What's happened to you?'

I swallow down my sobs. I have to keep it together. 'Mom, we were shipwrecked, in a storm.'

'Oh, honey. I knew you were still alive. I knew it.' Through the crackles on the line I hear her start to cry. 'I kept telling them, my baby's alive. I never gave up.'

'I didn't either, Mom.'

'Where are you?'

I hear the sound of movement downstairs and the top of the ladder starts to shake. I clamp the phone tighter to my ear.

'Mom, I need you to listen to me. This is really important. We're on an island, somewhere near Costa Rica. It's called Ile de Sang.'

The sound of the ladder creaking and tapping against the floor gets louder.

'Did you get that, Mom? Ile de Sang. A few hours south of Costa Rica.'

I see the top of Ruby's Afro slowly appearing through the hole in the floor.

'Are you OK, Grace?' Mom says, her voice suddenly tense. 'What's going on?'

'We're trapped here, Mom, we need help. Did you get the name?'

'Oh, Grace. Oh no –'

'Did you get the name?' I practically scream into the phone.

'Ile de Sang, south of Costa Rica.'

My heart pounds with relief. 'That's right. We need help. Urgently. I love you, Mom . . .' Tears start spilling from my eyes again . . . 'I love you so much.'

Ruby starts marching toward me, her face set in fury. I see a glint of silver in her hand. She's holding a knife.

'I love you too, honey,' Mom says in my ear. 'And don't worry – I'm going to get help.'

Ruby holds the knife up to me and gestures for the phone.

'I love you, Grace,' I hear Mom cry, before Ruby grabs the phone and terminates the call.

Chapter Twenty-eight

And suddenly, I'm back in my middle grade ju-jitsu class and my teacher, Mr Lewis, is telling me what to do should a knife-wielding maniac be about to attack. I launch myself at Ruby, grabbing her arm and twisting it hard. It's as if hearing Mom's voice has given me renewed strength. But Ruby is so much taller than me – when I try to throw her over she wriggles free and pushes me hard on to the bed. She leans over me. The knife is still in her hand. I bring both my knees into my chest, then launch them out at her. The force of my kick sends her staggering backward. I hear the clink of the knife landing somewhere on the floor.

'You – stupid – girl!' she gasps, rolling on to her side and clutching her stomach.

Keeping my eyes fixed on her I start crawling round in the dark, trying to find the knife.

'I called home,' I tell her defiantly. 'I told them where we are. I told them to send help.'

Ruby laughs. 'They'll never find us.'

'Why not?'

'Because no one can find us.'

I sit up straight and stare at her. 'What do you mean?'

'Hortense has cast a force-field around the island,' Ruby gasps. 'To keep people away.'

'But – but that's impossible.'

'Oh, really?' Ruby pulls herself up to a seated position. 'So how come no one found you already?'

'Well, how did your guests get here then?'

'Because they were invited. Hortense lifts the force-field for people who are invited.'

'What about the man? The man whose boat we found?' My voice is shrill with fear and defiance. 'We found a warning note from him too. He wasn't invited, was he?'

Ruby's face clouds over. 'He managed to slip through, when some other guests were arriving. It was a fluke. It never should have happened.'

I take a moment to mentally regroup. 'Well, what about us then? We definitely weren't invited.'

'Oh, you were,' she says quietly.

Her words fill me with dread.

'Are you her?' I say, stumbling to my feet.

Candlelight flickers on Ruby's face. 'Who?'

I swallow hard. 'Hortense.'

Ruby starts to smile. 'No.' There's a second's silence. 'If only.'

'If only?' I stare at her.

Ruby nods. 'Hortense is an incredible woman. I can only dream of being as powerful and wise as her.'

I feel the sudden urge to laugh hysterically. 'Powerful and wise?'

Ruby looks at me calmly. 'Yes.'

'But look at what she's done.'

Ruby winces as she stands up. 'What has she done?'

I think of the man's warning note and how he'd jumped to his death rather than face Hortense. And I think of the story Cruz told me when we first got to the island. 'Possessing people's bodies. Bringing us here.' I say, deciding to call Ruby's bluff. 'I know all about the bowls.'

Ruby continues staring at me, defiant. 'Really?'

'Yes. I know there's a spell on them.'

'And do you know why she had to cast that spell?' Ruby hisses. 'Do you know what happened to her before she came here?'

I shake my head. I want to hear Ruby's version of events. I want to see how it ties up with what I've been told.

'Over two hundred years ago, Hortense was brought to

America as a slave. She was just fourteen years old – a child. Do you have any idea of how slaves were treated?'

I nod. 'Some.'

Ruby raises her thin eyebrows. 'Really? Well, when Hortense was on the ship being brought to America her mother got sick with smallpox. Do you know what they used to do to slaves that got sick on board?'

I shake my head.

'They threw them overboard – alive. So before Hortense even got off the boat she'd seen her mother murdered, in cold blood.'

I gulp. 'I . . .'

Ruby places her hands on her hips 'Then, when she got to America, she was sold to a French plantation owner, François Buchet just outside New Orleans.'

I nod, recalling the story Cruz told me when we first got to the island.

Ruby looks over at the portrait on the wall. 'Hortense was a very beautiful young woman – Buchet became obsessed with her and he made her his lover.'

'But . . .'

'What?'

'How old was she?'

'I told you. Fourteen.' Ruby stares at me intently. 'Hortense wasn't the heartless witch she's been painted to be. She wasn't a marriage wrecker – she was a child – an orphan, stolen from her homeland and desperate for security. She loved Buchet with all her heart. But he didn't deserve that love. He was evil through and through.'

I look over at the painting. Somehow, the sorrow in Hortense's eyes looks even more pronounced. 'She got pregnant with his child, didn't she?' I whisper.

Ruby nods. 'Isaac. When Buchet's wife found out, she made him cast Hortense out.'

'And that's when she put a curse on him?'

'No!' Ruby yells. 'There was no curse. There was no reason for a curse. She had her son. Buchet had released her so she was no longer a slave. And her incredible powers meant that she was already becoming a well-respected voodoo queen –'

'But how?' I cut in. 'She was still so young.'

'She had been practising voodoo her whole life.' Ruby frowns at me, like I should know that already. 'Voodoo was the religion where she was from. Even as a child she had remarkable powers, but all she wanted to do was use those powers to help people. Even Buchet. She still loved him. She had no desire to cause him harm.'

'But I thought his crops failed, and his other child died.'

Ruby shakes her head. 'It was all just coincidence. But of course Buchet didn't see it like that.' She leans closer to me, her eyes glinting in the candlelight. 'He set fire to her house.

289

He killed their baby. He tried to kill her. He drove her from New Orleans, and told everyone she was a monster. He had so much power and influence they all believed his lies. He made sure it was too dangerous for her to ever return.'

I nod, thinking of the dream I kept having on the other side of the island – the choking smoke and the baby crying. Sadness starts mingling with my anger.

'But still . . .'

Ruby glares at me. 'What?'

'It doesn't justify what she's done since. Possessing other people's bodies as if they were – as if they were clothes.'

Ruby shakes her head. 'The people she possesses are chosen very carefully. They are always people with no ties. Loners. Orphans. People with no real family.'

I frown. 'That doesn't make it okay. She still takes their lives. She still kills them.'

Ruby sighs. 'Her body is over two hundred years old. She has to possess these others to be able to live any kind of life.'

'But why does she want to keep on living?'

'So that she can be reunited with Isaac.'

'What? But how?'

'Buchet took his remains and buried them somewhere in New Orleans. When Hortense was driven out she always vowed she would return and find him.'

'So why didn't she? Why didn't she go back when Buchet

died? He was older than her. He must have died way before she would have.'

Ruby frowns. 'Didn't you hear what I said? He poisoned everyone's minds against her. It would have been far too dangerous. To this day, her name is still said like a curse.'

I think back to how Cruz first came to hear of Hortense — as an evil voodoo queen in a book of spooky seafaring legends.

'And anyway, she had to wait,' Ruby continues.

'For what?'

'For her powers to get strong enough.'

'Strong enough for what?'

Ruby smiles. 'To bring Isaac back to life.'

Ruby's dreamy expression as she says this makes me shudder. I take a deep breath and try to compose myself. 'Okay, well why hasn't she gone back in one of the bodies she's possessed?'

'She hasn't been able to — until now.'

My heart starts to pound. 'What do you mean?'

'She's never been able to possess another body for more than a few weeks. And her magic is only strong enough for it to work within the force-field she's created here, on the island.'

'So, what did you mean by "until now"?' I swallow hard, dreading her answer.

Ruby leans forward and smiles menacingly. 'Well, now you are here.'

I instinctively step back. 'But why me? What have I got to

do with any of this? Just because my dad bought me that bowl.'

Ruby shakes her head. 'It's *why* he bought you the bowl.'

'I don't understand.'

'The only way Hortense can get off the island is by possessing the body of someone born under exactly the same astrological conditions as her.'

I look at her blankly.

'Somebody born on the same date and time and during the dark of the moon.' She looks at me. 'When is your birthday?'

I look back at her, too afraid to speak.

'February fourteenth,' Ruby says. It isn't a question. 'At one minute past midnight.'

I feel sick as I think of how my parents always love to joke about how I held on just long enough to be a Valentine's Day baby.

'During the dark of the moon,' Ruby adds. 'The time when the veil between the spirit world and the living world is at its weakest.'

'Live forever in the dark of the moon.' I whisper the words from the rim of the bowl.

Ruby nods. 'Exactly. When Hortense takes possession of you she will finally be able to live forever and go wherever she likes.'

'But . . .'

Ruby's eyes glaze over with a reverential joy. 'Finally, we will be able to bring her home.'

'We?' I ask weakly.

'Her followers.'

There's a sudden burst of laughter from outside. I look towards the shuttered window. 'You mean, they're all . . .'

'Part of her cult. And I am her priestess.'

'Are you – are you a spirit too?'

Ruby shakes her head and laughs. 'Of course not.'

'But how are you her priestess? You're so – young.'

Ruby laughs knowingly. 'I've only been priestess for two years. It passes down through my maternal bloodline. My great, great-grandmother's great grandmother was Hortense's closest friend. She started the cult after Hortense was banished. She was the first priestess.' Ruby steps toward me.

Fear cuts through the surreal haze in my head and I start backing away.

'For some reason, Hortense really likes you,' Ruby says with a frown.

'What do you mean, she really likes me? She doesn't even know me!'

Ruby looks at me like I'm demented. Then she starts to laugh. 'Oh, she knows you,' she says softly.

I feel a stab of anger. Just because Hortense was able to access my dreams and talk to me in my head it does not give her the right to claim to know or like me.

I start backing toward the ladder and feel something cold

and hard beneath my foot. The knife! I bend down and grab it, then point it at Ruby.

'She *doesn't* know me, and she isn't going to possess me.'

But Ruby doesn't bat an eyelid. She just stands there staring at me, calmly.

'Do you want to see Cruz again?' she asks, her voice now sickly sweet.

'What?' I grip on to the knife with both hands to try and stop them shaking. 'Where is he? What has she done to him?'

'He's at the altar – waiting for you.' Ruby smiles at me with the arrogant glint in her eye of someone who's just played their trump card.

I stay frozen to the spot. It could be a trap. 'How do I know you're not lying? How do I know he's there?'

Ruby takes a small digital camera from her pocket. She turns it on and steps close to show me the display screen. I see a picture of Cruz lying on the altar.

My stomach lurches.

'Oh my God! Is he dead? Has she killed him?'

Ruby continues smiling smugly.

'Is he dead?' I'm screaming now.

Still, Ruby smiles.

Anger descends upon me in a blaze of red. I pull my arm right back and sock her in the jaw.

Chapter Twenty-nine

I half climb, half fall down the ladder and on to the ground. The others are all still dancing. Through my tear-filled eyes their bodies have become one blurred, heaving mass. I stumble past them, heading for the woodpile.

Todd grabs my arm. 'Hey, wanna dance?' His voice is deep and slurred, his eyes glazed. I think of the punch. Did Ruby spike it with something after all? Then I notice the Flea, crashed out on the floor.

I pull my arm from Todd's grip. I hear him laugh and say, 'Whatever.' I run behind the woodpile and into the forest. I'm in such a state of panic and fear I go the wrong way at the red ferns and have to double back on myself. *Please, please, please, let Cruz be alive.* I say over and over in my head. And then I see a sight that makes me stop dead in my tracks. A white hand, tinged blue, is protruding from the undergrowth, palm upwards, as if reaching out to me for help. Slowly, I crouch down, squinting, hardly daring to look. I reach out and touch the hand – and instantly recoil. It's cold and hard as stone. I sit shaking, my eyes shut tight for a second. I don't want to look. I don't want to see who it is, buried there beneath the ferns. But I have to. Swallowing hard, and summoning all my courage, I open my eyes, lean forward and part the leaves.

'Oh no!' I hear my voice, disconnected, echoing up into the trees. Somewhere high above me, I hear the beating of wings. Michael is lying face up, his eyes staring blankly into space. I lurch backward, letting go of the leaves and they close on Michael like curtains. I look down at his hand. He's dead. Michael is dead. Although part of me had been worried about this from the start, nothing could have prepared me for it actually happening. Michael is dead. I think of Lola back at the camp, oblivious. And then I think of Cruz. I stagger to my feet and race on.

When I finally get to the track leading to the altar I see a blaze of light. I fight my way through the vines, not caring when they tear at my skin. A ring of torches is burning round the edge of the clearing, the flames licking at the night air like monstrous tongues. I see Cruz lying on the altar, his eyes closed. Hanging from the altar on either side of him are two dead chickens. Dark pools of blood stain the ground beneath them. Their throats have been slashed.

'Cruz!' I yell at the top of my voice.

He doesn't move.

I race over and hug his body to me. It feels cold and lifeless.

'No!' I start shaking him. His dark curls fall forward over his face. 'Wake up! Please!' I take a deep breath, then place my fingers on his neck. There's no pulse. I can't feel any pulse. Cruz is dead. It's like a nuclear bomb has gone off inside of me, wiping out everything.

I stand up and look around the clearing for Hortense, tears stinging my eyes. 'Where are you, Hortense?' I scream. 'Come out, you coward.'

I hear footsteps running down the pathway toward the clearing. I clench my fists and wait.

A figure bursts through the trees.

Lola.

I think of Michael lying dead so close to us. How am I going to tell her?

She halts. Then starts walking toward me. A terrible thought hits me. Why is she here? All of my earlier niggling doubts rush back into my mind: Lola's closeness to Ruby, the fact that she was the only one invited to stay in the house. The weird way she acted over the graveyard and how easily she calmed down over Michael disappearing. Then I remember how Michael had accused her of changing. Did she change because of her infatuation with Ruby – or was it because she'd been possessed by Hortense? I think back to what Ruby said in the house earlier. '*The people she possesses are chosen very carefully. They are always people with no ties. Loners. Orphans. People with no real family.*' Lola has no family. I stare at her, horror prickling beneath my skin.

'Grace,' Lola says softly.

I take the knife from my pocket and step toward her.

Lola frowns. 'What are you doing?'

'I know who you are!' I yell at her.

'Of course you do,' Lola says with a smile.

'Grace?'

I jump as I hear Belle's voice behind Lola.

'Get out of here, Belle. It isn't safe.' I cry. 'Go get Jimmy and Dan. Tell them I need help.'

Lola stares at me. 'What are you doing?'

'What am *I* doing?' I fight to keep my voice from trembling. 'What are *you* doing? What *have* you done?'

Lola takes another step toward me.

I thrust the knife at her, then see Belle come running up.

'Keep away!' I yell.

But Belle grabs Lola from behind and throws her to the floor.

I stare at her in shock. 'Belle, can you see?'

Belle looks up at me and nods, then sits on Lola before she has the chance to get up.

'Get off me! Let me go!' Lola starts wriggling about, trying to break free.

'Quick,' Belle says. 'Help me tie her up.'

I put the knife down on the altar and take off my belt. While Belle holds Lola down, I tie her hands tightly behind her back.

'What are you doing?' Lola screams.

'Pass that bottle,' Belle says, nodding to the glass bottle on the altar. I grab it and hand it to her. Belle splashes a few drops of the liquid inside on to her hand, then clamps it over Lola's face. Almost immediately, her body goes limp.

Belle sighs and gets to her feet.

I stare at the bottle. 'What was that?'

'I recognised it from when I was in the volcano,' Belle says. 'It's what they used to put me to sleep.'

'Oh.' I look at Cruz and my body starts to shudder. Then I look back at Belle. 'He's dead,' I gasp.

'Oh, Grace,' Belle whispers. Then she comes over and hugs me tight.

'He's dead,' I sob. 'She killed him.'

My body buckles against Belle's as the full horror of what's happened sinks in. All this time I'd thought Lola was my friend – I'd trusted her, confided in her – and all this time she was Hortense.

'Grace,' Belle whispers in my ear. But her voice sounds weird. I turn to look at her. She cups my face in her hands and wipes the tears from my cheeks. 'Thank you,' she whispers. Again, her voice sounds different. Familiar, but not Belle's. It's too deep for Belle's.

'But –' I begin.

'Love is the only thing that counts,' she whispers, and her eyes fill with tears.

'Belle?' Panic rises inside of me. I look down at Lola, then back at Belle.

'Don't worry. I won't hurt you,' Belle says. But it isn't Belle's voice – it's Hortense's.

'You!' I gasp. The ground seems to sway beneath me and for a second I think I might actually pass out from the shock.

She nods and grips my arms tight.

'But – how long – how long have you been Belle for?'

'Since the night before you left the beach. I possessed her body while she was asleep.'

I think of Belle's shallow breathing and how we'd thought she was having a nightmare. 'Is that why – is that why we couldn't wake her at first?'

Belle – Hortense – nods.

I think of the moment Belle finally woke up – and how worried we'd been when she said she was blind. But it hadn't been Belle at all. It had been Hortense.

'Were you just pretending to be blind?'

She shakes her head. 'I made a spell.'

My head feels as if it's about to explode with shock and confusion. 'But why – why would you make yourself blind?'

'So you wouldn't suspect me.' She gives a small smile. 'I hadn't thought that you would find the doll and break the spell.'

I think of Belle and I standing in the pool – and the head of the doll floating right by us. An icy chill runs down my spine.

'Did you – did you see the doll's head, that day in the pool.'

'Yes. You had broken the spell by destroying the doll.'

'So after that you were just pretending to be blind?'

She nods and gives a wry smile. 'It wasn't easy.'

'But how did you know what to do and what to say? Were you reading Belle's mind? I don't understand – I . . .'

Hortense shakes her head and smiles. 'You forget. I was watching all of you, all the time before, when you were on the beach. Most times, I knew what to say. Other times, I would guess, or keep quiet.'

I think of the closeness I'd felt with Belle that day in the pool; how I'd washed her hair, and told her about my mom and dad; told her about Cruz and how much I loved him. She'd seemed so caring. So understanding. I'd actually believed that we were friends. I look at Lola lying motionless on the ground in front of us and I feel sick to my stomach. 'Did Lola know about you?'

She shakes her head. 'No. She had been brought here for me to possess. But then you arrived, so I had no need for her any more.'

'Oh my God. Is Lola – is she dead?'

'Don't worry about her,' Hortense says.

I stare at her, almost unable to take it all in. 'But why – why did you possess Belle?'

A tear spills from her eye and snakes down her cheek. 'I really wanted to get to know you,' she whispers. She pulls me toward her. 'I'm so grateful to you. You're *the one*.' I try to break free, but she has me in some kind of vice-like grip.

'The one you're going to possess!' I exclaim.

I hear a shuffling noise. Over Belle's shoulder I see Ruby and her guests filing into the clearing, some of them are carrying drums. They start chanting something as they form a circle round us. I look around the clearing desperately. But there's no way out. I see Ruby smiling at Hortense – the knowing smile of a close friend – and I get a sudden flashback to the creaking sound I'd heard in her house. I look back at Hortense.

'Was that you? When I snuck into the house the other day? Was it you walking around above me?'

Hortense nods. 'That was the closest you came to catching me. I had to be very careful after that.'

I think of how I'd raced from the house into the kitchen and then seen Belle – Hortense – standing in the middle of the clearing. She hadn't come from the cabin – she'd come from the house. Then I think of how she'd told me she'd dreamt about the baby and the fire. I'd been so worried about her.

302

But it had all been a trick to throw me off the scent. My mind starts filling with all the conversations we've had. All the times I'd consoled her, all the times I'd confided in her and the bond we'd formed — or I thought we'd formed. My head swirls with confusion. Was that all just pretence?

'No,' she says softly, reading my mind. 'It was real.'

'Then how can you do this to me?' I'm crying now too.

'I have to be with my baby again,' she whispers, her face now inches from mine. 'I have to find him. That's why I made you have the dreams about him — so you'd understand.'

'But what about *my* family?'

The chanting is so loud now I can barely hear my own voice. 'Why did you have to kill Cruz?'

'You'll be together again,' she says with a knowing smile that makes me want to shake her.

'What? In heaven?' Panic rises inside of me. 'Thanks.'

'I'm sorry, Grace,' Hortense says and she pulls me to her and kisses me hard on the mouth.

I'm hit by a waft of her sickly sweet scent, and then everything goes black.

Chapter Thirty

The inside of my head feels like one of those old-style radios
that you tune with a dial. I keep catching random snatches of
sound, then it moves on to something else. I hear Mom saying,
'I love you, Grace.' Then chanting and drumming. I hear Ruby's
voice. 'Is it done?' Then Hortense. 'Yes, it is done.' A cheer.
More drumming. Someone crying – a girl. 'I love you, Grace.'
I try to say, 'I love you too, Mom,' but my body is paralysed. I
hear a man's voice saying, 'Put her here.' Then, someone else
saying, 'Let's go.' Footsteps running away. And then Hortense,
whispering in my ear, or is she inside my head again? 'Goodbye, Grace.'

I feel as if I'm dropping, down, down, deep into the
ground, my body heavy as lead. Part of me feels like I ought
to be struggling; like I ought to be fighting against this,

but it's too strong. And so I let myself fall.

Some time later — it could be minutes — it could be hours — I hear a loud squawk, followed by another. *Pesky parrots*, I think to myself and I instantly want to laugh. I feel drunk. Am I drunk? What happened? Where am I? *Open your eyes*, I tell myself. But my eyelids feel as if they're stuck down with glue. In the end I have to count myself in, like I'm starting a race: *one, two, three*. I wrench my eyelids open a fraction and squint at the bright sunlight. I'm lying on the ground. Why am I lying on the ground? Where the hell am I? I force my eyes wider and turn my head. And what I see almost makes my heart stop. Cruz, lying on the floor a few feet from me, his face pale and waxen. And all of a sudden I'm bombarded with memories.

It was Belle. Hortense was Belle. I look around for Lola but there's no sign of her, or the altar, or any of the things that were here before. I look at Cruz again and my eyes fill with tears. He's dead. Cruz is dead. But how am I still here? How am I still alive? Did Hortense's magic go wrong? Was she unable to possess me after all? And where are the others. I have to warn the others. But even the slightest movement feels like too much of an effort. I close my eyes to try to summon up the strength to move.

'Lola?'

My body jolts at the sound of Cruz's voice. I open my eyes. He's moved on to his side and is staring at me, dazed.

'Cruz?' My voice is barely more than a croak.

'Where's Grace?' he asks.

'I'm here,' I whisper. He's alive. Relief hits me like a sledgehammer. But can it be real? Am I seeing things? Am I dreaming? I try to sit up. But something feels very wrong. My body feels very wrong. And it's not just the aching tiredness – my limbs feel the wrong size somehow.

Cruz pushes himself into a seated position. He's looking at me, really scared. 'Where's Grace?' he says again, staring right at me.

I swallow hard to try and get some moisture into my parched mouth. 'I am . . .' I break off. What's up with my voice? 'I – am – Grace,' I say. I'm talking with a British accent. Why am I talking with a British accent? My panic seems to energise me and I manage to roll on to my side. I look down at my hands. There's a tattoo of a blue butterfly on my wrist – *Lola's* tattoo of a blue butterfly. My throat tightens. This must be a nightmare. A terrible nightmare. Maybe I'm dying after all. I bring one hand to the other and grip them tightly. I feel the tips of the fingers pressing on the knuckles. The hands feel as if they're my own – but they're not.

'What's happened?' I whisper.

'I don't know,' Cruz replies. He tries to get up but his legs buckle and he collapses on to the ground. 'I need to find Grace,' he mumbles.

I somehow manage to grab on to his hand. 'I *am* Grace,' I say, a bit louder this time, but even more British.

Cruz pulls his hand away and looks at me like I'm crazy. 'Why do you say that?' he says angrily.

'Because – it's – true.' There's so much I want to say to him. Words are jostling in my head, but my brain is still in such a fug I can't figure out how to order them.

Cruz stares at me.

'I thought – you – were – dead,' I gasp, just about managing to get the words out. 'I thought – I'd – never – s-see you – again.'

'Lola?' he says, frowning.

'No!'

Cruz gets to his feet.

'Don't – leave.'

'I have to find Grace.' He starts walking past me, out of the clearing.

'Come back! Please!'

But he's gone.

It takes everything I've got to heave myself up on to my feet. But as soon as I'm standing I'm stumbling back down again. Everything is off kilter. But my need to go after Cruz somehow propels me back up and I stagger out of the clearing.

Thankfully, he's obviously feeling just as rough, and has hardly made it any distance at all.

'Cruz!' I call after him in Lola's voice. 'Please!'

He turns and looks at me.

I stumble down the track toward him. I need to say something that will make him know it's me. 'Soulmates – in – every – life – time. Gazillion – kisses,' I call out to him. The effort is exhausting. I close my eyes, and drop to my knees to catch my breath. I hear his footsteps approaching. He crouches down next to me.

'What did you say?'

'We've kissed – a – gazillion times,' I stammer. 'You saved my life.'

'But . . .' he looks at me, confused. 'Grace?'

I make my head nod. 'Hortense did this.'

Cruz pulls me up and stares into my eyes.

Memories of him and me crowd my head. 'Milky Way,' I murmur. 'Imaginary girlfriend – Phoenix. See you – later – alligator.'

'In a while, crocodile,' Cruz whispers. His eyes go glassy and a tear rolls down his face.

'I love you,' I whisper.

He hugs me to him so tightly I can hardly breathe. 'I love you too.'

'I – I thought you were dead,' I gasp through my tears. 'I thought she'd killed you. What happened?'

He shrugs. 'I do not know. I don't remember anything after leaving to look for Michael.'

I have a flashback — a bluey-white hand sticking out from beneath the bushes.

'I think — I think Michael is dead,' I whisper.

Cruz lets out a gasp of shock. Then he takes hold of my hand, real carefully, like he still isn't sure it's really me. 'How are you in Lola's body?' he asks, frowning in confusion.

I shake my head. 'I don't know. Hortense must have done it. She was Belle. She was Belle all along.'

Cruz's eyes widen. 'What?'

'She possessed Belle's body — that last night on the beach — when we thought she was having a bad dream and we couldn't wake her up. Hortense had possessed her.'

'But . . .' he breaks off. 'What about the blindness?'

'It was so we wouldn't suspect anything. She made a spell with that doll we found.'

Cruz stares at me and shakes his head. 'This is all crazy. Nothing feels real.'

I take hold of his hand. '*This* is real,' I say, echoing his own words back at him. 'You and me. Us. We are real.'

His eyes fill with tears, but he starts to smile. 'Oh, Grace.' Then he kisses me with such intensity that I know he knows for sure that it's me. Finally, he breaks away.

'What do we do now?'

My brain actually hurts as I try to formulate a plan. 'We should look for the others . . . But we must be careful . . . Hortense.'

Cruz nods and very slowly, arm in arm, we start making our way back to the retreat.

When we get there all is ominously quiet.

Cruz heads straight for the well and gets us both a cup of water. As soon as I drink it I start feeling more human again — but even more disorientated as the enormity of what's happened hits me. I am inside Lola's body. I look up at the clear blue sky. The sun is disappearing behind the forest in the direction of the fields. I feel a jolt of shock as I realise that it's afternoon already.

'Let's go check out the house,' I say in my clipped British accent.

The house has been stripped bare.

We're on the second floor, just about to climb back down when I hear a voice from below. We go over to the window and peer out.

The Flea and Todd are coming out of the boys' cabin. They're rubbing their eyes and clutching their heads like they've got hangovers from hell.

I hear Todd say something about coffee and he goes over to the kitchen.

The Flea walks over to the girls' cabin. 'Ladies are you decent?' he calls out, before disappearing inside.

'What should we do?' I say to Cruz.

But before he can answer a shriek rings out from the girls' cabin. Todd comes running out of the kitchen. 'What's up?' he calls.

The Flea bursts out. 'It's Beau-Belle – she can see again!'

I'm frozen to the spot. Belle's still alive! But is she still Hortense?

The next second Belle comes stumbling out into the sunlight. 'Where are we?' she says, looking around in panic.

'We're at the retreat, silly,' the Flea says. 'Is it how you pictured it?'

'What retreat?' Belle says.

The Flea looks at the others, anxiously.

'It was pretty strong punch,' Dan says with a laugh.

'Damn right, if it can give the blind their sight back!' the Flea exclaims before hugging Belle and bouncing up and down.

Jenna and Cariss emerge from the cabin, blinking.

'What's all the commotion about?' Cariss snaps. 'Oh my God, my head is killing me.'

'Belle can see again!' the Flea says.

'What, really?' Cariss stares at her.

'Wow! That's awesome,' Jenna says, looking genuinely pleased.

Belle rubs her eyes. 'What do you mean, I can see again?'

The Flea touches her gently on the arm. 'You were blind, honey. Remember?'

311

Belle looks at him blankly. 'What are you talking about?'

The Flea turns to Dan. 'Do you think she's got amnesia?'

Dan shrugs. 'Looks that way, bro.'

'Can you please not talk about me as if I'm not here?' Belle snaps. 'Where's the beach?'

The Flea stands in front of her. 'What's the last thing you remember?'

'Going to sleep on the beach of course.' Belle looks at Jenna and Cariss. 'How did they get here? Where are we?'

'Holy moley!' the Flea exclaims. 'Have I got some explaining to do!' He looks over at Jenna and Cariss. 'Hey you guys, go get Grace. She's gonna love this.'

'Isn't she up already?' Jenna says looking concerned. 'She isn't in her bed.'

The Flea shakes his head. 'I haven't seen her. Come to think of it, I don't remember seeing her for most of the party.'

'I have this vague recollection of her going off into the forest at some point,' Todd says. 'But then again, I'm pretty sure I saw some pixies break-dancing over by the well too, so it may well have been a hallucination. What was in that punch?'

The Flea looks around the clearing. I want to run down and tell him that it's okay – I'm okay – but how can I?

'Shoot, you don't think she went looking for Cruz, do you?' Todd says, his face suddenly serious.

'Did anyone see Cruz last night?' the Flea asks. 'Did he ever come back?'

'What about Michael — and Lola?' Todd says.

'Who are Michael and Lola?' Belle asks.

The others all start looking round anxiously.

'Do you think we ought to go down there?' I whisper to Cruz.

'I guess so,' he replies. But before we can move the Flea lets out a cheer.

'Gracie! Thank God! We were just gonna send out a search party.'

My mouth goes dry as I watch the others all turn. I lean forward slightly so I can follow the direction of their gaze — and see myself strolling into the clearing, a beaming smile upon my face.

Chapter Thirty-one

I watch in horror as Jenna rushes over to me.

'Where have you been?' she says.

I feel Cruz tense beside me. He looks at me then back at 'Grace'.

'That isn't me,' I whisper.

'I know,' he whispers back, 'it's just . . .'

'I went to see the others off.' I hear my voice echo round the clearing. I get that weird, freaked out feeling I always get whenever I see myself on a cellphone video – but magnified a million-fold.

'What do you mean, see them off?' Cariss shrieks.

'Ruby asked me to go,' I reply – *Hortense* replies, cool as a cucumber.

'But what about us?' Jenna asks, her voice shrill with panic.

'Ruby said we were going to leave with them too.'

'Where is Ruby?' Dan says, looking puzzled.

'She had to go with them — she has some kind of family emergency back at home.'

'But why would they just leave us here?' Jenna says, looking round frantically.

I feel sick as I watch Hortense take hold of her arm. 'Don't worry — they've sent for the coast-guard to come get us.'

'But how have they sent for the coast-guard?' Jenna says.

For a split second, Hortense is silent. Then she starts to smile. 'There was a radio on the boat.'

'We have to go down there. We have to warn them,' I say, moving toward the ladder.

'No!' Cruz grabs my hand.

'But we can't let them go with her. We have to let them know who she is.'

'No,' Cruz says. 'They will think you are crazy.'

'But you could tell them too.'

'Then they would think we are both crazy.' He looks around the empty house. 'There is no proof. They've taken it all. We have to be smart. For some reason Hortense has let us live. We need to keep it that way.'

'What's that noise?' Dan calls.

Somewhere in the distance is a whirring sound. It's getting louder.

'It's a helicopter,' Todd shouts.

The others start shrieking. The noise gets so loud my ears hurt. A shadow falls over the clearing and wind from the blades whips through the trees and into the house.

I watch as it hovers over. Someone shouts something from the helicopter.

'Oh my God! We're going home!' the Flea starts jumping up and down, crying and grinning with excitement. Then his face falls. 'What about Michael and Cruz and Lola?' He runs over to the helicopter and shouts something up to the crew. Then he comes back over to the others. 'It's okay. There's another one on its way. They'll do a search for them.'

The others all look around at each other. I can tell from their faces they're not happy at the thought of leaving us behind.

'I say we stay and help them search,' Todd shouts.

Dan nods his head.

'Are you guys insane?' Cariss yells.

'There's more help coming,' Hortense says. I cringe as she touches Todd on the arm.

He looks at her, confused. 'But don't you want to stay and find Cruz and Lola?'

My heart starts to pound.

Hortense frowns. Then she clutches hold of her head.

'Grace, are you okay?' Todd says, instantly concerned.

I have to literally bite my tongue to keep myself from

yelling out to him, *She isn't Grace!*

'I don't know. I'm not feeling so good.'

Todd sighs. 'It was that punch. Okay come on, let's get you out of here.'

My heart sinks as he starts guiding her toward the helicopter.

The Flea comes over to Dan. 'The coast-guard are saying that we all have to leave. There's a proper search party on the way.' He points up at the sky. 'Look, here they come now.'

Dan follows his gaze and nods. 'Okay.'

I look at Cruz imploringly.

'We wait for the next one,' he says.

Then yet another awful truth dawns on me. I still can't go home. Not in Lola's body. I still can't see my mom and dad. And I realise something even worse. If Hortense is now me is she going to go back to my home?

'I have to stop her,' I yell and start scrambling for the ladder.

'Wait!' Cruz shouts after me. But I can't. I can't let her go.

I clamber down the ladder to the first floor. Half-way down I lose my footing and crash to the floor. I'm temporarily winded and it gives Cruz time to catch up with me.

'We have to let her go,' he says, gently.

'But what am I going to do?' I cry. 'How am I going to get my life back?'

'You will come with me — to Costa Rica. Then we will figure it out.'

I run over to the window and look out. The others are all gathered round a rope ladder that's been thrown down from the helicopter. I watch the Flea climbing up behind Belle. It's like my heart is being wrenched from my body.

Cruz comes up behind me and wraps his arms around me. 'You're still alive, and we are still together,' he whispers in my ear. 'We will figure out a way to get your life back. I promise.'

I watch in silence as Jenna and Cariss climb up the ladder followed by Todd. Dan gestures at Hortense to go up, but she shakes her head and nods for him to go first. Cruz moves away and starts pacing round the room.

I stare out of the window at this person in my body, about to fly off with my friends to my life. Why did Hortense bother keeping me alive if it was to be like this, living in this state of torture?

'*For love*,' I hear her voice whisper in my head. '*It's why I kept him alive too. Remember — love is the only thing that counts.*'

Then she turns, slowly, stares right up at me, and smiles.

'*Good bye, Grace*,' she whispers in my head. And then her voice is drowned out by the roar of the helicopter engine starting up again. She turns away and begins climbing up the ladder.

Epilogue

Hortense stares round the arrivals lounge, and her palms begin to sweat. It is all so big. And so noisy. And the lights are so bright. She takes a deep breath. Did she make a mistake, keeping Grace and the boy alive? Will her decision come back to haunt her? She shakes her head. By the time Grace gets back to LA she will be long gone. The first chance she gets she will be joining Ruby in New Orleans and then, finally she can be reunited with her baby. Part of her still can't believe that it has happened – that, after all these years of waiting, the spell has worked.

Next to her, the skinny boy, the Flea, points to a pale thin couple walking towards them. 'There's my parents!' he cries. He turns and hugs Belle. Then he hugs Hortense. She makes herself smile and hug him back.

'I'll call you later, Gracie,' he says, before running over to them.

Hortense feels in her pocket for her pendant and clutches it tightly.

She hears Belle scream and watches her run over to a plumpish woman wearing a headscarf. Her mom. They collapse to the floor in an embrace. Hortense smiles. It was worth keeping Belle alive just to be able to see this moment. She looks over at Jenna, staring anxiously around the hall, and feels the familiar prickle of hatred. She still can't understand why Grace would be so forgiving of her so-called friend, if it had been up to her — 'Grace!'

Hortense turns to see a woman with long, strawberry blonde hair running toward her. Tears are streaming from her eyes. A man is racing alongside her. He's also crying.

'Oh, Grace,' he gasps. 'Thank God you're okay.'

The woman reaches her first, and grabs her in a hug. Hortense makes her body relax and leans into her.

The woman is sobbing uncontrollably now.

Hortense thinks of Isaac to make herself cry.

The woman finally loosens her hold on her and stares into her face.

'I love you, Grace,' she gasps.

Hortense looks back at her and smiles. 'I love you too, Mom.'

Acknowledgements

Huge thanks as always to Ali Dougal and Jenny Hayes and the rest of the team at Egmont. Thank you also to all of the lovely bloggers and readers who got so behind *Shipwrecked* and made its publication so much fun – I tried to reward you with as many twists as possible in the sequel! I am so grateful also to all of my friends for doing so much to help me promote my books. Big shout out to my Nower Hill buddies – Lara, Lesley, Claire Gee-Gee, Gill, Michelle, Pete, Gra & Shirl, and 'Captain' Scarlett. And much love and thanks to Stevie O'Toole, Tina, Brenda, Charlotte, Marj, Wally, Jan, Sara, Lexie and Flynnie. And special thanks to Stuart Berry, for telling me how Agatha Christie came up with her plot twists and thereby making me rewrite the whole damn book! Much, much love and thanks to Jack Phillips. And Katie Bird. And the rest of my family. And to Aaron Daniel – for helping me become a 'dancing, doubtless daisy'.

MORE HIGH-VOLTAGE READING FROM
ELECTRIC MONKEY

Dear
Dylan...

SIOBHAN
CURHAM

'Funny, full of heart ... I couldn't get enough' Lauren's Crammed Bookshelf

WINNER OF THE
YOUNG MINDS AWARD

Finding
Cherokee
Brown

SIOBHAN
CURHAM

Everything changes when ... dare to dream ...

SIOBHAN CURHAM

'*TENDER, QUIRKY* AND *COOL.*
SIOBHAN CURHAM IS A NAME TO WATCH.'
CATHY CASSIDY

MORE HIGH-VOLTAGE READING FROM
ELECTRIC MONKEY

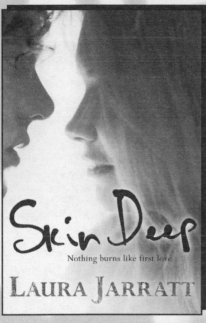

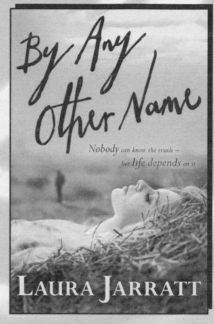

SHORTLISTED FOR
WATERSTONES BOOK PRIZE
2013 & ROMANTIC NOVELISTS'
ASSOCIATION'S YA CATEGORY

NOMINATED FOR
THE CARNEGIE MEDAL

LAURA JARRATT

'EDGE OF THE SEAT STUFF...
ABSOLUTELY TERRIFIC READING.'

BOOKS MONTHLY
ON BY ANY OTHER NAME

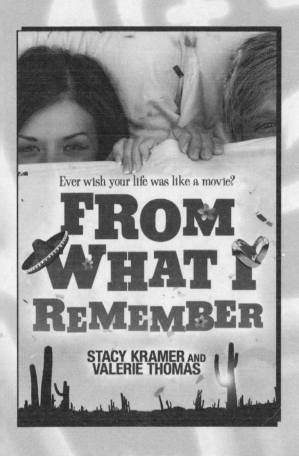

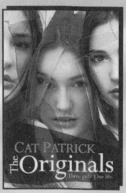